THE
SCALAWAGS

C. J. PETIT

C. J. PETIT

THE SCALAWAGS

Printed in the United States of America

First Printing, 2017

ASIN: B073VS2MWC

TABLE OF CONTENTS

PROLOGUE

November 11, 1861
Davenport, Iowa

"Texas?" Sam asked as he looked across the small tent at his fellow soldier.

"Yup. Mulberry, Texas. Just on the good side of the Red River."

"Why'd you come all the way to Davenport to enlist with the Union Army?"

"Some of us Texas boys weren't too happy with the whole secession thing, so we moseyed across Arkansas, hopped a steamer and came upriver. The only place that was forming up regiments was in Davenport."

"That's a pretty far piece to get involved in a war, Joe."

"It's not gonna be pretty, Sam. Despite what some of these fellers around here are sayin', I don't think it'll be over quick."

"I don't, either. Those rebels seem mighty pissed."

"I can understand it some ways. They're just all riled up by the politicians who are spoutin' off about the damned Federal government tellin' the states what to do. Now, in Texas, we don't cotton to it either, but I don't think cuttin' the country in half is gonna solve anything."

"Well, Joe, I'm glad to have you here."

Joe stood as best he could in the low tent and shook Sam's hand.

———

April 9, 1864
Battle of Pleasant Hill, Louisiana

It was a confused mess as battles often are. Nobody seemed to know what anyone was supposed to be doing or where they were supposed to be doing it.

Sergeant Sam Walker had his men in line, preparing to engage the Confederate flank with his bayoneted Springfield rifle in his hands. He was waiting for the signal from Lieutenant Brewster but couldn't understand the reason for the holdup. He kept watching and waiting as he stared at his commander, and Brewster seemed to be looking for a signal of his own from the captain. Sam wondered if he could see what every damned private in the line could see happening a few hundred yards away.

Sam saw the opportunity for a sure victory begin to fade as more rebel infantry moved into position…a lot more.

Joe stood beside him in the line and said sharply, "Sam, they're movin' in over there!"

"I know, Joe. Damn! We had them ten minutes ago, but now we'll get our butts kicked if they send us in."

"You know they're gonna do it. Those generals don't care about us all that much. They'll send us in and tell the folks how gloriously we died."

Sam kept his eyes trained on Lieutenant Brewster as he replied, "I know."

Sam hoped that their officers had seen the reinforced Confederate flank and just once, would call off what would now be a suicidal assault. For too many battles and skirmishes, by the time the generals' and colonels' tactical plans were put into motion, the entire situation had changed dramatically, but not once had they altered their original plan of attack. Sam doubted that this would be any different.

They may have seen the problem but again, they didn't call off the assault.

Lieutenant Brewster pulled his saber and circled it over his head to start the attack.

"Forward!" shouted Sam with an encouraging voice that he didn't feel.

Then, after hearing the lieutenant's shouted command, he finished the order by yelling, "March!"

The line stepped out along with the rest of Company C of the Fourteenth Iowa Volunteer Infantry Regiment, marching in a line abreast with three other companies as they began to take hits from a withering fire from a combination of muskets and cannon loaded with canister rounds.

The fire was vicious, but the line kept advancing at a quick step as men fell or were simply gone when a large round from one of the cannons blasted him from existence. Sam felt a Minié ball hit his cartridge pouch without setting off any of the gunpowder, so he said a very quick silent prayer of thanks and kept in step with the rest of the rapidly depleting line.

Corporal Joe Farrell was to his right as he always was and had been since they'd been together back in training. They were shoulder to shoulder as they kept moving as reserves filled the front line before a well-placed Confederate canister shot changed everything. A massive gap was created when eight members of the advancing line of bluecoats were eliminated by the whizzing mass of lead balls. The screaming was more disconcerting than the cannon shot, and untouched soldiers stopped and looked at their downed comrades before some knelt to help.

"Get back in line and keep moving!" Sam screamed, "If you stop to help, they'll pick you off!"

Some started moving, but others stayed behind anyway. Sam didn't pay them any more attention because he had to keep the line of soldiers moving at all costs now. They were just sixty yards from the rebel flank when Sam saw the lieutenant's saber suddenly point forward. It was time to make use of his musket's bayonet.

"Charge!" Sam yelled, lowering his Springfield and changing to a trot, feeling Joe running beside him.

The firing and screaming created a deathly cacophony unmatched in any other arena of human endeavor as they plunged forward to kill the enemy.

They got within fifteen yards of the Confederate line before Sam fired his one shot, and Joe fired his a second later. They were screaming loudly as they crossed over the rebel rampart, trying to impale a man in gray. when suddenly, Sam's battle was over.

The sight of a Confederate soldier swinging his musket was the last thing that Sam remembered.

———

February 8, 1865
Camp Ford Prison Camp, outside of Tyler, Texas

"Joe, you feel warm. Are you all right?" Sam asked.

Joe laughed weakly, then replied, "Just be grateful for the heat, Sam. I remember how cold it was up in Iowa in November. I'm just glad that most of this damned war was fought where it wasn't so blasted cold."

Sam sat with his back against Joe's back as they usually did because they needed the heat.

"I didn't think it got this cold in Texas," Sam commented.

"It's not as bad as you Yankees get, but it can get chilly."

"Why did you have to go and mention food? I could use a hot bowl of chili."

Joe snickered before saying, "I didn't mention food at all. But now that you brought it up, I sure would like some of my mother's pecan pie."

"There you go again with that pecan pie. I never heard of such a thing. A pie made out of nuts. Why can't you just have apple pie like everyone else?"

Joe chuckled lightly, then said, "She makes a great apple pie, too. But her pecan pies are even better."

"I'd eat a pecan tree right about now, Joe, bark and all."

"You think them rebs are just trying to starve us to death?"

"Nah. Except for Sergeant Malarkey, those guards are almost as skinny as we are. You give them some of these blue rags and they'd fit right in. I think Malarkey eats all their food, too."

"He is an ornery cuss. He beats his men as much as he whips on us."

"You sure you're all right, Joe?" Sam asked as he felt Joe shudder.

"Just the usual trots and things. I'll be all right."

"You know, I can't wait to get home. Barbara Jean is waiting, but I'm gonna spend the first month eating everything in sight and then I'm gonna marry that girl and have sixteen kids."

"Julia was still mad at me when I left. Seems like she forgave me, though. Her last few letters were nice. If I'd have known that she was pregnant, I probably would have stayed around. But at least she's got my sister and brother to keep her company."

"Did you want a little girl when you found out she was going to have your baby?"

"Nope. Wanted a boy, but the more I think about it, the more I like havin' a daughter."

"You gonna go back to ranching when you get home, Joe?"

"What else? You sodbusters have to wait for things to happen. I like bein' on the back of a horse and makin' things happen. You goin' back to farmin'?"

"I don't think so. I don't think I'll ever be able to do something that's so tame again."

"You oughta come down to Texas and stay with us. We could always use another hand. Besides, my little sister, Mary, should be a right pretty woman by now. I told you before that she's the one for you."

"You forget I'm gonna get married to Barbara Jean, Joe."

"That's what you think. Mary is the only girl for you," he said before he laughed then started hacking.

Sam was seriously worried for his friend as he asked, "Joe, are you sure you're okay? I can feel your chest rattling right through my back."

Joe was unable to reply as he continued to cough. Sam would have stood and then checked him out, but he simply didn't have the energy anymore, so they just stayed that way, back-to-back, huddled together in the light snow under cloudy skies and a stiff breeze. Even with the cold weather, if the sun had been out, it would have been a lot better, but it wasn't.

Sam and Joe had been captured together on that ill-timed charge at Pleasant Hill, then a week later after a long march, they'd been brought to the prison camp. It had been built to hold four hundred men but now held four thousand. Some prisoners had already been exchanged and the rumor was that the war was almost over. Of course, that rumor had been around for two years, but this time there was substance to the rumor. General Grant had Bobby Lee on the run out of Richmond and Sherman was chasing down Joe Johnston's army in the Carolinas. The only question was would they surrender or fight a long guerilla war.

Sam optimistically said, "Joe, you need to hang on. I don't think we have much longer here."

"Sam, I'm tryin'. I really am. I want to go back home and see Julia and our little girl. She's almost three now, and I ain't ever seen her. I'm so close now, I swear I could hear her voice last night."

"You'll see her, Joe. You'll have some of your mother's pecan pie, too. You'll get so fat on pecan pie you'll have to be fed in the hog pen."

Joe laughed again which resulted in a deeper, longer coughing spasm.

"I'm sorry, Joe. I shouldn't make you laugh."

Joe coughed for another minute before saying, "Sam, if I don't make it outta here, go and make sure my Julia and our little Beth are all right. Take care of them for me."

"You can do it yourself, Joe. We've only got another month or so. I can feel it."

"I know. Sam, I'm just sayin' that if I don't get better, go to Mulberry and make sure they're okay and tell Julia I'm sorry for leavin'."

"Alright, Joe. But I still think you'll make it."

"Maybe. I just want to be sure they're all right. Besides, you'd get to meet Mary. She's the right one for you, Sam, not that Barbara Jean. Mary is the only one."

"I told you a thousand times, Joe. I'm gonna marry Barbara Jean."

Joe hugged his chest as he said, almost in a whisper, "You never know, Sam. You never know."

11

They were the last words Joe Farrell ever spoke. He and Sam stayed back-to-back for another hour before Sam woke from his unintended nap and noticed that Joe hadn't coughed in a while. He also felt the lack of heat from Joe, and with a panic that he hadn't felt in years, Sam sucked in every bit of energy he could, then struggled to his feet. When he did, Joe fell over backward, his blank eyes staring into the gray sky.

Sam looked down at his best friend and brother-in-arms, and in a hushed voice only meant for his own ears, he said, "Joe, we survived Shiloh and a lot of other battles and now you leave me in this godforsaken place. I know you're in a better place now, Joe. It's nice and warm and bright, and you've probably got a slice of pecan pie in front of you. Enjoy your pie and watch over Julia and Beth. I'll go to Texas when I get out of here to make sure that they're all right."

He then shuffled away from Joe's body and notified the guard, who followed him to where his corpse lay as snow continued to drift onto him. As the guard bent over to grab Joe's ankles to drag Joe from the compound, Sam started to protest, but spotted Sergeant Malarkey walking towards him, his hated hickory club swinging at his side.

When he was close, he smiled at Sam and said, "What, blue belly, your boyfriend didn't want your kisses no more?"

Sam just glared at him. There was no point in saying anything and giving him the satisfaction of clubbing him with his favorite toy.

Then, to try to goad Sam into doing something stupid, the sergeant of the guards kicked Joe's lifeless body before he cackled and walked away. Sam apologized to Joe and swore he'd get even with Malarkey one day and assumed it would be on the day that he was a free man again and Malarkey was the prisoner, but that didn't happen.

Sam remained a prisoner until he was exchanged in August, and Malarkey had deserted long before that happened. The Confederates took him and others by wagon across Arkansas and put them all on a steamer to New Orleans.

The Union Army medical team took him and some of the other prisoners to Saint James Army Hospital where they kept him until July of 1866 when his weight had returned to an acceptable hundred and fifty-two pounds, which was still almost fifty pounds less than he had weighed when he enlisted. He was discharged from the army on the 17th of that month and given a steamer ticket to Davenport, Iowa.

CHAPTER 1

May 13, 1867
Davenport, Iowa

"Papa, it'll be all right."

"Sam, your home is here," his father argued, knowing that it was probably futile.

"I know that, Papa, but I don't fit in anymore. I feel like it's a different world now."

"Give it some time, Sam. You haven't even been back home for a year."

"Papa, for the entire time I was away, I dreamed about coming back home. We all did. Each one of us believed that when the war was over, we'd return to our homes and everything would be perfect. I'd marry Barbara Jean, we'd have children, and I'd get to eat mama's wonderful cooking. But I learned soon enough that things aren't ever the same. For almost four years while I was away, I imagined perfection, but that's not possible. It's not fair to expect it really, but it still eats at you."

"Sam, don't go getting upset about Barbara Jean now."

"No, Papa, I'm not in the least upset. She and Frank are married, and that's the end of it, but that's not why I'm leaving. I just don't belong here anymore. I'm a misfit."

Earl Walker sighed. He hated to admit it, but Sam was right. He really was different now. When he had first returned to the family farm, they had all been shocked by his appearance. His six-foot-two frame was like a rail and he weighed around a hundred and fifty pounds. At first his mother had tried to shovel the food into him, but it had made him sick. It took six months to get him to his normal weight of around two hundred pounds, but it wasn't just the lack of weight that had made him different. He seemed out of place and distant. He would sit and just stare toward the horizon as if he was expecting someone.

Sam still worked around the farm once he could physically handle it, but his heart just wasn't in it anymore. When he was a teenager, he'd worked with enthusiasm and even joy, but now it seemed like drudge work to him.

"You're still planning on going down to Texas?" his father asked.

Sam nodded and replied, "I promised Joe I'd make sure his wife and daughter were being taken care of. He had a brother and a sister, so their ranch should be fine, but I promised. I don't know what else to do anyway, so maybe I'll find out down there."

"How will you get there? It's a long way."

"It's not bad, really. I'll take a steamboat down the Mississippi to Columbia, Arkansas, and then ride across Arkansas and a few miles of Texas. It'll only take a week or so."

"Why don't you take the train? It's faster and can get you closer."

"It's a way of honoring a friend. Joe had ridden from Texas, crossed Arkansas and took the steamboat to Davenport. It's kind of going home for him because he never had the chance."

"Do you have enough money?"

"Yes, sir. I've still got all that army back pay they owed me for the time I was in prison and then in the hospital. That, plus what I've saved in the last year gives me over five hundred dollars."

"Well, if you need any more, send me a telegram."

"Yes, sir."

Earl stood up and shook his son's hand, then said, "Sam, if you ever start to feel like you can come home again, please come back. Your mother will miss you something fierce."

"I know, Papa."

Father and son left the sitting room and walked to the kitchen, where Rose and Anna Walker were cooking dinner.

"I don't suppose you were able to talk him out of it, were you?" asked Rose.

"No, Rose. I couldn't. If you couldn't, what chance did I have?"

"Papa, Sam will be all right. Won't you, Sam?" asked Anna, her blue eyes sparkling as she looked at her older brother.

Anna was Sam's biggest heartache about leaving the farm. His only sister had been the focus of his young life, even while he was visiting Barbara Jean. Now that Barbara Jean had married his older brother, she was all that he had in the way of female companionship.

"I'll be fine, Anna," he said as he grinned at her.

"You sure have enough guns."

"I sure hope so."

"Why so many, Sam?" asked Rose.

"Well, I bought the Spencer and the two Colt pistols from army surplus. The pistols take a while to reload, so I bought the spare. The Winchester is brand new and it's a lot better than the Henry. It's always a good idea to have too many than not enough, Mama."

"You sure have been scaring the cows with all that practicing, Sam," Anna said.

"I didn't see any milk falloff, though. The chickens all seemed to be pouring out the eggs, too."

"You never did let me shoot one of those pistols either," complained Anna.

"Anna, it was only because I didn't want you to make me feel bad by shooting better than I could."

She smiled at Sam, then quickly changed to a more solemn visage as she said, "I'm going to miss having you around, Sam."

Sam stepped close, gave his sister a hug then kissed her on the top of her head.

"You'll stop missing me when one of those boys who have been hanging around the house wins you, Anna."

"One may win me, Sam, but you'll always be the first one in my heart."

"And you'll be in mine, Anna."

He didn't doubt that Anna would be married soon. She had stunned Sam when he had returned. When he had gone, she was still a skinny girl with ribbons around her pigtails and freckles on her face. When he had walked in the door, he didn't know who she was at first until he saw those same smiling blue eyes. She had developed into a pretty young woman with long brown hair and a way about her that marked her as special.

Rose had dinner ready, so they all sat down and had their last dinner as a family. Frank and Barbara Jean lived on the farm, but in their own house that their father had built when they had gotten married two years earlier.

Sam still remembered the letter from his mother telling him of their wedding and had been surprised that it hadn't bothered him that much. At the time he was much more concerned about Joe Farrell's death and about food. Even when he saw them together for the first time, it hadn't upset him at all. He had wished them well, but he felt that they both were uncomfortable with his presence. It was one of the many reasons he felt out of place on the farm. Frank still worked the farm with his father, and they had two other full-time hands as well. It was a prosperous farm.

After dinner, Sam and his father walked to the sitting room again where he asked, "Do you need anything else, Sam?"

"I don't think so, Papa. The steamer leaves Davenport at 8:40, so I'll have to leave early to get there. It's a good forty-minute ride."

"Sam, before you go, I have to ask you something. I didn't bring it up because it wasn't my place. But in the year that you've been back, you've never talked about that camp. Why is that?"

"I don't know, Papa. I just want to forget it, I guess. But I will tell you one thing. Aside from the lack of food and the disease that was everywhere, what made it all worse was the boredom. If you're hungry or sick and have nothing to do but think about being hungry or sick, it makes time slow down. It made leaving such a thrill because it gave us something to occupy our time other than talking or thinking about food."

His father just nodded, having just a tiny glimpse of how miserable it must have been in that prisoner camp, and that was after years of war and horrible battles. He wished that he could help his son but understood that any help had to come from himself.

————

Sam was up when the first rooster announced the sun's arrival and had already packed what he needed. His horse, a light-reddish-brown gelding named Rusty, was in the barn with his Spencer and Winchester already in their scabbards. He had his first saddlebag packed with nothing but ammunition. When he had bought the Spencer, he had bought ten boxes of ammunition as well. It hadn't cost much. The cartridges were ten cents a box and the Spencer was seven dollars. The Winchester though, had set him back twenty-four dollars, and the six boxes of ammunition were another three dollars. He had purchased the two Colt New Army pistols for five dollars each from the army. Like the Spencer, neither had ever been fired. He had bought a large pouch of paper cartridges and percussion caps for the pistols. He also had a flask and two pounds of powder as well, but the paper cartridges made loading faster. After the cleaning kits had been added, the saddlebags were full and heavy as sin.

He packed a second set of saddlebags with his spare Colt pistol, extra clothing, his shaving kit, some soap, a sewing kit, a hairbrush, a toothbrush and powder, and two towels. He wouldn't worry about food until he got to Columbia. He had $455 in his money belt but kept the rest in different pockets. He had already bought his ticket on the *Northern Swan* to Columbia and had his assigned cabin.

He finished dressing and put his gunbelt on but wasn't wearing a hat. The only hats available in town would have marked him as a Yankee, and he'd rather go bareheaded than let the still angry Southerners think he was a carpetbagger.

He walked out of his room wondering if he'd ever see it again and found Anna waiting for him in the hallway. She took his arm as he walked to the kitchen but didn't say anything.

Sam was surprised to see Barbara Jean and Frank sitting at the table with his parents as they entered the kitchen.

"Morning, Frank and Barbara Jean. How are you?"

"We're fine. Didn't think we'd let you leave without saying goodbye, did you?" Frank asked with a smile.

Sam returned the smile and said, "I appreciate it, Frank," but noticed that Barbara Jean wasn't smiling.

Barbara Jean Ledbetter had been his girlfriend since they were thirteen. She was tall, even at that age, and had finally

19

topped out at five foot nine, just an inch under Frank's height. She was always the most vivacious, lively member of the class and when she blossomed into a frighteningly pretty young woman, the other boys would watch Sam enviously.

But after Sam had gone off to war, she had become lonelier than she had expected, and when Sam had been listed as missing, she didn't waste much time in setting her cap for Frank. Frank was like a slightly shrunken version of Sam. Handsome and smart, Frank had his pick of the young women, especially after so many men had gone off to war, but it had been Barbara Jean whom he had chosen.

For obvious reasons, he never had confided in Sam about his desires for Barbara Jean while he was on the farm. But once Sam was no longer a competitor, Frank had stepped in and courted Barbara Jean, marrying her just a few months after Sam had been declared missing.

Even after his parents had received a letter from Sam saying he was a prisoner, Frank didn't feel any remorse for his decision to steal Barbara Jean from his brother. Whether Barbara Jean had any regrets no one knew, but a few months after they were wed, Frank did have some regrets.

He discovered that Barbara Jean, the wife, wasn't the same woman as Barbara Jean, the unattached female. Barbara Jean became a bit of a nag and would quickly and pointedly call out his shortcomings or mistakes. His biggest surprise came in the bedroom where he discovered that the vivacious and flirty Barbara Jean was a prude, crushing all of Frank's premarital fantasies.

Sam hadn't known any of this, of course, but it didn't matter. They seemed happy, and he was leaving.

He sat down to breakfast next to Barbara Jean, ironically. She never smiled at him or even said a word to him. She ate her food as Sam chatted with Frank, Anna, and his parents.

After they'd eaten, Sam finished his coffee, stood, then walked to his mother and kissed her on the cheek. He shook his father's and Frank's hands and then leaned over and kissed Barbara Jean on the cheek before he set his empty cup down in the sink and turned to Anna.

He wrapped her in a giant hug and kissed her softly on her forehead as he said softly, "I'll write to you, Anna. Don't write back until I have my address."

Anna nodded and wiped the tears from her eyes as she tried to force a smile that she didn't feel.

Sam released his sister, pulled his second set of saddlebags off the floor, and hung them over his shoulder.

He then turned to his brother, grinned and with no ill intent, said, "Frank, let me know when I'm an uncle."

Frank turned red and nodded before Sam left the kitchen heading for the barn where he saddled Rusty and put both set of saddlebags in place. He led Rusty out of the barn, mounted and waved at the family, who were standing on the back porch. They waved in return, and Sam rode out of the farm heading east toward Davenport and the beginning of a journey with an unknown purpose.

He arrived at the dock of the *Northern Swan* in plenty of time and led Rusty on board, where he was directed to the livestock area. He pulled the Spencer, Winchester and both saddlebags from Rusty and headed for cabin eleven where he soon reached his temporary lodging, opened the door and smiled. He'd barely fit in the small room, but it didn't matter.

He set both saddlebags and both long guns in the corner, then took a deep breath and briefly thought about the upcoming journey to Texas before he turned to tour the boat. He had been issued a key when he bought the ticket, so he locked the door and began to explore the boat. The last time he had ridden on a stern-wheeler was when he had left the prison. The Confederates had transported the exchanged prisoners by wagon to the Mississippi. Once they were in the control of Union doctors, they had been fed enough to satisfy their hunger, but nothing more. The medical corps had learned from experience that letting the emaciated men from other prison camps eat as much as they wanted was a mistake. They had to reintroduce their systems to food gradually.

The ride up the Mississippi had been on the overcrowded *Mississippi Rambler*, which had broken down twice. The trip took six days, but this part of his trip should be much shorter, but even the cross-country trip to Texas shouldn't be nearly as long as the one he'd taken when he last saw the state because he'd be riding his horse, not sitting in a slow-moving wagon with a bunch of other filthy, half-starved men.

Sam walked around the upper deck and stopped at the bow, gazing down the wide Mississippi as it flowed south eventually reaching the Gulf of Mexico.

"Looks nice and wide, don't it?" asked a gruff voice behind him.

Sam turned to see the captain standing behind him, his hands clasped behind his back.

"Yes, sir. It does. But I have a feeling that there are a few hazards out there," he replied with a grin.

"That's a fact, son. Every twist and turn in that watery snake has sandbars, logs, rocks, and all sorts of things that can keep me up nights, but I know most of 'em, and the ones that I don't, the pilot does. That river is sneaky, though. It'll change things, and if a captain gets too uppity, the river will take him down a peg mighty fast."

"That's why riverboat captains are famous and train engineers aren't."

The captain cracked a broad smile before he said, "Aye. That's true. Any moron can sit in one of those steaming monsters and make it follow those steel guides. Where are you headed, son?"

"Down to Columbia, and then I'll be riding across Arkansas to Mulberry, Texas."

"There are a lot of unsavory sort down there, so you'd better keep your powder dry."

"I plan to."

"You any good with that Colt?"

"I'm better than most, but I'm a lot better with the rifle, though."

"Don't trust anybody."

"I appreciate the information, Captain."

"You're welcome, young feller. Well, I'd better get this boat ready to go."

He waved and returned to his bridge and Sam noticed that smoke had started pouring out of the two stacks as the fire was building up in the boiler.

He left the bow and headed around the other side of the deck to watch the crew cast off as other passengers were doing the same. The passengers were almost exclusively men; the only two women he noticed seemed to be farm wives. If he had a hat, he would have tipped it to them as he passed, but instead, he just nodded and passed a pleasant, 'good morning'. He also noticed that he was one of the few men who carried a pistol, which surprised him.

Sam walked down the starboard stairway, reached the lower deck then walked to the first door and checked out the large dining room that would convert to a floating saloon when meals weren't being served.

As he explored the vessel, he began to review his upcoming journey. He'd be riding about two hundred plus miles once he left the boat. That would take him about five days if he kept a decent pace. He'd pick up some food in Columbia but wouldn't be making any fires on the rest of his ride. He had his bedroll and a slicker and would stop in towns for most nights.

Twenty minutes later, the lines were cast off, the paddles began turning, and the *Northern Swan* began to creep away from the dock. After another ten minutes, the boat was making good time going downriver.

Sam stayed on deck and watched the scenery slide along on both banks. A few people came to the banks to watch the boat pass and waved, so he smiled and waved back. Most of the folks seemed to be farmers, as he had been before he had enlisted. As he watched them fade behind the boat, he wondered what he was now. He wasn't a farmer, nor was he a soldier or a prisoner or patient. *What was he?*

————

Around noon he walked into the dining room, found an empty table and took a seat. He didn't have to order anything, as they only made one meal, so just a minute after sitting down, he was brought a plate of roast beef and boiled potatoes. He finished his lunch before most of the passengers arrived to eat, then stood, left the table and returned to his cabin, where he laid down on his bed to relax, but the monotonous thrumming of the steam engine coupled with the rolling of the boat soon lulled him to sleep.

When he awakened, he was initially confused, then remembered where he was, before he pulled out his pocket watch and found that it was 2:35. Well, he wanted to keep a low profile while on the boat, and you can't get any lower profile than staying in the cabin and sleeping.

He stood, stretched, then opened the door getting blasted by the bright sunshine. It wasn't as warm as he expected for May, but it was still comfortable. He guessed that the sternwheeler was making around seven knots, so they were about fifty miles from Davenport with only another six hundred and fifty miles to go on the Mississippi, all of it south. It would be warmer by the time he reached Columbia though, and including stops, they should arrive in three days.

Sam left his room and locked the door behind him, leaving his gunbelt with his other weapons so he would blend in better.

Sam became comfortable on the steamboat that day, and it stayed routine until the boat docked at Saint Louis the following afternoon.

He was leaning on the second-deck railing watching passengers, cargo, and livestock leave the boat, then followed the loading of coal and supplies on board before allowing oncoming passengers to cross the gangplank.

Sam noticed a significant improvement in the number of gentry in this group compared to previous stops. They were probably heading to New Orleans and guessed that the saloon would become much more crowded and that the previously rarely used poker tables would be filled. In addition to the higher class of the passengers, there were also several attractive women being escorted on board by well-dressed gentlemen.

The boat pulled away from Saint Louis in mid-afternoon and resumed its southern journey. Sam stayed in his cabin but was treated to the sounds of occupation on both sides of the thin walls and wondered if those sounds would be more animated at night.

Sam left his room at five o'clock to have an early dinner to beat the crowds. When he arrived at the dining room, he was surprised to see that many of the others had the same idea, and he had to wait for an open table. He still managed to leave the dining room by six o'clock, well before the late-supper crowd. Those were the folks that would stay in the room and gamble and drink, two vices that Sam felt were a waste of money and time.

———

The next morning, Sam was standing on the stern rail of the upper deck, almost hypnotized by the turning of the paddle wheel churning the Mississippi and the water cascading back down like miniature waterfalls. He noticed a couple standing almost directly below him and shifted his attention to watch.

The lady was a very handsome woman in her upper twenties, he guessed, of medium height with blonde hair and a full figure. The man she was pointedly arguing with was a few years older than she was and he was curious about their relationship. He only caught snippets of the dispute, and they didn't make much sense.

The man pointed his finger just inches from her face and said, "I'll pick him."

Then she angrily replied, "You didn't do so well last time."

The man put an end to the argument with a stern, "I'm sure of this one, and that's all I want to hear."

Sam turned and left the stern, not wanting to be noticed for some reason, then headed for the bow of the boat as the sun set. He stayed on the bow for almost an hour before stretching and deciding to go and visit Rusty. He had an apple in his pocket that he had saved for him.

He jogged down the port staircase and entered the livestock deck where h found Rusty looking at him as he pulled out his pocketknife and cut the apple in two, handing one half to his horse.

He rubbed Rusty's neck as he fed him the second half of the apple.

"Just two more days, Rusty, then we'll be heading west to Texas. You can use up some of that fat you've been adding just standing around."

Sam checked his watch again and decided to go and have a beer before turning in. He may not drink heavily, but a nice cold beer sure sounded good right about now.

He left the livestock deck and headed for the other crowded area on the boat, only with people and no critters. After reaching the saloon, he entered the doors to the steady cacophony of conversation, glasses clinking, and chips being tossed onto tables. He thought about just turning around and heading back to his room, but the desire for that cold brew was too strong, so he headed for the long, dark bar at the other end of the dining room.

He arrived and made eye contact with the bartender, ordered a beer and exchanged a nickel for his sudsy mug. He turned with the heavy glass in his right hand and put his back against the bar as he studied humanity in motion as they fought to lose their money. There were six poker games going, with a few observers standing nearby, a roulette table and a spinning wheel of chance.

He sipped his beer and noticed the woman who had been arguing with the man on the stern earlier and, aside from the fact that she was worth watching, he was curious about what she and her male companion had been discussing. She was standing at the side of a poker player with her hand on a man's shoulder, but he wasn't the same man from the argument.

Sam spotted that man at another table, which struck him as odd. There were three other women in the room. Women, as a rule, weren't allowed in saloons, but he guessed that riverboat dining rooms that converted to saloons were an exception.

He was impressed with the woman. She was wearing a low-cut dress, showing more cleavage than would be considered acceptable in the streets of Saint Louis. Sam enjoyed the show as he continued to sip his cold beer and was almost finished when the woman leaned over, giving Sam an even better night's entertainment, and whispered something to the poker player, who turned suddenly to her and smiled. Then he tossed his cards down and picked up his chips.

The blonde hooked her arm through his, and they walked to the cashier where the man cashed in his chips and stuffed the bills in his pocket.

Sam smiled, knowing what was going on. He had never witnessed it, of course, but one of the officers in his regiment had told the story of a woman suggesting a quick romp on a riverboat and letting the man take her to his cabin. After getting her partially undressed, her enraged 'husband' would magically know where she was, barge into the room and accuse the man of adultery and demand satisfaction. The patsy would offer a monetary substitution for either an arrest or a duel and the offended 'husband' would sullenly accept his money to soothe his honor. Sam was enjoying himself. This was the only fun he'd had on the trip so far.

The well-endowed woman was giggling as she and her victim left the saloon. Sam finished his beer, waited a few seconds, crossed the floor, then stepped up the starboard stairs behind them as the man and woman reached the second deck. Sam made note of the patsy's room, number thirteen, which was just two doors down from his own cabin.

He unlocked his door, then stepped inside leaving his door partially open and pulled on his gunbelt. It was difficult to avoid hearing the opening round of the wrestling match two doors down as he sat on his bed and waited.

The noise from the cabin was surprisingly loud but was suddenly joined by the staccato sound of rapid footsteps pounding up the starboard stairway.

Sam was almost laughing as he listened to the offended fake husband's arrival. He saw the shadow of the man pass by his doorway and stood but stayed in his cabin until the drama played out in room thirteen.

He listened as the door to the very occupied cabin was yanked open, which was then followed by a loud gasp of surprise and the expected cry, "It's my husband!"

Sam had to restrain his laughter at the terrible acting but knew that it was far from a charade to the victim.

He heard the wounded husband shout, "How dare you, sir!", which was followed by loud defensive cries of, "Wait! Wait! I didn't do anything!"

Sam had heard enough, so he took two steps out of his cabin and turned right where he saw the man still pointing into the cabin.

"What's going on here?" Sam asked loudly.

The 'husband' turned to Sam and was momentarily stunned, but then recovered, pointed into cabin thirteen and loudly replied, "This man has assaulted my wife and I demand satisfaction."

Sam stepped over to cabin thirteen, then glanced past the still-pointing man. If he'd been entertained before, this was act three and there was lot of soft skin on display.

Sam pulled out his pistol, which startled the 'husband', then Sam looked at the partially undressed gentleman in the room and asked, "Well, John, did you want me to arrest them or did you want to handle it?"

The man outside the cabin was confused as he turned to look at Sam and asked, "What are you talking about? That man is the adulterer! He needs to be arrested."

Sam pointed at the victim and said, "That man, sir, is Special Agent John Hopkins of the Pinkerton Detective Agency. I'm

Sam Johnson. We've been assigned to find the team pulling this scam on passengers and it looks as if we've got them. John, did you want to bust 'em?"

Luckily for Sam, the half-dressed man was quick to pick up on Sam's playacting, then nonchalantly pulled up his trousers, stood and replied, "I'll take care of it, Sam. Thanks for backing me up. Did you get anything else?"

"I sure did. I heard these two arguing a little while ago. She was mad because he picked the wrong victim the last time that they played their little game. He said he had picked the right one this time and to shut up," then Sam grinned and asked, "I guess he picked wrong again, didn't he?"

"He sure did," the victim said with a laugh, "Let me get my cuffs."

The 'husband' made a quick evaluation of the sudden shift in his situation, then suddenly burst into a dead run to the starboard stairs and raced down the steps so quickly that Sam thought he was going to take a nosedive onto the lower deck.

"Halt!" Sam shouted, and pointed his pistol at the quickly descending scam artist but didn't bother to pull the hammer back.

Sam watched as he raced along the deck, leapt from the side of the boat, and splashed into the Mississippi, disappearing beneath the brown, swirling water.

"Do you have any idea where we are?" Sam asked as he turned to face the victim.

"Not a clue. Who are you, anyway?" he asked.

"Sam Walker."

"You aren't really a Pinkerton, are you?"

"No. I was a farmer until a couple of days ago and a soldier before that."

The still semi-dressed woman looked at Sam with a stunned look on her face, so Sam looked at her and smiled as he said, "Sorry."

Then she surprised them both by bursting into laughter. After he recovered from her reaction, he began to laugh as well, and soon all three were raucously laughing at the sight of the man's hasty departure from the steamboat.

When Sam finally slowed down, he said, "Ma'am, you might want to get dressed before someone gets the wrong idea of your profession."

She started laughing harder and Sam watched her, amazed with her reaction but still enjoying the show.

When everything had calmed down, the woman finally began pulling her clothes back on as neither man could resist watching the closing act. She didn't seem to mind at all.

When she was decently dressed again, or as decently as she could be in the clothing she was wearing, she asked, "So what happens to me now?"

Sam looked at the victim, and said, "That's up to Mister...I never did get your name."

"Henry Washington. I live in New Orleans. I'm a cotton broker."

"Well, Mister Washington, it's up to you what happens to the young lady."

Henry looked at her and asked, "Tell me how you got into this scam."

She was still buttoning her dress as she replied, "I was a prostitute in Saint Louis, and the man who just jumped into the river, Freddie Custer, was our minder. He kept us from leaving and seeking business on our own. He decided to branch out into this line of work, and he chose me to be one half. I think he did it just so he could enjoy my services as his make-believe wife. I

31

don't have much money, so I could just go back to Saint Louis, or maybe I could work in New Orleans."

"Do you like doing that?" he asked.

"Would you? Until a year and a half ago, I was the wife of a dock worker. We didn't have much money, but a lot of folks were worse off than we were. We ate regular and had a roof over our heads. Then he missed a footstep going over to the boat on the plank with a load and dropped straight into the river. He couldn't swim and was swept downriver by the current. I lasted six months on food brought in by the landlord. You can guess how I had to pay him. Then his wife found out about the arrangement, and I was tossed out. That's when Freddie found me and put me to work, first in the brothel and then, after six months, doing this."

Sam wished he could help, but this wasn't his decision.

"What's your name?" asked Henry Washington.

"My real name is Elizabeth Taggart."

"Elizabeth, let me ask you something. Do you want to come down to New Orleans and stay with me for a while until you can make up your mind about what you want to do?"

She smiled and replied, "Does that mean I have to keep pretending to be a wife?"

"No, not at all. I find you to be a very interesting person. When you laughed at the situation, I was surprised because I thought it was funny too, but thought you would be outraged."

Sam saw no reason to stay, so he turned to go back to his room.

Henry saw him leaving and just said, "Thanks, Sam. I owe you."

Sam waved, entered his room, closed the door and kicked off his boots. As he stretched out on his bunk, he thought it had been a very interesting evening. He heard the door to cabin thirteen close and a few minutes later, round two of the interrupted wrestling match began. He was reasonably sure that it wasn't an act this time, especially after hearing the continued loud cries to the deity echo through his room.

———

The rest of the river journey was uneventful. Sam bumped into Henry and Elizabeth fairly often and found them behaving like newlyweds. *Who knew what their real status was?* Maybe the captain had performed an impromptu wedding ceremony, but he doubted it. He was curious if anything real came of it after they reached New Orleans. As far as he knew, Henry could be married with eleven children waiting for him. Even if he wasn't married, bringing a former prostitute to your home might be frowned upon, unless no one knew her past.

———

On the morning of the fourth day, Sam knew that Columbia, Arkansas, was only a few miles away, so he began packing his things. His door was partially open when he heard a light knock.

He swung the door open the rest of the way, smiled and said, "Good morning, Henry, Elizabeth. Going to breakfast?"

"In a few minutes. You'll be leaving the boat at Columbia?"

"Yep. I have a long ride ahead."

"Sam, we both owe you a lot for your help that night."

"It was kind of fun, really. No offense, Elizabeth."

She smiled and replied, "None taken."

Henry then said, "Now, I cashed in all my chips last night, Sam, and I figure I owe you some of the winnings."

"I'm all right for money, Henry."

"I'm sure you are, but it never hurts to have a little more. I would be insulted if you didn't accept this. Realize it's not costing me a penny. This is all courtesy of the bad poker players on the boat."

"Well, in that case, I won't feel so bad."

Henry handed him an envelope, and Sam just slid it into his pocket before Henry shook his hand as Elizabeth opened her purse. Sam thought she was going to give him more money, but he was wrong.

"Freddie gave this to me last month to make sure that the victim paid. I don't need it anymore, so I want you to have it," she said as she handed him a Remington derringer.

"That's a nice little gun," Sam said as he accepted the small pistol.

"And here's the ammunition he left in the cabin," she said, giving him a box of .41-caliber rimfire cartridges.

"Thank you, Elizabeth. This may come in handy."

"I hope it doesn't come down to it, Sam," she said before leaning forward and kissing Sam on the cheek.

"Thank you, Sam," she said as she smiled.

Henry and Elizabeth then turned and walked arm-in-arm down the stairs as Sam returned to his cabin and closed the door. He opened the envelope and pulled out the cash, then whistled. That must have been some high-stakes poker game. There was $1,250 in the envelope, so he quickly moved it into his money belt, wondering if Henry had been honest about it all being poker winnings. He doubted it but knew that he'd be insulting Henry if he had asked. Besides, if he could afford it, maybe it really didn't matter to him, but having that much more money gave him a lot more options.

He then checked the derringer, found that it was loaded, so he slipped it into his pants pocket and added the box of cartridges to his ammunition bag.

He left everything in his cabin and walked downstairs to have his last breakfast on the river.

An hour and a half later, he was standing on the dock holding Rusty's reins and waving goodbye to Henry and Elizabeth as the boat began pulling out of Columbia.

He watched the boat until it made a turn a couple of miles south, then mounted Rusty and rode into town. He'd need some supplies before he headed west, so he stopped at the dry goods store and bought some jerky, dried beef, hard tack, and a compass so he wouldn't go astray. After paying for the order, he asked the proprietor if the road went straight across Arkansas to the Texas border and was assured that it did. It wasn't much of a roadway, really, but it was a path that he could follow.

Sam had been expecting some hostility from the folks in Arkansas so soon after an unsettled peace had been reached. Things were still very tense as Northerners had been drifting down into the South to either help them rebuild or take advantage of depressed land prices. But the storekeeper didn't seem to hold a grudge, especially when Sam paid in very welcome greenbacks.

Sam loaded his supplies on an overloaded Rusty, mounted, then turned west on the crude roadway, knowing he had a long ride ahead and not having a clue what awaited him at the end other than Texas.

CHAPTER 2

Sam left Columbia shortly after ten o'clock in the morning and knew that he should have stayed around for lunch at a café but wanted to get on the road. Besides, he had eaten a good breakfast on the boat.

As he rode, he scanned his surroundings and evaluated the soil as all farmers did without even realizing it. It was good in some areas and too much clay in others. It was pretty country though, with a lot of pines and hills. The road actually worsened after he left town, but it gave him direction. He verified the direction with his compass and found it was usually due west as advertised but would sometimes dip southwest.

He was making good time and hoped to get to Hamburg before sundown, then Eldorado, Calhoun and Lewisville, and then he'd be in Texas. There were quite a few streams and creeks to cross, and then there was the Red River, his only real obstacle on his route as all the swamps were farther north. That didn't mean that the mosquitoes and other bugs weren't here though, and he soon found them already happily willing to accompany him on his journey. He assumed there would be a ferry across the Red if he stayed on the roadway.

The journey through Texas would include Boston, Clarksville, Paris, and then Bonham. He might make it sooner if he decided to stretch his rides and would need to get Rusty reshod again somewhere along the way, but Sam felt as if he was almost there. Just a few hundred miles of country full of folks that were still a tad hostile to Northerners. Luckily, Sam had spent so much time with Joe that he could mimic his mild Texas twang and his manner of speech.

Sam smiled as he recalled how Joe would fail miserably at trying to copy his nonaccented Iowa speech patterns. He missed Joe. For four years they had shared the same tent, meals, and stories. He would talk of Julia, and Sam would talk of Barbara Jean and Anna and Joe would give him grief for talking about his sister as much as he did his girlfriend.

Joe had died before Sam got the letter about Barbara Jean's marriage to Frank. It wasn't unusual to get letters a few months old as they had to be censored, rerouted and exchanged under a flag of truce. But each envelope from home was gratefully accepted and read so often that the paper usually failed within days. He wondered if Joe would have used that letter to extoll the virtues of his sister, Mary. He had done that enough as it was but had never said what she looked like. But then again, he had no idea how much Anna had changed while he was gone, either.

Joe had made Julia sound like she was Venus, or at the least Helen of Troy. Of course, Sam had done the same for Barbara Jean. After they had been in prison camp for a month, their topics still included their women, but to a much lower degree. The longer they had been there, the more they had talked of food and of the much-anticipated return home; a return home that meant food in their bellies.

Joe had one other worry that Sam hadn't had. His home was in the South and he didn't know what to expect when he finally returned to the ranch he'd left behind. Granted, Texas wouldn't be as hard hit as the Deep South, but it would be subject to a measure of devastation. Despite Joe having served in the Union army, he expected to find problems at home, not all of which were Yankee related. Many of his neighbors had expressed their displeasure at his departure to join the Union forces, but he hadn't expected them to really do anything about it other than to make noise.

This trip down the Mississippi, across Arkansas and East Texas, was as much about Joe as it was about Sam's restlessness. Joe was more of a brother to him than Sam's own brother.

Sam was still angered that despite the two of them surviving all those battles with nothing more than minor wounds, his best friend had died while waiting to go home. It was just six months after Joe's death when Sam had been exchanged and he still felt almost guilty for everything that had happened to his best friend.

Sam was a rarity among the prisoners as he had never contracted any of the diseases that dominated everyday life in the camp. Disease was the big killer, even in their army camps. They lost almost ten times as many men from disease as from enemy fire, but neither he nor Joe had had anything more than a passing cold or a bad case of the trots until they had been captured. They had been together for four years and just when it looked like they'd be heading home, Joe had died. It wasn't fair and Sam sometimes wished that he had died, so Joe could reach home to his wife and unseen daughter and enjoy one of his mother's pecan pies.

Sam was wrapped up in his thoughts of Joe and had been drifting when he snapped back into an alert state, knowing what a mistake it was to start woolgathering. Out here on the roads, there were ex-Confederate soldiers who were desperate to make a living and the only way some found was to prey on travelers like him. Sam couldn't afford to let himself drift like that again and quickly scanned his environment and his back trail. It was all clear at the moment, but he was still angry with himself.

He pulled over around noon and let Rusty graze and water, while he had some smoked beef, hard tack, and water. Twenty minutes later, he was back on the road.

THE SCALAWAGS

Sam reached Hamburg well before sunset, arriving around four o'clock, left Rusty at the livery and asked to have his shoes checked. He left the livery taking his rifles and saddlebags to the hotel where he checked in and was given a key. It was a small thing, but he felt better being able to lock his door. He left all his things in the room then left the hotel to find someplace to eat, which wasn't difficult. He found a decent diner and had a filling dinner. He wasn't quite sure if it was rabbit or possum, but it tasted good.

––––––

Early the next morning, he returned to the diner and had a more standard breakfast of bacon and eggs that arrived with a helping of grits. He tried them and decided he'd pass.

He was on the road with a newly shod Rusty shortly after breakfast. When he left Hamburg, he noticed that three men had seemed to take interest in his departure, but he kept a good pace and hoped that he'd build up such a gap that there wouldn't be any trouble.

Sam checked his backtrail every ten minutes or so and began to relax after an hour. He continued to ride, and late in the morning he picked up riders behind him. *How had they gained on him when he was keeping a good pace?* He estimated that they were two miles back and gave a brief thought of setting a harder pace to see if they'd still follow but knew that Rusty had endured a full day's ride yesterday and didn't want to push him that hard. But he needed to get away from those men and needed to do it quickly or he'd never even see Texas.

Sam began looking for someplace to hide. There were plenty of trees, so that would be his best bet, but he wanted a curve so he could just disappear and for once, luck was against him. There had been curves galore until he needed one. He checked on the approaching riders again and saw that they had gained on him even more. *How was that even possible?*

39

Sam had no choice now, so he nudged Rusty up to a fast trot, and when he found a good spot, turned quickly to his right and fifty yards later rode into the trees.

————

Behind him, John Everlast, Jake Warton, and Dennis Flaherty saw Sam make his turn into the trees.

"We got him now, Jake!" shouted John.

"I don't like this one, Jake," yelled Dennis, "That boy had too many guns."

"He can only fire one at a time, Denny. We've got three, we know the territory, and he doesn't."

Dennis shook his head. He had a bad feeling about this but neither of the others seemed to share his concerns. None of them had taken a good look at the guns he was carrying when he was in town. They saw the stocks sitting in the scabbards and his pistol on his waist, but none of them knew about the Winchester.

They each had a pistol, and Jake had a Spencer. The one thing they did know was that their horses were all better than what he was riding. After the war, they had been returning to Arkansas when they had come across an untouched horse ranch in southern Missouri that was tucked away in the Ozarks and had good stock. They had liberated three of the animals and two saddles. so Dennis had had to ride bareback until he could steal a saddle from a nearby farm. It wasn't a great saddle, but it was the best he could do.

But the horses had served them well. They'd been able to run down several travelers who'd thought they were safe once they left the town. Travelers were good picking because nobody noticed when they went missing.

After entering the trees, Sam began scanning for someplace to hide Rusty and didn't have to look long. There was a hollow

40

not a half mile into the forest, so he stepped Rusty into the depression, dismounted, hitched him to a small shrub, then grabbed the Winchester and opened up the saddlebag with the ammunition and took out a box of the rimfire .44 cartridges. He emptied the box into his two jacket pockets and crawled up the side of the hollow, then reached the edge and waited. The trees posed a problem. If he shot one of his pursuers, the other two could just stay behind trees and keep him pinned down, so he had to come up with some way to bring them closer.

After a minute of thought, he left the Winchester where it was and slid back down the hollow to the bottom, pulled the Spencer out of its scabbard, then climbed the bank to the rim of the hollow again, about twenty feet from the Winchester. He left the Spencer on the edge and returned to the Winchester, cocked the Winchester's hammer and slid it down from the edge just a few feet and left it with its muzzle just a foot from the top of the hollow. The Yellowboy would be his ace in the hole. He returned to the Spencer and quickly cocked its hammer, then waited for the three riders.

The three highwaymen easily found Sam's tracks where he had entered the woods but stopped short of the trees and tied off their horses on branches. Jake pulled out his Spencer, while John and Jake drew their pistols. They all cocked their weapons at the same time, making a combined loud click.

Sam had heard their horses' hoofbeats and knew they were there. When he first spotted them, he'd fire the Spencer once and then slide down and cross over to the Winchester. If he was lucky, he'd be able to get a clean shot at the second one. The third one would be iffy. He didn't know what they had for firepower either.

The three men spread apart as they followed Sam's trail and Sam caught quick views of two of them, knowing that the third one couldn't be far off. The next question was who would fire first. Sam didn't want to waste a shot in warning. If he shot, it would be to kill as it had to be. *But how to get them to open fire without exposing himself?*

Jake was getting nervous as he usually did when they were close to their target. He was in the center, about three hundred yards from Sam.

"What if he kept riding through, and he's back on the road?" Jake asked Dennis.

"He didn't. He's in there. He'd have risked us seein' him if he tried to get back to the road."

In the silence of the forest, Sam heard the short conversation and while he didn't know what they said, he knew they were close. He got glimpses of one or the other as they passed through gaps in the trees and was still debating about warning them to back off. He doubted if it would have any impact on them and knew it would give his position away. Then he smiled at the realization that it would most assuredly give his position away.

He waited another minute and then shouted, "I know you're out there. You'd best leave. I don't want to kill all of you!"

Jake jerked in surprise, as did John and Dennis. They were about fifty yards out, and the shout startled them. Victims didn't do that.

"There he is!" John said in a normal voice and raised his pistol.

Jake drew his Spencer level and Dennis followed with his pistol and soon, all three muzzles were pointed at Sam's location.

Sam saw them all aiming at him and ducked as their guns all erupted in flame and smoke. The ground where he had been exploded in dirt and dust as he quickly returned, slid his Spencer into position, aimed quickly at Jake and squeezed the trigger. The Spencer rammed against his shoulder, but Sam didn't waste a second waiting to see the results before he slid the Spencer back down the hollow and scrambled across to the Winchester.

Sam's large .56 caliber missile struck Jake low in the right inner thigh, ripping muscle and tissue from his leg as he screamed in pain with blood pouring from his femoral artery.

John and Dennis glanced at Jake and made a huge error in judgement. Instead of returning to safety behind the trees, they let their anger and firm belief in their own invulnerability override any common sense as they screeched a rebel yell and began to run toward Sam.

Sam had reached his Winchester and popped up just as they began to yell. The hairs on the back of his neck stood up and a chill went down his spine at the familiar sound, but it didn't affect his accuracy at all.

John and Dennis had each fired a second round toward where they thought Sam was until they saw movement to their right and began to shift in that direction. They were only thirty yards out when Sam fired his first Winchester round at Dennis. It struck him just below the ribs on the right side and crossed diagonally past his spine and exited his body. He spun once, then twirled to the ground with a loud grunt rather than a scream, then planted his face into the pine-covered Arkansas soil as Sam levered his second round into the chamber.

John fired his third shot at Sam, but his gun's barrel was bouncing as he ran, throwing his shot wildly off target. Sam wasn't running and placed his sights on the oncoming shooter before he fired his second and final round into John's chest, smashing through his heart and left lung. He hit the ground just twelve feet from Sam then slid to a stop as his life's blood pumped into the dark earth.

Sam turned and vomited down the hollow at the sight. There had been no need for this, none whatsoever. If those three had asked for some money, he would have given them some, but they had to try to kill him. This hadn't even been hard for him to do. It was like target practice, only easier. They had almost run into those bullets and the too-recent memory disgusted him.

He slid back down the hollow and took his canteen to wash the foul taste from his mouth. He had killed before on the battlefield, and he hadn't reacted this way. *What was different about this one?* They had fired first and attacked. *Was it because he was so much better equipped for this fight?* He just didn't know but kept returning to how it was all so unnecessary.

He picked up his Spencer and put both guns back into their scabbards, then led Rusty out of the hollow and wondered what he should do about the bodies. He approached the nearest one first and picked up the dead man's pistol. It was a nice Colt New Army which he shoved back into the man's holster and hooked the hammer loop in place. He did the same for the second man before walking to the first one that he'd shot. The one with the Spencer he wouldn't even examine for the time being. He mounted and rode Rusty out to the trees where he found their horses.

Once he saw them up close, he realized how they had been able to ride him down. They were magnificent animals. He wondered how the men had managed to find such beautiful animals. All three were geldings without brands, so they weren't army horses, not that the army ever gave horses like this to the cavalry. Generals would get horses like these.

He untied the horses and fashioned a trail rope from one of the men's ropes. They all had rope and Sam realized he had missed getting rope in his own fitting out. Well, he had some now, he thought as he stepped back onto Rusty and led the three horses into the woods.

Before putting the bodies on the saddles, he checked their pockets and found that the three men had a total of $6.20 on them, but none was in useless Confederate money which was still in circulation in some parts of the South. Their saddlebags had some spare ammunition but not much and no identification could be found anywhere. It took him half an hour to get the bodies slung over their saddles and tied down before he led the three loaded horses out of the trees just an hour after he had entered them.

He had to get rid of the bodies. Eldorado was next, but it was still another thirty miles away. But one thing he was certain if was there would be a U.S. Army post somewhere before he reached the town. The army was everywhere in the South. He'd passed one post after leaving Columbia and had been surprised that the army would station so many colored troops in the South. He knew that a lot of Southerners deeply resented having their former slaves watching them with rifles in their hands. Maybe that was why they did it. It was like poking a finger in their collective eye. He had been impressed with the troops' discipline and hadn't heard of one incident of colored soldiers taking revenge on their former masters.

He'd never fought with any colored units, but he'd talked to other soldiers who had. Almost universally, he found that they'd been found to be brave and well-disciplined. He wondered if it mattered to the white folks of the South. Most didn't seem to care one way or the other as their lives didn't seem to revolve around issues like slavery. The rebels who he'd talked to couldn't care less about the matter and told him it was only the landed gentry that wanted slavery. He shared some good moments with many of the captured Southern boys, talking about farming.

He rode with his cargo for two more hours before taking a short lunch break. He was moving much slower now because of the cargo.

Forty-five minutes later, he saw an American flag in the distance over a collection of hastily built buildings and knew that it was an army post. Twenty minutes later, he arrived at the post and found a private on guard duty when he pulled to a stop.

"Private, could I speak to the officer of the day?"

The man looked up at Sam and said, "I see you had some trouble."

"These three chased me down into some trees. We had a shootout and they lost."

"You spend time in the blue?"

"Four years with the Iowa Fourteenth, including a year in a rebel prison camp."

"We're supposed to muster out in a couple of months. Follow me."

The private turned and led Sam through a main thoroughfare of sorts to a larger building with a HEADQUARTERS sign hung on the front. Sam stepped down and hitched Rusty to a hitching rail.

The private waited until he neared the building before opening a doorway and Sam followed him inside.

"Captain, this man had a shootout with some highwaymen and brought three bodies in tow."

The captain, who had been writing a report, turned and looked at him, then looked at the soldier and asked, "Excuse me, Private Green, what did you say?"

"This gentleman, who served four years with the Iowa Fourteenth, was waylaid a few miles east of here and has three bodies outside."

"The hell you say! That is good news, Private. Those bastards have been raising hell around here for months."

He stood, looked at Sam and asked, "What happened?"

"Like the private said, sir. I was riding along and picked them up trailing me, so I headed for some trees hoping they'd leave, but they didn't. They came into the trees with guns drawn. I shouted at them to leave, and they opened fire instead. I shot them all. You'll find their wounds in front."

"Why the hell did you shout? Why didn't you just shoot first?"

"I wanted them to shoot first. Once they did, I could shoot them all without having a guilty conscience."

"If they had their guns drawn, you didn't have to wait, but let's go look at them."

The captain walked outside, followed by Sam and Private Green, then when he reached the horses, he examined the three bodies.

"Can I guess that the first one was the leg shot?" he asked as he stared at the massive wound.

"It was. I needed to move to get to my Winchester for the other two."

"How many shots did you take?"

"Three altogether. One with the Spencer and two with the Winchester."

"That's some good shooting."

"It was almost point-blank range, Captain. After I shot the first one, I thought the other two would be smart and head for the trees, but they must have been enraged, because they both screamed the rebel yell and came at me firing their pistols."

"There are a few of them running around, ex-Confederate soldiers with nothing left. There are bigger groups of them back east though and some amount to small armies."

"Well, I've got to be moving on, Captain. Can I leave the bodies here?"

"We'll take care of them. You want their horses and guns? You're entitled to them."

"I'd appreciate it."

"Come and join me for lunch. Private Green, have these bodies removed, put their gunbelts and pistols in their saddlebags and then bring the horses back around."

"Yes, sir."

Sam and the captain went around to the mess tent. It was a bit early for lunch, but the cook made sure that they were fed. Sam found that the captain had been at Shiloh as well, and they discussed that mess and a few other shared army complaints as they ate.

"So where are you headed?" the officer asked after swallowing a healthy bite of steak.

"A town called Mulberry, Texas. My best friend in the army was a Texan named Joe Farrell. He came all the way north to Davenport, Iowa to join up just to keep the Union together. We survived the whole war and got captured at Pleasant Hill, which was another stupid decision. He died in February of '65 and never got to see his little girl. Before he passed away, he asked me to check on them to make sure they were all right. I promised that I would."

"I don't know what it's like in that area, but the whole South is on edge right now. There's a lot of anger under the surface about us Yankees being down here and anger against neighbors that supported the Union like your friend. I hope you find them okay."

"So, do I, Captain. I've got to get going."

"Thanks for clearing up that little mess of ours, Sam."

"Glad it served some use."

They shook hands, and Sam left the mess building and headed for Rusty. The bodies had been removed from the horses, but still had their canteens, ropes, bedrolls, and saddlebags, in addition to the saddles.

Sam stepped up onto Rusty and headed out of the post for Eldorado, trailing three fine geldings behind him.

He arrived at Eldorado shortly after five o'clock. The pace had been slower again, but he stopped at the livery and asked to have the three geldings' shoes checked and replaced as needed. He left both Spencers with the horses and said he'd pick everything up early in the morning. The liveryman told him he'd have them all saddled and ready to go at seven before Sam paid for the boarding and would pay for the new shoes that may be needed in the morning.

He kept his normal saddlebags and left the heavy saddlebags with the horses. Eldorado was a good-size town, and liveries were usually safer than banks when there was more than one which provided competition. Their whole reputation was at stake if anything a customer left with them went missing, but in smaller towns with just one livery, that wasn't always the case.

Sam found a nice café, had a good roast pork dinner and guessed the beef would show up once he crossed into Texas. His only experience with cows was with the milk cows on the farm. They had to have a pair of bulls, of course, because milk cows only gave milk after they had calved, but the rest of the cattle business was foreign to him. It did appeal to him though and wondered how many cattle the Farrells' ranch had.

He went to his room, spent a nice, quiet night sleeping and was back on the road early the next morning after having a big breakfast. He did have to pay for new shoes for the three additions and whether it was necessary or not didn't matter. Knowing that they were well shod was worth it.

The rest of the trip across Arkansas was without any excitement at all, which he regarded as a true blessing.

He crossed the Red River on a ferry and was soon in Texas, not that he could tell the difference. When he arrived in Texas, there was no difference in the landscape, but after he arrived in Boston, he discovered one noticeable difference. The men all seemed to wear Stetson hats, or Confederate caps.

Sam was also was still wearing his army boots, so after reaching town he headed for the dry goods store and bought a pair of nice cowboy boots and a light-gray Stetson, both of which made him feel more Texan. He wasn't about to buy a used Confederate cap.

He left his horses with the liveryman, keeping his old boots in one of the spare sets of saddlebags. He'd taken to riding each of the geldings in turn and found one, a handsome chestnut gelding with four white stockings, especially pleasant. He had a smooth gait and seemed to have plenty of reserve. Sam decided to make the gelding his primary ride and named him Fire.

It was an inside joke to him. Fire meant *four* in Norwegian, and he now had four horses. He only knew that because a Norwegian private in his company kept counting cadence as 'one, two, three, fire'. He never could get it right. Sam had told him one day he'd get the entire regiment to shoot a volley unintentionally.

Sam kept to his schedule, reaching Clarksville, Paris, and then Bonham on successive days.

When he reached Bonham, he decided to take a little time to get a read on the area as Mulberry was just twelve miles northwest of the town and he didn't want to arrive at the ranch so late in the day. He'd leave Bonham early tomorrow morning, so he'd be able to meet Joe's family.

After having a good chicken dinner at Chilton's Diner, Sam got a room and after pulling off his new, still-too-tight boots and his new hat, he stretched out on the bed and studied the ceiling.

After he fulfilled his promise to Joe and making sure his family was okay, what would he do next? He had plenty of money and had already found that many ranches had gone into default because of the deaths of their owners or failure to pay taxes. Maybe he should buy one and have his own ranch. But even that idea didn't solve his biggest problem: he was lonely. For all those years at home in Iowa, he'd never been alone. Then he had his army friends, especially Joe. Even after returning to his family, he felt an incredible sense of loneliness that had surprised him. He couldn't understand it and wondered if it would ever leave.

He continued to just ruminate in silence as he tried to imagine a life that didn't make him feel so alien. He didn't come up with any solutions before he drifted off to sleep.

CHAPTER 3

Sam slept in on the last day of his journey, or at least sleeping in as he thought of it. The life of a farm boy, then as a soldier, didn't make sleeping past sunrise an option. But today, he didn't roll out of his hotel bed until well after the sun was up. He cleaned up from his trip and even took a bath before returning to his room, strapping on his gunbelt, then pulling on his new Stetson, snatching his saddlebags before leaving the room. He dropped off the key and left the hotel for the café.

After his breakfast, he returned to the livery, mounted Fire and led Rusty and the two unnamed geldings down the street heading northwest. He had asked the waitress about the Farrell's Bar F ranch and was told it was northwest of Bonham about eight miles, so it wasn't that far from a nice town. He didn't know how big Mulberry was or if it was nice either, but he did like Bonham.

He felt a mixture of excitement and dread as he rode along and both for the same reason. He was reaching the end of his trip and still had no idea what would happen today or the days that followed. *What if the Farrells blamed him for Joe's death somehow? Did they even tolerate Yankees?*

It really didn't matter much, he supposed. If they told him to get the hell out, he'd leave, at least temporarily. He would feel as if he had let Joe down, and that would never do. He'd fulfill his promise to make sure that his wife and daughter were safe even if they didn't want him around.

He was walking his miniature herd rather than moving at his normal pace to give him time to study the surrounding fields. He'd already passed two entrance roads to ranches but hadn't seen anyone. He'd heard cattle in the distance but hadn't seen any animals. There seemed to be plenty of grass for the critters and with the Red River so close, he imagined that the streams and creeks that fed it would make water plentiful. But it was so quiet and empty, it was as if someone was throwing a giant party nearby and everyone had gone.

After another hour of walking the horses, he found the Bar F Ranch and turned down the access road as he kept scanning. He was halfway to the house when he saw his first sign of human activity. It looked like a boy walking from the barn to the house and he must have spotted Sam because he quickly stopped, then bolting into the house's back entrance.

Sam kept the horses moving as he approached the ranch house, but before he reached it, people boiled out of the front door. One was armed with a shotgun, and it was pointed in his direction.

"Good morning!" Sam shouted as he stopped about thirty feet short of the house then put his hands out to the side.

The man with the shotgun jerked the muzzle a bit to make his point and shouted, "What do you want?"

"Mister Farrell? My name is Sam Walker. Joe was my best friend in the army, and he asked me to come by and see how everyone was doing."

"I don't give a damn who you are. You turn those animals around right now and get off my property!"

Sam was stunned, even though he had already suspected that it might be their reaction. But when facing two barrels of a shotgun, continued conversation was out of the question. He turned and began walking his horses back down the access road, his heart pounding as he expected to hear the shotgun's roar before being pelted by the pellets. He turned left toward Bonham when he reached the road, grateful that he was still alive, but it gnawed at him.

Joe had described his family in detail, and Sam had the impression that they would welcome him with open arms. But the more he thought about it, he began to realize Joe had seldom talked about his father and maybe there was a reason for his terrifying welcome.

As he walked Fire along the road, his next question was lodging. He didn't want to return to Bonham or go on to Mulberry and stay in a hotel, either. As he rode south, he noticed a ranch entrance road on his right. It was only a half a mile from the Bar F's entrance road. The sign said Circle W, but it was hanging at an angle and looked ready to fall. He turned down the road wondering if this was one of the abandoned ranches he'd heard about. It sure was quiet. He saw the ranch house in the distance and thought that it was a nice size but needed a new coat of whitewash. The big barn needed paint too, but the bunkhouse seemed solid. He rode toward the house and stopped thirty feet short and shouted the mandatory, "Hello, the house!"

Then he waited. After two minutes, he stepped Fire forward to the house and dismounted, wrapped the reins over the hitching rail and went inside.

The main room was still furnished but everything had a thick layer of dust. The fireplace looked in good shape, if you discounted the bird's nest. There were no eggs though, so it must be temporarily uninhabited.

The bathroom still had a large tub, which Sam thought was a plus. There were three bedrooms, all still furnished, and they even had quilts and pillows.

The kitchen was in better shape than the other rooms. The previous owner had left all the cookware and kitchenware and it all made him seem a bit creepy, as if he was walking in a graveyard.

"They must have wanted to leave quickly," Sam said aloud.

He left the kitchen via the back door and headed toward the outbuildings. There was one large building almost as big as the barn. It looked like a smokehouse, but it was too big.

He found the barn in decent shape and Sam could see that some repairs were necessary, but he found the tools nearby to do the work. The tools needed to have the rust removed, but that was all. The sharpening wheel was nearby, so he could put an edge on everything. There was a wagon and harness, although the harness was cracked and probably should be replaced. After leaving the barn, he walked to examine was the bunkhouse. It was small with only four bunks, but it was in better shape than the barn.

Finally, he walked out the last building and opened the door and discovered that it was a smokehouse after all. A huge one, at that, and still in good condition. He closed the door and went around behind the smokehouse and discovered a large collection of pens.

Sam quickly recognized them as hog pens without the hogs. There were twelve roomy pens and knew what the previous owner raised on the ranch, and that they didn't have horns, nor did they moo. At least the stink was long gone. There was even grass growing in the pens and he knew that if he modified the rails, the pens would make good corrals.

He returned to the horses and stepped up on Fire. The Circle W, if he could buy it, would make a good spot to hang his hat, but didn't know what he would do if he stayed. He could almost see the Bar F from there and from the barn he could get a full view of Joe's family ranch. He'd be able to keep his promise to Joe and maybe get a fresh start on his broken life at the same time.

He turned south and trotted his caravan toward Bonham, arriving shortly after eleven o'clock and headed for the bank. It took him ten minutes to open an account and deposit thirteen hundred dollars. The clerk seemed very happy to have him for a customer especially with all of those Yankee greenbacks. Sam's adopted Texas twang helped by not marking him as an outsider. Sam was given some blank drafts along with his bank book and after stepping out to the boardwalk, he scanned the town and headed for the county offices where he knew he'd find the land office.

As he entered the small office, the only clerk looked up at him and asked, "Howdy. What can I do for ya?"

"I was ridin' from Mulberry and noticed a few ranches that looked kinda empty. I've been lookin' for a place for a while and was wonderin' about the Circle W."

"I should think so," he said before he snickered, "The Circle W is barely a ranch. It's only two sections and is kinda tucked in around the bigger ranches. Couldn't raise any good-size herd on that small a place."

"Why is it small?"

"Because Henry Williams didn't need a lot of room 'cause he didn't raise cattle. Raised hogs."

"That's what I figured. I saw a lotta pens out back."

"Yes, sir. Had a couple of hands workin' for him and had more'n a hundred of those critters on the ranch. Could smell them all the way to Mulberry, but had himself a good business, too. Built a big smokehouse and supplied the whole area with ham and bacon. When the war came, those hogs went walkin' with the army in '62. He was left with nothin', so he walked with the army, too. His wife, Lizzie, had died just before the war, so he just left it. The smell is gone by now, I reckon. You interested in somethin' that small?"

"I just need someplace to hang my hat until I get my feet back under me."

"Well, the back taxes are all you'd have to pay. The others are all on the market still lookin' for buyers, but there just ain't too many buyers yet. I guess we'll start gettin' more carpetbaggers down here soon enough."

"I reckon. How much are the back taxes?"

"Let me look it up," he replied before he turned and walked back to his only file cabinet, pulled out a drawer and then selected one set of records and returned to the counter.

"The back taxes on the ranch are ninety-four dollars and sixteen cents. I went up for auction a while back, but nobody wanted it 'cause it was too small."

"Well, I figure it'll work for me, but I sure won't raise any hogs, neither."

The clerk laughed then said, "That's a bonus."

The clerk kept a smile on his face as he watched Sam digging into his pockets. Getting a delinquent ranch back onto the tax rolls was always worth at least a smile.

Sam rummaged around in his pockets and seemed to be scratching together the funds, so the word didn't get out how much cash he had. He placed the crumpled bills on the counter then counted out a hundred dollars.

The clerk gave Sam his change and then did some paperwork before he finally gave Sam his copy of the deed to the Circle W.

"The brand is still available, if you want to register it."

"That's a good idea. I don't need to change it with my last name bein' Walker."

"Did you want to fill out the application form?"

"Sure. I'll do that."

Sam filled out the short form and handed it to the clerk.

"The application fee is one dollar. You can check back in another week and see if it's been approved, Mister Walker."

Sam handed him the enormous fee, shook his hand and said, "The name's Sam, and I'll see you in a week."

"Good to know you, Sam," the clerk said, "I'm Harvey Greenway."

They were still shaking hands as Sam replied, "Glad to meet ya, Harvey."

They finally stopped their handshake, and Sam slipped the deed into his pocket for the time being, then left the land office a ranch owner. No wonder the Yankees were coming south in droves. He imagined that even the big spreads could be had for pennies on the dollar. He'd been very fortunate to find such a nice setup for just the back taxes. He wondered why it hadn't been looted over the years and wondered if there was some fear of the place for some reason. Superstitions had a powerful effect on some folks.

Whatever the reason for his windfall, he planned on working on the ranch and staying until he at least found out about Julia and Beth. If he stayed much longer maybe his accent would become permanent.

He stopped by the livery on the way back to the bank, wanting to see if there were any horses that could serve as draft horses for the wagon. He examined the stock in the corral and found a couple of nice geldings that he liked for the work. But there was one tan Morgan mare with a black mane and tail that he liked just because she was so pretty, so he went inside.

"Howdy!" he shouted.

The liveryman stepped out of a stall where he had been brushing down a customer's horse and asked, "Howdy! What can I do for ya?"

"I need some horses and saw a couple of geldings that I liked."

"Well, let's go look at 'em."

They headed for the corral, and Sam pointed out the two healthy, yet not spectacular, geldings. He wouldn't use his nicer animals to pull the wagon and he owed Rusty the exclusion as well.

"Yes, sir. Good horses. One's five and the other is six. Both newly shod, too."

"What's the story on the Morgan mare?"

"She's a pretty one, ain't she? She's a youngster, too. Only four."

"What kind of a deal can you make on all three?"

"Well, now, I'll tell you what I'll do. Seein' as how you want all three, I'll let 'em go for eighty dollars."

"Eighty? Now, we both know that horse prices have dropped something fierce since '65. I'll give you sixty-five dollars for all of them."

"I can't do that. A man's gotta eat. I'll go to seventy-five dollars, but not a penny less."

"You ain't gonna get a better offer for a while, but I'll go up to seventy dollars if you include the bridles and make me a trail line. We're talkin' good Yankee money, too."

At the mention of real currency, the liveryman knew he wouldn't get a better deal anytime soon, but said, "Mister, you're drivin' me to the poor house, but I suppose I'll do it."

"You don't have any pack saddles, do you?"

"Two of 'em. You want one? It'll cost you another twenty dollars."

"Well, seeing as how I almost broke ya on the horses, I'll give you the twenty if you'll set it up on one of those geldings."

The liveryman didn't say another word, but just grinned and shook Sam's hand. He headed to a dry room and picked out one of the packsaddles and Sam helped him saddle one of the two geldings.

Sam counted out the ninety dollars, then the liveryman set up the trail rope for the three horses and led them to Sam.

"What's your name, Mister?"

"Sam. Sam Walker." ·

"Harry Beecher."

They shook hands again, and Sam led the horses out of the livery, tied off the trail rope to Fire, then took Fire's reins outside the bank and headed to Parson's Dry Goods where he tied Fire to the hitchrail before entering the mercantile.

Sam walked down to the clothing section and picked up a pair of heavy work gloves, two more pairs of britches, four more shirts, some underpants, and six pairs of socks, then walked up front and set them on the long counter.

The owner, John Parson, was stocking tins of carrots, saw Sam, then stepped over and asked, "Will that be all, sir?"

"No, sir. I need a couple of panniers and a bunch of supplies."

John grinned and said, "Well, I'll be happy to help."

Sam began getting food and other supplies and bringing them to the counter while the storekeeper had the two panniers on the floor and was filling them as Sam brought the items up front. When the order was completed, Sam asked what the damage was.

"Sixteen dollars and fifty-five cents."

"Coulda been worse," Sam said as he grinned.

Mister Parson smiled as Sam paid the bill, then helped Sam carry the two panniers outside where Sam hung them on the pack saddle, making sure the basket of eggs was securely on top.

"Goin' for a long ride?"

"No, sir. I just bought me a ranch up north a bit. The Circle W and aim to be a regular customer."

"Glad to have you join our town. What's your name?"

"Walker. Sam Walker."

"John Parson."

They shook hands, then the proprietor walked back into his store while Sam stepped up on Fire. It was time to go to his new home.

———

After he arrived at his new ranch, he put all the horses in the corral and filled the trough, then had to hunt down some hay to toss inside as well.

He left the panniers on the back porch while he cleaned the place. The previous owner had left a broom along with pretty much everything else he needed, so he began sweeping out a couple of years of dust from the kitchen. After that, he had to prime the kitchen pump and get water flowing again, then found some old towels and used them to remove the last vestiges of dust from the table, chairs, and counters.

Then he began unloading his panniers and soon had the kitchen's larder and cold room stocked before he finally answered his stomach's call and ate some smoked beef and drank some water to quiet it down for the time being.

He pulled all the bedding out and carried them out back where he shook the dust from the top quilts then hung all of the bedding over the clothesline. Everything sagged until the quilts almost touched the ground, then he let the light breeze and the sun work on getting out the musty smell. There were three bedrooms, which gave him lots of space for his things. He just didn't have a lot of things to fill the empty space.

61

But he did have his guns: five Colt New Army pistols and gunbelts, two Spencers, one was a rifle, the other a carbine, and his Winchester. He also had enough ammunition to sink a canoe.

He brought all his guns and ammunition into the bedroom closest to the kitchen and set them on the floor for now. He'd have to build a cabinet for them when he had time. He looked disarmed, but he always kept Elizabeth's derringer in his pocket and wondered what Henry and Elizabeth had done when they had arrived in New Orleans.

Next up was the cookstove and then the fireplace. The cookstove was still rust free, so he just added some wood and set a fire going to burn out any critters that might have decided to call it home. The iron racked and popped as it heated, and after he had the fire going, built another one in the fireplace, leaving the nest in place as kindling.

With everything more or less settled, he returned to the kitchen and made himself dinner on the still-hot stove. He felt pleased with himself as he drank his first cup of coffee in his new home. He'd never had a place that he could call his own before, and that seemed to wash away some of the loneliness and lack of direction. This was his home and he decided at that moment that he was going to be a Texan from now on, regardless of what happened on the ranch less than a mile away.

The rest of the day was spent cleaning and more cleaning. Sam had never seen so much dust. While he was finally cleaning the kitchen, he found a set of keys to the house in the empty tea canister. The bathtub would be handy in bad weather, but he really would prefer a nice swimming hole where he could dive under the water as he'd loved to do as a boy. Maybe the ranch didn't have any water at all, and that's why the previous owner had abandoned it. With the Red River so close, he found that hard to believe. There was a nonworking windmill near the house that he'd have to repair to let it pump water into the large cistern at its base. He assumed it had been used to water horses, since it was too tall for hogs.

As the sun began to set, Sam moved his bedding back into the house and made three beds which wasn't an army-taught skill. It was a Mama Walker taught skill.

He had finally had enough for the day and crawled into bed around nine o'clock, expecting another good night's sleep. He drifted off, and forty minutes later, found himself back in the prison camp. There was only one other prisoner, Sergeant Malarkey. It made perfect sense to the dream Sam because Malarkey belonged there, but prisoner Malarkey had a big club and was grinning at him.

"Looks like only one of us is goin' back, Yankee. I'm goin' back to Iowa and kill that little sister of yours, but first I'm gonna have my way with her, and there ain't nothin' you can do about it."

"I'm gonna kill you, Malarkey!" dream Sam screamed as he reached out with his huge hands to crush the dream Malarkey's fat throat.

But his hands wouldn't move, and Malarkey laughed at his failure. Sam was panicking in his inability to help. *What was wrong with his hands? He had to get away! He had to warn Anna!*

Sam turned away from the hideous cackle coming from Malarkey and started to run toward the wide-open camp gate. He was almost there! He knew without turning that Malarkey was right behind him. His feet felt like giant rocks as he moved ever closer to the gate and freedom with Malarkey's foul breath hot on his neck. Sam's feet seemed stuck in thick mud as he struggled to reach the gate. It was so close, yet he knew it was an impossible goal.

Then he saw the shadow of Malarkey's enormous club swinging toward his head and knew he was about to die.

Sam woke with his scream still echoing through the empty house. Sam sat shaking, with his heart threatening to explode in his chest as he looked around him in panic. *Where am I?* It took several seconds of confusion to remember he was in his own bedroom in Texas.

He dropped back down in his damp bed, his back still soaked with sweat. He lay with his eyes open, reliving the nightmare, as he usually did. Like most nightmares, it made no sense once he was awake. *Why would he dream about Malarkey?*

Malarkey had never hit him. He'd hit other prisoners, of course, including Joe. Two he'd beaten so severely that they'd died. But for some reason, he had left Sam alone. He had never shown up in any of Sam's nightmares before, but maybe it was because he was so close to the prison camp that had finally brought him into his nightmare.

He stayed awake for another two and a half hours before he finally drifted off to a dreamless sleep.

———

When he finally awakened the following day, he set about getting his ranch in order. After a nice breakfast of eggs and bacon washed down with half a pot of coffee, he began to work.

By ten o'clock, he had the windmill turning and pumping water again. It had an automatic float shutoff valve to keep it from overflowing the cistern, but when he looked in the dry cistern, he noticed a large opening in the bottom. Now he knew how the hogs had been getting their water. He returned to the pens and found that centered in each group of four pens was a circular trough. At the bottom of each was a hole. Even as he watched, the troughs began to fill with water from the turning windmill.

Mister Williams may have been a pig farmer, but he was pretty clever. The pens must be on slightly higher ground than the house, maybe two feet. That had allowed him to make troughs that the hogs could use, and that meant that Sam's horses could use them as well once he turned the pens into corrals. Sam smiled as he returned to the windmill and the filling cistern.

He saddled Fire to begin his inspection of his ranch, which he realized that he should have done before he bought the place. He found the grass to be plentiful, if not overgrown. There was fencing along the borders comprised of posts with three strands of wire, which surprised him because the hogs were penned in.

There were a few spots that needed repairs, but overall the fences were in good condition. He rode for almost a mile before he found water when he spotted a nice creek running from south to north toward the Red River. He crossed over the stream and rode another half of a mile before finding the back of the ranch. It was a small ranch by Texas standards, one section north to south and two sections east to west. Two full sections, or two square miles of North Texas, which worked out to over twelve hundred acres. He followed the western edge of the property and approached the creek again. Sam found a rocky patch that measured a good half acre, which he thought would be a good place to build his swimming hole, but not today. Today he'd have to get to the barn and start his repairs there. He needed to get the tools that were already inside cleaned and sharpened.

Two hours later, after a quick lunch, he was doing just that as he sat in front of the grinding wheel and put new edges on the two axes, the machete, and scythe. He had to grind away some rust on the other tools as well.

He found an almost full reel of wire for fencing and a fencing tool in the corner, so he'd be able to repair the fence. He might need to add a couple of new posts, too.

He spent the rest of the afternoon repairing the stalls in the barn, and at one point, he climbed up into the loft, walked to the loft door and opened them wide. He looked out and could see the Bar F house in the distance, about a mile away and figured if he had a good set of field glasses, he'd be able to see what was going on.

He was still a bit irritated with Mister Farrell's reaction, but perplexed as well. *Why would he be so hostile? Did he blame him for Joe's death somehow?* He also wondered if the rest of the family felt that way, or even if they were still there. He hadn't paid attention to the rest of the family once he'd seen that shotgun. *How could he help Julia and Beth if he couldn't see them?* He'd give it some time to see what happened because he still had a lot to do.

After dinner and some more repair work, Sam washed off his accumulated dirt in the cistern. He'd ride into Bonham tomorrow and see if he could hire someone to paint the house and barn.

That night, he wrote a long letter to Anna, telling her what had happened and how he had become a ranch owner. He told her how much he missed her and how special she was. He'd post it tomorrow when he went to see about getting the house and barn painted.

Six days later, his newly whitewashed house and red-painted barn almost glowed in the sunlight, Sam finally got around to digging his swim hole. It took three days to do it right because he didn't want just a big bathtub, he wanted a real swimming hole. When he finished digging, he'd created a crater in the earth that measured almost twenty feet long, ten feet wide, and eight feet deep. He finally broke a small part of the dam holding back the creek on the southern end and let it fill. Once it was full, he created another breach in the northern end to let the water return to the creek. While the silt settled, Sam used some of the rocks to build a small patio for him to use as a changing and drying platform when using the swim hole.

He had to wait another day before the silt had cleared well enough to use, but as the sun was setting for the night after a long day's work, he finally made use of his creation. He felt exhilarated as he dove into the cool, but not cold water.

He returned to the ranch when it was almost dark, had dinner, and crawled into bed, expecting a dreamless sleep after the first soothing swim in his man-made pond, but it didn't work out that way.

Sam bolted awake two hours after he'd closed his eyes. He hadn't screamed this time but was sweating and his heart threatened to rip from his chest. It was his fourth bad dream since he'd been on his ranch, and all of them included Malarkey. The sudden emergence of Malarkey as a regular inhabitant of his nightmares caused him some concern. *Did it have any significance at all?* Maybe it was punishment for having the gall to decide to live in his home state. Malarkey used to brag about being from Texas as he belittled the other guards from other southern states, paying special attention to the boys from Louisiana.

Two days after his swimming hole construction, Sam was returning from Bonham, leading his packhorse, who was loaded with oats for the horses and some fresh produce and eggs for himself, when he saw a wagon approaching with an outrider. He pulled off the hammer loop on his Colt, just to be safe, but really didn't expect any problems.

When the wagon was within a hundred feet, Sam recognized the driver as the same ornery Farrell who had pointed a shotgun in his direction on that first day. He hoped that the man wasn't going to be as hostile on the open road, and after making sure the shotgun wasn't in his hands, felt a bit safer.

They took up the entire road, so Sam led his packhorse off to the side and waited for them to pass. As they rolled by, he tipped his hat to Mrs. Farrell and a very pretty young woman sitting beside her on the driver's seat that he assumed was Joe's fabled sister, Mary, the girl that Joe had repeatedly told him was the only woman for him.

As he looked at her, he caught a glimpse of a slight smile from Mary but a glare from her father. The outrider, Joe's brother, Max, nodded his silent greeting. Max would be twelve years old now, but there was no Julia or Beth. Sam wondered if they were back at the house. The wagon seat was full, so maybe they were staying home rather than riding in the wagon bed.

After they had gone, Sam gave them one last look and headed to his ranch and soon crossed under his recently repaired Circle W sign twenty minutes later. He had received approval of the brand transfer the week before and had held off repairing the sign until he was sure the brand would stay.

Today, Sam would be building his gun cabinet after weeks of being annoyed seeing his weapons haphazardly scattered about the empty bedroom. He would be using scrap boards and the tools on hand, so it wouldn't be a fancy piece of finished furniture that he could have bought in Bonham, but it would serve its purpose.

He was in the barn and after two and a half hours of cutting and planing the boards to a smooth finish, he was ready to assemble the home for his guns. He wasn't going to be crude and use nails to hold it together, though. He was going to use wooden pegs and some glue he had bought in Bonham which would make it stronger. He had created some pegs and was getting ready to assemble the piece when his ears picked up the unmistakable sound of hoofbeats coming from the front of the house and knew that he had a problem. All of his guns were inside the house except for the derringer.

He walked out of the barn and saw a stranger approaching the house riding a dark sorrel with a white back end marked with dark brown spots.

"That's a bad horse if you were involved in a shootout," Sam thought.

As Sam walked out of the barn, the man noticed him, then turned his horse in Sam's direction. As he drew closer, Sam studied his cold face and the Colt on his right hip. The man's hammer loop was in place, so he didn't intend to use it, yet the man still almost screamed trouble.

Sam stopped and waited for the stranger to reach him and vowed never to go anywhere without a serious weapon from now on.

After pulling his horse to a stop just fifteen feet away, the stranger smiled and asked, "Mind if I step down?"

"Go ahead. What can I do for ya?"

"Just stoppin' by. I saw someone fixed the sign out front and did some checkin' and found out that someone bought the place. You must be Sam Walker."

Sam wondered why he had been 'checkin', but replied, "I am. Who are you?"

"Name's Jimmy Toomey. I'm from Mulberry."

It was the first person he'd met from Mulberry and quickly thought that maybe he should pay that town a visit.

"Well, what are you needin' exactly, Jimmy?"

"Just checkin'. We got a lotta Yankees driftin' down this way and some of us don't appreciate carpetbaggers or scalawags."

"I reckon so. You boys doin' anything about it?"

Jimmy stared at Sam, tilted his hat back and replied, "Maybe we are and maybe we ain't. Where you from?"

"East a 'ways. Out near Tyler, but things got a bit crowded and I wanted a ranch of my own."

"Ain't any up your way? Heard there were a few."

"Needed to get far enough away from my pappy. He's an ornery ol' cuss."

Jimmy snickered, then asked, "You ride with the gray?"

"Nope. Texas shoulda stayed outta that mess. Shoulda stayed the Republic of Texas," Sam answered without answering.

Jimmy snickered again before saying, "You're all right, Sam. Maybe I'll come by and see you again sometime. Just to let you know, you got a family of scalawags for neighbors."

"You ain't joshin' me, are ya?" Sam asked with his eyebrows raised.

"Nope. Them Farrells at the Bar F had a boy go off with the Yankees. Died for 'em, too. But we'll show 'em that it ain't right to turn your back on the cause."

"Well, don't that beat all," Sam said, sliding his Stetson back and scratching his head, "I got neighbors like that after all."

"They got a good-lookin' filly over there, too. I got my eye on her, scalawag or not."

"She ain't got a sister, does she?" Sam asked as he smirked appropriately.

"Kinda. She had a sister-in-law, but Mike already lassoed her. She sure is one handsome woman and Mike didn't seem to care if she was a scalawag."

"Who's Mike?" Sam asked as he scratched the right side of his chest.

"Mike Malarkey. He's kinda the boss. You wanna meet him?"

Sam's stomach did a full somersault as he tried to maintain his composure, but quickly replied, "Nah. I ain't got no time. It'll take me two more months to get this place workin'.'"

Jimmy did a quick scan of the place and said, "Looks like you're doin' okay, though."

"Workin' my butt off."

"Well, I've got to be headin' back. Good to meet ya," he said, offering his right hand.

"Likewise," Sam replied as he shook his hand.

After Jimmy Toomey boarded his horse, he looked down at Sam and said, "One more thing, Sam. It ain't wise to go around unarmed like that."

"I hear ya. I suppose I gotta get me a pistol one of these days."

"That'd be smart," he said then grinned before wheeling his horse and riding away.

Sam's heart was still pounding as he watched the man turn north onto the road to return to Mulberry. Mike Malarkey was in that town and he had Julia with him? *What about Joe's daughter, Beth? What happened to her and* how the hell did that happen? The group that Jimmy Toomey was with sounded as if they were planning on doing something about the local scalawags, the Farrells. He felt incredibly isolated with the sudden revelation, but knew he was far from helpless.

But he felt like he had learned a lot without giving up any information. Jimmy will report that Sam was on their side and a good son of Texas. Thank you, Joe! If he hadn't learned to mimic Joe's soft drawl, he'd probably be dead by now. But then there was the whole Mike Malarkey problem. *Would he recognize Sam?* Sam was ninety pounds heavier than when he had left the camp and was well over two hundred pounds now. His hair was longer, too. Malarkey was a big man, but now Sam was bigger and stronger. He doubted if Malarkey could handle a pistol as well as Sam either as few other shooters could. But he was a serious threat, as was his little group of rabble-rousers.

If he was going to become a Texan, then he'd have to deal with Malarkey and his followers in Mulberry; the boys who were planning on dealing with the scalawags that lived less than a mile north from where he was standing.

Sam was going to go back and finish his cabinet when he remembered that the Farrells were headed into Bonham more than three hours ago and should be returning soon, which might give him a chance to at least warn them without having to face that shotgun again.

He walked to the cistern, took off his Stetson and his shirt, and dunked himself in the water. He threw back his excessively long hair and ran his fingers through it to get it straight, more or less. He supposed he should get a haircut one of these days, but it was beginning to grow on him...literally. It was already over his shirt collar.

He pulled on his shirt, trotted back to the barn, saddled Fire and stepped into the saddle. He hadn't seen that shotgun anywhere on the Farrell's wagon, but it might have been in the footwell, so he figured he might need some more firepower of his own, just in case. Besides, it was his new rule.

Sam trotted Fire to the house, dismounted and quickly entered through the front door. After reaching his gun-filled bedroom, he strapped on his preferred Colt, snatched the Winchester and returned to Fire. After slipping the rifle into the scabbard, he mounted and turned Fire toward the road.

He figured that if the family had taken the wagon to Bonham, they were probably buying a lot of supplies, so it was likely they were still on their way back, but he might have to find them in town if they stopped for lunch.

Sam kept checking his backtrail to make sure that Toomey wasn't following but was pretty sure that he had been convinced that Sam was a good ol' boy and no threat either. After all, Jimmy knew that Sam didn't have a pistol.

He'd just returned his eyes to the front when he picked up a large dust cloud in the distance. It wasn't moving fast, so it might be the Farrells. He soon noticed that it was a wagon and a trailing rider, which pretty much assured him that the Farrell family was on its way back to their ranch.

He really didn't care what the old bastard, who was actually probably only forty-five or so, said to him this time. He had to find out what had happened to Julia and warn them about the threat posed by their fellow Texans.

He had purchased a good pair of used field glasses in Bonham on his last trip into town when he wanted something to watch the Farrell ranch a bit closer. It was a bit of ironic because they were surplus Confederate issue but had been made in England and had excellent optics.

He kept the same speed until they were within a thousand yards, then he slowed Fire and when they were just four hundred yards away, Sam pulled to a stop but didn't give up the road. They'd have to stop and talk to him.

As the wagon approached, he could see that Max was nervous. He wasn't armed, but Sam hadn't done anything with his weapons either. He didn't want to appear to be a threat, because he wasn't.

When the wagon finally stopped about twenty feet away, Sam spoke before Mister Farrell could launch a tirade.

"Good afternoon. You were more than rude to me the last time I saw you, Mister Farrell, and I don't know why. Your son, Joe, and I were closer than brothers and I was with him when he died in that Confederate prison camp. He knew that he was

73

too sick and was probably never walk out of that camp and had me promise to look after his Julia and Beth.

"Now, I aim to keep my promise to my best friend. I left my family in Iowa and rode across Arkansas to come here just to do as he asked. I'll look after your family as well, whether you want me to or not, because you just aren't ready for what's coming.

"I was working at my ranch a little while ago and was paid a visit by some sneaky bastard named Jimmy Toomey. He took me as a kindred spirit and told me things, things that bothered me. He told me that Julia had been claimed by a man named Mike Malarkey. Is that true?"

"That ain't any of your damned business!" shouted Earl Farrell.

Sam was a bit surprised by his vitriolic response, but firmly replied, "It is exactly my business, Mister Farrell. It's the reason I traveled fifteen hundred miles. I am going to keep the promise I made to Joe. Do you know who Mike Malarkey is?"

"I told you, it's none of your business. Now, give us the road!"

"Mike Malarkey was Sergeant Mike Malarkey of the Confederate States of America. He was the head guard at that prison where Joe died. He beat and killed prisoners, including Joe. When Joe died and was being taken away for burial, that cold-hearted bastard kicked him just to get me to say something so he could beat me with his club.

"That's the man who has Joe's Julia and Beth now, Mister Farrell. Now maybe you don't give a rat's behind about it, but I do. Oh, and one more thing that Mister Toomey mentioned that you might find interesting. He said that my new neighbors, the Farrells, were scalawags and that his little group would make them sorry for what Joe did when he went to Iowa.

"I'm going to give you the road now, Mister Farrell, then I'm going to return to my ranch and make plans to try to help Julia and Beth. I owe it to Joe."

Sam took one more, long hard look at Joe's glaring father, then wheeled Fire to the north and set off at a gallop, not because he was worried about being shot in the back, but because he was incredibly angry. *How can a man be so callous about his own daughter-in-law and granddaughter?*

After a mile, he slowed down to a fast trot, and patted Fire's sweaty neck as he apologized. He'd have to go into Mulberry tomorrow, get a read on the town and learn what he could about Julia and Beth. Knowing Mike Malarkey, the odds of her being treated well were almost nonexistent, and he wondered why she was even there. *Did she go with him voluntarily? What if she was so angry with Joe for leaving her that she hated the Yankees and had thrown in with Malarkey's crowd?* There was always that chance. If he found out that it was that way, *what would he do with his own ranch? Would he stay or just pull up roots again?*

He did know that if Julia was now Mike Malarkey's woman by choice, it would put a dagger into his heart. He couldn't imagine Joe being so much in love with a woman and now seeing her with that monster.

Sam reached his ranch and turned down the access road, still deep in thought about Julia and Beth. He had missed lunch, so he figured he may as well eat something once he'd taken care of Fire.

After unsaddling his big gelding, he brushed him down and gave him some oats and water in his stall. He usually kept Fire and the tan Morgan mare in the barn but kept his other four horses in the expanded corral.

He had never ridden the mare but walked over to her and brushed her down as well. She was such a pretty thing. When he had first bought her, he'd watched her trailing behind and admired the way she moved with her almost perfect gait. Since she'd taken residence on his ranch, he'd found her to have a very pleasant manner.

75

He suspected that the other reason that he'd bought the small horse was to give to Julia when he found her, or maybe to Mary, if Joe had been right about her. She sure was a pretty young woman and despite just the short few seconds when she'd smiled at him, he could see the quick mind behind those eyes.

After making sure his two barn horses were content, he walked outside to check on his four geldings, including his neglected friend, Rusty.

When he reached the corral, he did a quick evaluation of its current state. He had added two rows of rails to the ex-hog pens by removing some dividing rails which converted eight giant pigpens into two enormous corrals. There were still four more pens that were attached as well, and they had access to the automatically filling troughs.

He talked to Rusty and the other three horses for a few minutes, then turned around and was walking to the house when he decided to finish the gun cabinet after all.

He took off his gunbelt and Stetson and began the assembly, pounding pegs into the holes and then gluing the open pegs before lining them with the holes in the boards and tapping them into place with the mallet.

Once the assembly was complete, he stepped back and admired his work as it lay flat on the barn's floor. It needed some varnish, but it looked solid and would be a good home for his weapons. It was heavy for pine too, and once the guns and ammunition were stored, it would be a lot heavier.

Sam left the barn and headed for the house to finally get something into his stomach. He left the back door open for some air, then opened the cookstove's firebox door and after adding some kindling and a splash of coal oil, ripped a match across the cast iron then dropped it onto the small pile of kerosene-soaked sticks. The tiny funeral pyre exploded to life, then he added the split wood, slammed the door closed and walked to the sink to fill his coffeepot.

As he prepared to cook his late lunch and early dinner, he was still thinking about his place in this torn community. Financially, he was in great shape, even with the purchase of the ranch and the horses and getting it repaired, he had still not dipped into his bank account. He still had over two hundred and fifty dollars in cash, too. It was the other, troubling aspects of his new home that bothered him. He could understand the resentment, but the war was over, and it was time to get on with life. Obviously, for a man like Mike Malarkey, this kind of behavior was his life.

He had baked some biscuits the day before, so he heated them up and fried a steak. As the steak was sizzling in his frypan, he walked into the cold room, grabbed the crock of butter then after leaving it on the table, poured himself some coffee.

He turned the steak over, still ruminating about that confrontation on the road. Even as he was sitting at his table, cutting into the meat, he ate in a foul mood. *How had that cantankerous Earl Farrell allowed his daughter-in-law to get involved with Mike Malarkey in the first place?* He should have been protecting her and his granddaughter from the likes of that bastard, unless she had gone off with him by choice. If that was true, maybe that was why he was so angry with the world.

He finished his dinner and cleaned up afterward, then decided that what he really needed was a trip to his swimming hole. He grabbed some clean clothes and a bar of white soap. He didn't bother Fire, but figured he owed his old friend and headed to the corral. He led Rusty out of the corral and rode him bareback to his swimming hole.

Minutes after arriving, Sam was stripped naked and under the warm water, before he stroked to the patio, grabbed his bar of soap and began lathering his hard, muscular body. Once he was sure that he hadn't missed any spots, he tossed the soap onto the stones, then dove back under.

After another thirty minutes of soothing swimming, he left the water, but splashed some of it onto those rocks to cool them off before he lay on his rough patio under the hot Texas sun. He had his eyes closed as the hard light pounded on his skin and he thought about possible directions his visit to Mulberry could take after he arrived in the town.

He really didn't come up with any definite plans by the time that he dressed in his clean clothes and climbed back onto Rusty.

After leaving the red gelding in his corral, he was walking past the barn headed for the kitchen when he heard the nicker of another horse out in front of the house. He was unarmed and cursed himself for the repeated mistake, figuring that Toomey had returned to do some more checking, but at least this time, he could correct his lack of firearms.

Sam blew out his breath and quickly crossed to the back porch, walked into the kitchen, then stopped in his bedroom, tossed the dirty clothes into his basket and put on his gunbelt. He felt better as he strode across the main room and opened the door to ask Toomey what he wanted, but when his eyes revealed his visitor, he knew it was most assuredly not Jimmy Toomey.

Sam smiled and said, "Good evening, Miss Farrell. What can I do for you?"

Mary Farrell had been sitting on the porch steps and stood when she heard Sam's footsteps approaching.

She didn't return his smile, but said, "Hello, Mister Walker. I was wondering if I could talk to you."

He noted her serious face, so he just replied, "Sure."

Sam stepped out onto the porch and sat on the steps with Mary just two feet away. It would be inappropriate for her to go inside.

She looked down at her folded hands as she said, "Mister Walker, I want to apologize for my father. Ever since Joe left all those years ago, he's been this way. He blames the Yankees for taking him away and for causing his death, and none of us can tell him any differently."

"That doesn't bother me, Miss Farrell. What does is his apparent lack of concern about Julia and Beth. That infuriated me. I know Mike Malarkey. He's a heartless, cold bastard who likes to inflict pain on those he can control. I'm worried about Julia and Beth, and I was wondering if she had gone with him willingly. It keeps me awake nights. She didn't, did she?"

"No, she didn't. Except for my father, we all are worried about her. He never liked Julia. But you need to know that Beth is dead, Mister Walker. She died in October of '64 from pneumonia."

Sam closed his eyes as he felt the pain that Joe would have felt if he ever knew, but Joe never knew because he had never even met his daughter. He wanted so badly to see his little girl, but maybe it was better that he had died before returning home to this.

"Joe, maybe you're seeing her now," he prayed silently.

He then turned to Mary and stammered quietly, "Joe…Joe, he never knew."

"No. Julia didn't have it in her heart to put that kind of news into a letter. She hoped he would return, and we could all be there when she had to tell him."

"He wanted to see his little girl so much," Sam said.

Then after a short pause where he let out a long breath, added, "I'm sorry. That was quite a shock."

"I know. But I had to tell you."

"Thank you for that."

Mary exhaled herself, then said, "You have to understand just how much my father despised Julia. He wanted Joe to marry a girl named Joan Anderson, who was the only child of Carl and Sarah Anderson of the Rocking A ranch that joined our ranch on the eastern edge. My father thought he had had it all set up until Joe met Julia in Mulberry. Joan Anderson had no chance after that.

"My father was furious and did everything he could to make Julia look bad, but none of it mattered. After Joe died, my father practically threw her out of the house. We tried to help her, but she was getting desperate.

"Mike Malarkey had money, but no one knew how he'd gotten it. He bought a lumber mill outside of Mulberry and then a flour mill. He offered her a home and security, so she accepted his offer and married him. We haven't heard from her since. We would really appreciate it if you could find out about her."

"I will, Miss Farrell. I have to fulfill my promise to Joe."

She finally smiled and asked, "Could you call me Mary, please?"

"I will, Mary. And please call me Sam," he replied as he managed a small smile, still upset about what she had told him.

She kept her smile as she replied, "Thank you, Sam."

"You're welcome, Mary."

"Joe wrote to us a lot about you, Sam," said Mary quietly, "Father never read the letters, but mama did and let us read them, too. You two spent the whole war together, didn't you?"

The memories of those days with Joe rekindled a warm smile as Sam answered, "We spent every day and almost every hour together; from the first days in Davenport to the final ones in the prison camp. I don't believe that we were ever apart for more than two days in a row. That's something that only marriage and war can make happen."

"Sam, how bad was it?" Mary asked quietly.

Sam trained his eyes on hers as he replied, "Mary, the whole war was one confusing mess after another. We were in some horrible fights and the worst was Shiloh. But I'll bet that altogether, we spent maybe twenty days out of the entire time we were in the war actually fighting.

"Most of the time we were waiting or moving. It was just boring, and we were fighting to stay healthy more than firing guns or trying not to get shot or stabbed. The camps stunk to high heaven and then there were those hospitals with the stacks of severed limbs outside. I guess it's the smell more than anything else that will stick in my mind."

Then, after a short pause, he continued, saying "In the battle where Joe and I were captured, if the officers had just let us go when we had the chance, we would have rolled their flank and would have won the engagement, but they hesitated. While our commanders debated, they reinforced their flank, so by the time we received the order to march, we knew we were walking into a hornet's nest.

"When we were taken to the prison camp, it was already overcrowded, and they kept bringing in more prisoners. From what I learned from the doctors, ours wasn't even the worst of them. It made our worst day in our own camps look like a picnic. Food was so scarce that even our guards didn't get enough. You can imagine how little was left for the prisoners. Sanitation was almost non-existent, and the entire camp was like one massive latrine. The smell was overpowering, but we didn't even notice it after a while.

"At first, we talked about home and families, like we did when we were in our own camp, but after a month or so, all we thought about was food. When we did talk about family, it always included some reference to food."

Sam then laughed lightly before saying, "Once, Joe said how it was getting chilly outside, and I asked him why he was bringing up food because I could use a hot bowl of chili.

"That was when the snow was falling on the day that I lost him. Joe and I used to sit back-to-back to keep ourselves a bit warmer and to keep someone from sneaking up on us from behind to take our shoes or our heavy blouses. All we had was each other, me and Joe. It was that way from the day we met in Davenport. He was more of a brother to me than my own brother, and I still think of him every day. I miss Joe, Mary. I really miss him."

Sam felt his eyes beginning to water, so he quickly wiped his eyes with his shirt sleeve as he looked away in embarrassment.

Mary could feel his pain and understood more about Sam Walker than she had from all of Joe's letters where he'd extolled his courage and other fine traits. She'd always suspected that Joe had been exaggerating to try and convince her that Sam was the only man she should wed, but now, after just a few minutes talking to him, she didn't think her brother had done Sam justice.

Mary was curious about another of Joe's Sam stories and asked, "Did you leave your wife to come down here, Sam? Joe said you were going to get married as soon as you got home."

Sam turned his face back to Mary, smiled and replied, "No, ma'am. My brother married my girlfriend while I was in the army, so I had no entanglements in Iowa."

"She married your brother?" Mary asked in surprise.

"She did. I think my brother always fancied her, and once I was listed as missing in action, she was fair game."

"Did you get angry when you found out that she had married your brother?"

"You would think so, wouldn't you? But when I finally received the letter from my mother telling me about it, I was still so depressed about Joe's death that finding out she had married meant nothing to me.

"Joe was everything to me by then. We were best friends and brothers. We had been through hell together and he was the one who had borne the brunt of Satan's punishment. He was family and Barbara Jean was just a distant memory, an ideal. With Barbara Jean, I had imagined her as prettier and sweeter than she was, as most soldiers did about their sweethearts back home.

"It was the same about everything we held dear about our hopes for after the war; our families were all perfect and the grass was always green. We turned our memories into impossible dreams that would always disappoint us when we did get home.

"After the letter arrived from my mother, I recalled the times when we were together and let reality replace those dreams. I came to realize that even before I had enlisted, Barbara Jean had been nothing more than an image, an empty shell. There was nothing there, nothing to latch onto. I actually became more concerned for my brother, Frank once I did return.

"He probably discovered too late that the package means little in the long run. I knew then that what I wanted in a wife was a woman with substance, a woman who can keep me intrigued even when I'm old and bent. If the packaging is nice, that's just a bonus."

Mary tilted her head slightly as she asked, "So. you didn't even look around when you returned to Iowa? You were home for a while."

"It wasn't on my mind at all. After I had put my weight back to what it should have been and still hadn't done anything about settling down, my parents began to act as matchmakers, inviting one prospective daughter-in-law after another to the farm for dinner. But even though most were pretty and very nice, they just weren't right.

"Of course, it was made worse by having Frank and Barbara Jean there sometimes. My parents had built a house for them on the farm, but they'd eat at the family house a few times each week. It made an awkward evening when Barbara Jean would sit there with this stern look on her face while some sweet young thing would make doe eyes at me."

Mary smiled as she asked, "Was she jealous, do you think?"

"You know, I never thought about it. It was plain to see that Frank and Barbara Jean didn't get along, but I almost didn't pay any attention."

Mary laughed as Sam smiled and asked, "Do you know what the really odd part was, Mary?"

"I'm sure you'll tell me."

"Whenever I'd even mention Barbara Jean to Joe, he'd talk to me about you. He'd tell me that I had to forget about Barbara Jean, return to Texas with him and marry you."

Mary didn't blush as Sam expected, but quietly said, "I know. He wrote the same thing in his letters. He wrote one just to me telling me to explain that I shouldn't go looking for a beau. He wrote that you were the finest man he'd ever met and the only one who was good enough for me."

"That sounds like Joe. I thought Joe was the finest man I ever met, and I doubt if I'll ever meet his equal. But why haven't you married, Mary? Surely you've had your opportunities."

"Not as many as you might think. I didn't attend church socials or barn dances very often. I'm just not cut out for such

84

things. I'm a bit of a tomboy. I like to ride horses and work around the ranch. I've always been a bit headstrong and most boys don't like it. My father has called me a shrew on more than one occasion."

Sam looked at her almost angelic face, then said, "I would think that having a woman who tells a man when he's screwing up would be a good thing. As long as she doesn't start belching at dinner to prove a point."

Mary laughed as Sam looked at the rather sorry gelding standing at the hitching rail and asked, "Is that your horse, Mary?"

She shook her head and answered, "No. That's Max's horse. I don't have one. I'm a girl, and my father believes that I should only wear dresses and ride sidesaddle. I won't ride that way and he said I can't have a horse until I start acting properly."

"Come with me," Sam said as he stood.

Mary rose, said, "Alright," then they started walking toward the barn.

As they stepped along the hard dirt, Sam noticed that Mary was tall for a woman at five foot seven and had the same light-brown hair and blue eyes of the entire family. She was very pretty but leaning toward cute more than beautiful. Even though she was wearing a baggy shirt and oversized britches, he could tell that she was well formed. But it was her demeanor and personality that intrigued Sam.

They had only been talking for a few minutes, yet he felt he had known her for years. Maybe it was because Joe had talked so much about his little sister, although she was far from little anymore. Mary Farrell was a very strong-willed and impressive young woman. He wondered if she was that way before Joe left Texas because he'd never mentioned her strength of personality and had always describing her as cute and sweet. She may be cute, but Sam wasn't sure about the sweet part. It wasn't important anyway because Sam would prefer to have a woman who would be a challenge to his mind and spirit.

They reached the closed barn doors, then Sam swung the left door open and stepped inside as Mary followed.

"What do you think of her?" he asked, pointing at the mare.

Mary didn't answer, but slowly stepped up to the mare and began rubbing her neck. The mare's pleasant manner showed itself, as she nickered and almost smiled back at Mary, which Sam thought was impossible for a horse.

Mary turned with a big smile and said, "Sam, she's the most beautiful horse I've ever seen. What's her name?"

"I never named her. When I bought her, I only bought her because she was so pretty, and didn't want some yahoo buying her and treating her harshly. I've never ridden her or named her, though. I just felt like she belonged to someone else, and I'll admit that even when I bought her, I thought that I'd give her to either Julia or to you. After talking to you, I'm sure that she was meant to be your horse."

Mary didn't make any phony, 'I can't take such a gift' protests, nor did she worry about what Sam would ask in exchange because she already understood that he would do no such thing.

She just smiled softly at the horse, then turned and said, "Thank you, Sam. She's the greatest gift anyone ever gave me."

"Mary, I don't think I gave her to you. I think she was born for you. I think that you and she are kindred spirits, independent yet still with a good nature."

Mary was even more pleased after what Sam said because it told her that he seemed to accept her for who she was and not who her father wanted her to be. When she looked into the mare's eyes and saw that kinship of spirit and marveled at her new friend.

She then turned back to Sam and said, "Sam, can I leave her here with you? If I take her home, my father might give her away to prove to me that I shouldn't have a horse."

"Sure. I have plenty of saddles too, so I can set one up for you. If I'm not here, just take her out for a ride."

"Thank you, Sam," she said, her voice barely above a whisper.

"Now you've got to come up with a name for her, Mary."

"I already have a name for her. I knew that if I ever had my own horse, I'd name her Venus. The Roman goddess of love and beauty."

"What if she had been a gelding?" Sam asked with a smile.

Mary turned to Sam with a smile of her own and replied, "That's not possible, Sam. She was born for me."

Sam nodded, then said, "Yes, Mary. She was."

"I suppose I've got to get back. Father doesn't appreciate my riding around at all. He'd be seriously angry if he found I'd ridden here."

As they turned to walk back, Sam recalled the conversation with Jimmy Toomey and said, "Mary, before you go, I have to warn you about something that Jimmy Toomey said. He told me that he had his eye on you."

Mary stopped immediately and turned to Sam with wide eyes as she said, "Not him. Tell me you're joking, Sam."

"No, Mary. I'm not joking. I wish I was."

"He hangs around with Mike Malarkey. Julia asked me to be a witness at her marriage to Malarkey and Toomey was Malarkey's witness. While we were signing the forms, he put his hand on me and it wasn't an accident. I felt a chill down my back when that happened. The man scares me, Sam."

Sam reached into his pocket, pulled out the Remington derringer, then held it out to her and said, "Take this, Mary. It may look like a toy, but it's got some serious firepower. I've hit targets from thirty feet with that. All you need to do is pull the hammer back and pull the trigger. Don't aim it, just point it. If you need a second round, just do it again. It's already loaded with two cartridges. You shouldn't have to worry about someone like him."

Mary took the small pistol and slid it into her pocket as she said, "Thank you again, Sam."

He nodded again, then they began to walk out of the barn.

"Sam, how come Jimmy Toomey told you all those things? You're a Yankee and he hates Yankees."

"I can thank Joe for that, among other things. I used to mimic his Texas twang almost from the start, but he never could copy my Midwestern accent, because there isn't one. It's really boring, to tell the truth. I did it so often, that I can slide into it easily. When I saw him approaching, I just started talking that way. An accent, I notice, that you don't have."

"No, I'm the family oddity in that respect as well as the others. Julia didn't, either. Can you tell me something like a Texan?"

"Well, I sure can talk about that purty filly you got in the barn, ma'am. She's a might handsome critter and I ain't never seen nothin' quite so purty."

Mary laughed and shook her head as she said, "It's a bit overboard, don't you think?"

"That was just for you. I rarely go to that level."

"I've really enjoyed talking to you, Sam. Do you mind if I come by from time to time?"

"I'd thoroughly enjoy your visits, Mary. I feel as if I know you a lot better than someone I've only talked to for a short time. I guess it's because of all the time that Joe talked about you.

Anyway, if I'm not here, and Fire is in the barn, then I'm probably in my swimming hole in the far western pasture."

"You have a swimming hole?"

"I made it myself. I go out there at least three or four times a week and it sure beats filling the tub, not to mention it's a lot bigger so I get to dive and swim around."

"I have to admit, I'm jealous," she said as she grinned.

"Tomorrow, I'll be going into Mulberry to see what I can find out. I probably won't see Julia, but I want to find out as much as I can."

"If you see a very beautiful woman with dark hair, about five foot five, that's probably Julia"

"Thank you, Mary."

They reached the horse, and Mary mounted her brother's gelding.

"Thank you for everything, Sam, the gun and Venus. But mostly thank you for the most interesting conversation I've had in years."

"You're welcome, Mary. I enjoyed our talk as well."

She smiled one more time and turned the horse east toward the road, then waved one more time before heading north toward the Bar F as Sam waved back.

After she'd gone, Sam knew that Joe was probably right after all. He'd never met anyone like Mary before, but much more importantly, he felt as if they meshed like the gears in a fine watch.

Sam returned to the house with a lighter step. Now he had a reason to stay that didn't involve gunfights.

———

As Mary approached the Bar F access road, she knew that Joe had been right after all. Without question, Joe had been right. She knew even as Sam was talking about her lost brother that Sam Walker was definitely the man she'd been waiting to meet.

———

Just north of the Bar F, in the Slash D's abandoned ranch house, five men sat around the kitchen table.

"All right, Jimmy, what did they do?"

"They took their wagon to Bonham. They were loading up supplies."

"We can't stop 'em from buyin' in Bonham, but I'm surprised they had any money. They haven't been able to move any cattle for two years now."

"Must be gettin' low. Hey, Mike, I met a new feller today. Bought the old Circle W."

Mike sat back, glared at Jimmy and asked, "A carpetbagger bought the pig farm?"

"Nope. This feller was from back around Tyler. Said he had to get away from his old pappy."

"Got a wife with him?"

"Didn't see one, but I wasn't there long."

"What's he look like?"

"Big feller. Long, dark hair. Friendly enough, though."

"Was he packin'?"

Jimmy giggled before replying, "Nope. I told him he should wear a gun, and he said he should go and buy himself a pistol."

"Well, he ain't gonna matter none. Enough about him. Back to what I want to talk about. I want to push them Farrells outta here."

"We gonna go on another night shoot, Mike?" asked Pat, Jimmy's younger brother.

"I don't think that's enough anymore. I'm thinking we burn 'em out; their house, barn, even the bunkhouse."

"Want us to scare 'em out of the house first, Mike?" asked Reggie Anderson.

"Nah. Let 'em burn. Serves 'em right."

The last member of the group, Paul Hooper squirmed, and Mike noticed.

"You got a problem with this, Paul?"

"Boss, I ain't got a problem with scarin' 'em, but killing women is bad."

"Just tell yourself they'll be getting out of the house."

"Alright," replied Paul, unconvinced with Mike's attempt at logic.

"We'll do it tomorrow night. There won't be any moon, so you'll be able to ride straight across the south pasture and take care of it. Set the barn and house burnin' first. Get the bunkhouse later."

"Okay, Mike. We'll head over that way around nine o'clock tomorrow night. We'll get there just after they all head to bed."

"Come on back to my house and tell me how it went, even if it's late."

"Your wife won't mind?" Jimmie asked as he laughed.

"She does what I tell her if she knows what's good for her."

"We should be back sometime before midnight, I reckon."

"I'll leave a lamp burnin'."

———

91

That night, Sam had another Malarkey nightmare. In this one, Malarkey gestured him toward an open gate. All the other prisoners and guards were gone, and Sam knew he shouldn't go near Malarkey, but he did. As he walked closer, Malarkey kept smiling and waving him closer, pointing toward the open gate, letting him know that freedom was close.

Just before he reached the open gate, Malarkey slammed it closed and started laughing. Sam turned to leave, but his feet were stuck. He looked down and was terrified when he saw water filling the ground around his feet. *Why couldn't he move?* As he watched in horror, the water kept rising past his knees. He was panicking as he hurriedly scanned the empty prison camp. *Why wasn't the water going out the through the wire fences?* He looked back at the grinning Malarkey as the water reached his chest, and Malarkey started laughing.

He could feel the chilling wetness reach his chin, and knew he was about to drown as it passed his nose. He exploded into the real world with his heart pounding and the sweat pouring from his face as he swung his feet around to the floor, then sat on the edge of his bed with his wet forehead in his palms.

When his heart and breathing had returned to normal, he rose and walked out to the kitchen. There was still coffee in the coffee pot, so he filled a cup halfway and walked out to the back porch, then stopped and looked into the star-filled night sky.

Will the nightmares never end? He sipped the bitter, stale and almost cold coffee, but none of that mattered. He began to believe that the only way to end the horrible dreams was to finish Mike Malarkey himself.

He returned to the house, emptied the cup and put the coffee pot into the sink before returning to the bedroom and sitting on the bed, debating whether to try to get some more sleep or start his day a little earlier than normal. After two minutes, he sighed and slipped back under the quilt, then fell asleep faster than he expected.

CHAPTER 4

Sam felt surprisingly well rested when he left his bedroom for the second time that day. After a trip to the privy, he fixed himself breakfast, cleaned the dishes, then washed and shaved. He had worn a beard for most of the time he'd been in that prison camp, so he thought it would be more difficult for Malarkey to identify him if he was clean shaven.

He was dressed and ready to go to Mulberry by eight o'clock but held off for another hour. He put on his gunbelt and Stetson then went out to the barn and saddled Fire but took a second to say good morning to Mary's Venus. He decided to let her out to the corral so she could get some exercise and moved her before mounting Fire. He didn't have a long gun in his scabbard because he didn't want anyone to know about his Winchester, which was still a rare weapon in this part of the country.

He rode out of the Circle W and turned north, passed the entrance to the Bar F a minute later and wondered how Mary was doing. He wished she'd stop by later to find out if his reconnaissance in Mulberry yielded any results.

He reached Mulberry an hour or so later and headed for the dry goods store, figuring that he may as well pick up a good pocketknife while he was in town and should get a haircut, too. Just like his beard, while he had been in Malarkey's little corner of hell, he'd worn his hair long and thought a trim was a smart thing to do. Besides, barbers were a good source of information.

He stepped down, tied Fire to the hitch rail, then walked inside and let his eyes adjust to the lower light level. He walked to a display case that had a number of pocketknives, then found one that he liked that had a can opener. He asked the proprietor for one of the knives, paid for his purchase and slipped it into his now derringer-less pocket, he noted. He was heading for the exit when he stopped and turned back to the counter. He had been used to carrying the little derringer he had given to Mary and missed its added security, so he headed for the gun display, and spotted three boxed derringers.

He looked at the proprietor and said, "Let me have one of those Remington derringers and a box of ammunition."

"Yes, sir," the storekeeper said as he slid one of the Remingtons from the short stack and then pulled a box of cartridges from the shelf beneath the pistols.

He slid them onto the counter as Sam rummaged through his pockets, handed him a ten-dollar note and received his seventy-five cents in change.

He left the store feeling better and headed for the barbershop across the street. When he arrived, he was the only customer and was ushered into the chair immediately by the short, but friendly and impeccably groomed barber.

Once he was in the bright red leather barber's chair, he explained that he had let his hair go and needed a good haircut. But just as the barber was preparing to make his first cut, Sam, who had been staring out the window, noticed a very beautiful, dark-haired woman strolling on the boardwalk across the street from the barbershop and was almost sure that he was looking at Julia.

"Hold it!" he said loudly as he pulled off the apron, "I'll be right back."

The barber was stupefied as he watched Sam grab his Stetson, then jog out of the barbershop and head across the street.

Sam almost got run down by a passing rider but managed to avoid the accident by stepping back as the rider colorfully

94

expressed his displeasure before Sam continued to the other side.

He made it safely across the street and stepped onto the boardwalk. The woman had heard the commotion and turned to see what had happened just as he stepped onto the worn wooden surface.

"Excuse me, ma'am," Sam said, as he smiled, "You wouldn't happen to be named Julia, would you?"

Julia was startled. *Who was this man?* He didn't appear threatening, yet his smile and kind eyes marked him as very different from the others she'd had to avoid.

"Who are you?"

"My name is Sam Walker. I'm Joe's friend."

Julia felt her knees weaken, and Sam thought she might pass out.

But she regained her balance and asked quietly, "What are you doing here? Why aren't you in Iowa?"

"Joe made me promise to come here and make sure that you are okay."

She looked at Sam for a few seconds, then said, "It doesn't matter. You can't help," and began to turn away.

Sam knew he had just a short time to convince her and quickly said, "Julia, it really does matter to me, and I know that I can help. I have a ranch a few miles south of town now. I promised Joe and it's the only reason I left my home. I owe it to Joe."

"So much information!", Julia thought as she sighed, then turned and asked, "Sam, may I call you Sam?"

"Of course."

"Sam, this is a dangerous situation. I really wish you could help, but it wouldn't be fair."

"Julia, fair has nothing to do with it. Joe was more of a brother to me than my real brother. I would have given my life for him and I know that he would have done the same for me. That man that you married was the sergeant of the guards in our prison camp. He would beat the prisoners, including Joe. When Joe died, he even kicked him after he was dead. I know what he is capable of doing and I can't let you come to any harm. I'll do whatever I have to keep you safe."

Julia's mind was racing. *Could this be real?* She knew the name Sam Walker well, and based on the way Joe had described him, he was capable of doing what was necessary. He was even more impressive in person than he had been in her imagination, but she had made the mistake of marrying Malarkey, and it was too late to change that. The revelation of his position in the prison camp was a shock that was still racing through her mind.

After a few seconds, she replied, "I'm married to him now, Sam. I can't change that."

"Is it worth the risk, Julia? Sooner or later, that madman will hurt you badly. He has no soul."

Julia chewed on her lower lip, then said, "Sam, can you let me think about it, please? I live in town, just a few hundred yards from here. I'll come to the dry goods store tomorrow at ten o'clock if I choose to leave."

"I'll be here, Julia and I'll have a buggy waiting. If you want to come with me to the ranch, I can hide you there. I can send you to stay with my parents in Iowa if you'd like. You'd be welcomed and could live in peace and be happy. I can't offer much more than that."

Julia looked into his sincere eyes, then glanced behind her before she said, "I've got to go, Sam. If I decide to leave, I'll see you tomorrow."

"Goodbye, Julia."

"Goodbye, Sam."

Julia walked down the boardwalk to the store, watching Sam cross the street to return to the barbershop. Sam Walker was more than she had imagined since Joe's death. Joe had written to her telling her that if he couldn't make it, he'd send his best friend, Sam Walker, to help her.

Sam Walker had been her dream ever since she had learned of Joe's death and been ejected from the Farrell home. Now he was here in the flesh. She was still worried about the whole marriage problem, but she knew she had to go with Sam, especially now that she knew what Mike Malarkey had done to Joe. She didn't know if she'd be able to hide her rage and that might get her killed.

Sam returned to the barbershop to finish his haircut, wondering where he could get a buggy as he climbed back into the tall chair.

When he was thinking about what he would do next, the barber began to cut and talk.

"Mister, do you know who you were talking to?"

"It turns out she wasn't who I thought she was. I used to know a cute little gal down in Bonham and hadn't seen her in years. Her name was Barbara Jean. Boy! Was she a looker! Always regretted not visitin' her, too."

"Well, you're lucky. That was Mike Malarkey's wife."

"Who's he?"

"Nasty piece of work. Beats folks if he don't get his way and somebody needs to take him down a peg."

97

"Glad I don't live here, then."

"Sometimes I wish I didn't when he sends his boys around lookin' for his protection money."

Sam's eyebrows arched as he asked, "You tellin' me that he charges folks for not beatin' 'em up?"

"Or for not breakin' windows or settin' fires. You name the threat and him and his boys cover all the angles."

"How many boys does he have?"

"Well, there are the Toomey brothers, Reggie Anderson, and Paul Hooper. That's four and I don't think he's got any more."

"Sounds like a mess. What's with the sheriff?"

"Malarkey's got him in his pocket, so he's no help at all. I figure he's kinda afraid of Malarkey, too."

"So, if Malarkey and his boys just went away, things would be better in Mulberry?"

"Mister, if that happens, there may be a town party."

"Good to know. Say, you wouldn't know where I could rent or buy a buggy, would you?"

"Sure. Everybody knows that Willie down the livery has been tryin' to get rid of his buggy for a while now. He used to rent it out, but nobody does anymore. He'd probably give you a bargain price, too."

"Well, maybe I'll mosey down that way."

The barber finished with Sam's hair, and Sam paid the ten cents and added a nickel tip. He left the shop and felt the breeze on the back of his suddenly naked neck, crossed the street one more time, stepped up on Fire and turned him east toward the easily seen livery. After reaching the barn, he dismounted, soft tied Fire to the hitching rail and entered the large barn.

Willie Barton was near the front of the livery when Sam entered, so no shouting was necessary.

"Afternoon. What can I do for ya?" he asked.

"Barber tells me you have a buggy you'd like to get rid of."

Willie tried to hide his excitement but failed as he grinned and asked, "Yep. Out back. Wanna check 'er out?"

"Sure. Let's go see it."

They walked behind the barn and Sam did a quick appraisal of the buggy. It was dusty but overall seemed in decent shape.

"Looks a bit rough," said Sam, beginning the negotiations.

"Just dust is all. Wheels are all well-greased, and the pin is new and greased, too. Even the harness is in good shape. Just clean 'er off and she's as good as new."

"I'm not sure I really need one. I'm just thinkin'."

"I'd make you a good price, mister."

"I don't wanna use my big gelding to pull this thing. What do you have for horses?"

"C'mon over to the corral. Got six in there right now. At least two would make good pullers."

They headed for the corral on the other side of the barn and Sam liked two of them right away. One was a dark, almost-black gelding with a brown mane and tail. The second was a slightly taller gelding with a lighter coat and black mane and tail.

Those were the two that Willie wanted to show him, as it turned out.

"Now, these two were recently shod and would make either good ridin' horses or buggy horses. I could let you have one for thirty dollars if you get the buggy for another thirty dollars."

Sam thought about it. He still had $172.70 in his pockets and that $1,300 in the bank in Bonham.

"Tell you what, I'll give you seventy-five dollars for both horses and the buggy."

Willie made a pained face as he replied, "Mister, now that's downright cruel. I can't let those two and the buggy go for that. I'll make you a package deal for eighty-five dollars."

"We meet in the middle and I'll pay you cash right now. Eighty dollars."

Willie acted like he had to think hard, but both of them knew that he didn't.

"All right. I'll do 'er," he said while he grinned and shook Sam's hand.

Sam handed him the eighty dollars and they led the two geldings around to the buggy. Willie harnessed the buggy while Sam went around front and untied Fire, then led him to the back of the barn and hitched Fire to the right back rail and the other gelding to the left.

"Appreciate the business, mister. You got a name?" Willie asked as he stepped back.

"Last time I checked. Name's Sam Walker."

"Willie Barton."

They shook hands again, and Sam boarded the buggy, then waved to Willie before he drove around the barn and down the street. He felt a bit unmanly but after he turned onto the southern road and left town, the feeling vanished as he headed for his ranch.

He had to admit that it was a comfortable ride. The gelding had them moving at a good pace as he headed south and began to think of what tomorrow would bring. *Would Julia get in the buggy and let Sam drive her away from town?*

There was one thing he knew for sure. Joe had always said how beautiful Julia was, and Sam thought he must have been exaggerating. If anything, he had understated just how beautiful Julia was. She was one of those rare women that could take your breath away if she looked at you with those big brown eyes.

For an admittedly obvious reason, he wondered if she had the depth of personality that he had seen in Mary. Mary and Julia had obviously gotten along, so she wasn't some shallow flirt like Barbara Jean. If she did come with him, he'd already made up his mind that she'd live in the house, and he'd sleep in the bunkhouse. He'd done the minimal repairs to the bunkhouse that were necessary and even bought new bedding for the four bunks. The heat stove was in good shape, too. He had filled all the lamps in the house with more kerosene, including the one in the bunkhouse. It was a lot better than he'd spent many of his nights over the past six years.

He passed the Bar F and glanced that way, hoping to see Mary riding, but she wasn't. He was somewhat surprised by his infatuation with Mary after just a short conversation, but not entirely. It wasn't like he'd been struck by a lightning bolt or anything. He just felt so incredibly comfortable being with her, and it all came back to that meshing effect that he had already recognized.

There wasn't a hint of phoniness or protective facades in her. Mary was just an honest person who he was sure would be exactly the same person after he got to know her better. She reminded him a lot of Joe in that respect. He and Joe had met in Davenport, and even though Joe had arrived with four friends from Texas, he'd spent most of that first day with Sam. They had become close friends very quickly and stayed that way until that spirit-crushing day in February of 1865.

"Joe, I hope you're up there helping me. I don't want to screw this up," he prayed aloud as the Farrell ranch slid from view.

He turned his new buggy into the Circle W and headed for the barn. After taking care of all three horses, he rolled the buggy into the barn near the wagon, then took an old rag and began removing the dust that hadn't been blown free on the ride along with the new amount of Texas that had accumulated. That took almost twenty minutes.

He headed for the house, realizing that he had skipped lunch again and pulled out his watch. It wasn't too late for lunch after all, so stepped inside and made a quick lunch that was little more than a snack of ham and biscuits, before walking to the corral to ask for Rusty's help to head to the swimming hole.

When he walked behind the barn, he noticed that Venus wasn't in the group, so Mary must have stopped by for a ride after all.

Same smiled when he realized that it meant she'd be coming back.

He led Rusty out of the corral, closed the gate, then hopped onto his back and set him to a slow trot to the swimming hole. He was about a quarter mile away when he noticed that Venus was hitched to a scraggly bush near the hole and almost pulled Rusty to a stop in surprise, but then he did a quick scan and couldn't see Mary anywhere.

His good mood about spotting Venus vanished and was replaced by a sudden concern for her safety and was almost ready to return to the house to get his guns when Mary's head popped up from the pool's surface.

She saw Sam, smiled broadly and waved. Sam waved back and wondered if he should turn back and give her some privacy, but also wondered how she could be waving and staying above the water that was over well over six feet deep where she was. He finally determined that if she was that worried about it, she wouldn't have waved but instead would have gestured for him to go away, so he set Rusty to a slow trot again. He had to avoid putting Mary into the same category as other girls and women.

As she had told him yesterday, she was a strong-minded woman.

After he dismounted and dropped Rusty's reins, he stepped toward the patio, dropped to his heels and said, "Hello, Mary. I didn't expect to see you here."

Mary was treading water as she smiled and said, "I could tell when I saw your face. I think you were ready to run away. Weren't you?"

Sam smiled and replied, "I'll admit that the idea crossed my mind, but I remembered that you said you were headstrong, and I figured that when you waved, you wouldn't mind if I showed up."

"Good for you. I only got here a little while ago. You aren't going to kick me out, are you?"

"No. I'll wait my turn," he said and didn't know if he was grateful for the still brown-tinted water or not.

"Good. This is incredible, Sam. What a wonderful idea!"

"I like it."

"How did it go in Mulberry?" she asked as she paddled slightly closer so her feet could touch the muddy bottom.

Sam stood and walked toward the pool, so he didn't have to raise his voice, but looked away as he sat on the rocks, in case she decided to come any closer. The water wasn't that muddy.

"I found Julia right away. I was in getting a haircut and saw her across the street, so I went and talked to her. I don't think she's happy, Mary. She's afraid and I think Malarkey has been beating her, too. She told me to leave because she couldn't get away, but after we talked a little more, she told me to come back at ten o'clock tomorrow morning after she had time to think about it."

"Sam, do you mind turning around? I'll get dressed then we can talk."

Sam smiled, then said, "I guess you aren't quite the tomboy you claimed to be," as he stood, then faced back toward the house.

Mary laughed then stepped out of the water onto the hot rocks of the patio, and tiptoed to her clothes as she said, "How do you deal with these molten rocks?"

"I always splash water on them before I step out, then I can lay on top of them and let the sun dry me off."

Mary glanced at him as she quickly dried herself, then as she began to dress, asked, "How long do you lay there?"

"It varies. Sometimes it's only a couple of minutes, but I have been known to stay here for almost an hour. I have to be careful about falling asleep though. I'd turn into a piece of overcooked bacon if I did."

Mary laughed again as she sat down and pulled on her boots.

Sam's imagination wasn't doing him any favors since he'd heard her step out of the water, and it wasn't getting any better after hearing her dress, either.

Once she was sitting on the stones, with water dripping onto the rocks from her hair, she said, "You can turn around now, Sam."

After he took a seat on the rocks nearby, she asked, "So, what are you going to do, Sam?"

"Tomorrow morning, I'll drive my new buggy to Mulberry and see if she's waiting. If she gets into the buggy, I'll drive her back to my house. She can stay there until I take care of Malarkey and his boys. I was told that he has four, but it might be one or two more. It'll be as if I'm offering her sanctuary."

Mary wasn't surprised by what he'd just told her, but said, "Sam, that's really dangerous."

"I know it is. But it's more dangerous for Julia if she stays with him. Joe asked me to take care of her, Mary, and I have to do that."

"You're one hell of a good friend, Sam."

"Would you do any less for Julia, Mary?"

"I'd do what I could, but I can't do as much as you can."

"I know. If she comes here, she'll probably want to see you."

"She will see me. I'm becoming a bit more of a rebel at our house. I showed up last night, and my father demanded to know where I had been. He forbade me from taking another horse today, so I walked. It's less than a mile, so it didn't take long. That's why you were probably surprised because there wasn't a horse outside the house. If Julia is here, could I move in with you, too?"

Sam assumed that she understood that Julia would be alone in the ranch house, and answered, "That would be perfect, Mary. But how much grief would that cause for you at home?"

"With my mother and brother, none at all. I talked to my mother last night about coming over here. She understood and was happy for me. It was all of the letters from Joe that made it acceptable to her, you see. She had been so worried that you might not come at all. Then after my father greeted you with the shotgun, she was afraid that you'd leave. But she told me that after she saw you on that horse in front of the wagon, she knew that Joe was right."

"Joe was right about us, you mean?" he asked with raised eyebrows.

Mary's blue eyes held his as she simply replied, "Yes. About us."

"It's strange, isn't it, Mary? I was convinced that I was going to return to Iowa and marry Barbara Jean, but Joe never let that get in his way. He kept telling me that you were the only one for me and said it so often that I began to ignore it. But his last words to me were to come to Texas and take care of Julia and Beth. He knew that he wasn't going to last much longer, but he added that once I met you, and I'd know that you were the only one who was right for me. I told him I was going to marry Barbara Jean, and he just said, 'You never know.' They were his last words."

Mary sighed then, said, "Ever since we were little, Joe was always there for me. He'd watch out for me, like most big brothers, but he never treated me like a girl. He treated me like a person. We shared everything, and he'd tell me things that he'd never tell our parents, and I'd do the same.

"When he was going to join the army, he asked me to take care of Julia. But then we found out he'd died, and my father lost all reason. He cut off Julia and ordered her out of the house. His own daughter-in-law! I failed her, Sam. I failed Joe, and I was so ashamed of myself."

"You know, Mary. You remind me of my sister, Anna. She's younger than you are, though. She just turned eighteen when I left to come down here. We shared things just like you and Joe did. There's nothing about Anna that I don't know. She'd never keep secrets from me, and I wouldn't keep any from her.

"She told me that I shouldn't marry Barbara Jean before I left, but I didn't see Barbara Jean as she did. I'll be eternally grateful to Frank for marrying her, though. I probably would have had to marry her out of a sense of honor or something if she had still been unmarried when I did return. Do you know what Anna told me about Barbara Jean that really surprised me when I was home recovering?"

Mary looked at Sam with her lips and eyes smiling, almost already having an idea of what it might be, and asked, "What bit of knowledge did Anna pass your way?"

"Now, you have to understand that Barbara Jean was always a flirt. She'd wink and sashay very provocatively around the boys. I always thought it was just her personality and didn't let it bother me when I was young, although I admit I did appreciate it. Well, it sure worked on Frank, too, and I'm sure that he, like me and all the other boys thought that she was one of those women that would be, well, um, busy, once she was married.

"Well, after I returned, during one of our private conversations, Anna told me that Barbara Jean had confided to her before the wedding that she dreaded her wedding night and that the thought of having to be naked with Frank gave her the shakes. Anna was more than just a little surprised, and at first, thought that Barbara Jean was just trying to be funny.

"Everybody thought Barbara Jean was a borderline floozy, yet here she was confessing to Anna that the thought of being bedded disgusted her. It turned out that she hadn't been joking at all and confirmed it with Barbara Jean a month after the wedding."

Mary laughed and said, "That must have been a royal shocker for your brother."

Sam joined her in laughter, then said, "When Anna told me, she was laughing and reminded me of her warning before I had gone. I asked her why she had done that, and she said that the girls all thought that Barbara Jean was just too empty for me."

"I'll bet those same girls didn't think that about you."

"No, I'll be honest, and admit that they didn't. But Anna had spoiled me for all of them after I returned. I wanted a girl, and now a woman, who I could share everything with. Someone who I could talk to and listen to and not have to wonder if she meant something else."

"So, I have Anna to thank for your current marital status?"

Sam glanced at Mary and said, "Anna and my poor, deprived brother, Frank."

She laughed as she said, "Yes, I'd forgotten about Frank. That's a shame, isn't it?"

"What is?"

"Marrying someone and then acting like making love is a sin or something to be ashamed of?"

"My, my, Miss Farrell. You astonish me yet again. A fair young maiden such as you speaking of carnal lust? But yes, I agree with you in your perspective about that part of a marriage. It's part of life, a very big part, but just another piece that makes for a happy marriage."

"So, are you going to go for a swim now?"

"Not if you're sitting here watching."

"I'll give you the same consideration that you gave me. I'll turn my back until you're in the water."

"Alright. You turn and look at the barn and I'll let you know when I'm in the water."

"Fair enough," she replied as she turned and sat facing north.

Sam quickly kicked off his boots, then pulled off his shirt and pants.

Mary was still staring off to the north but wanted to turn around and surprise him. That conversation they'd just passed had filled in the few blanks that she had in her image of Sam and was reasonably sure that he understood her as well.

Sam smiled, took a short step back, made a short run, and cannonballed into the water, sending a giant plume of water into the air, soaking Mary.

She jumped up and turned quickly to the swimming hole and waited for Sam to surface, her hands on her hips of the dripping riding skirt.

When he did slowly rise from the brown water, he grinned and said, "I didn't say how I'd let you know I was in the water."

She started laughing, and Sam joined in from the pool as he treaded water.

As Sam looked at her, laughing as she stood in her soaked clothes, her wet hair still hanging down, there wasn't a doubt in his mind any longer. Joe was right. Mary was the only one for him. And just as Mary had believed, that recent sharing of information had let him know that she felt the same way. He'd spent less than thirty minutes talking to Mary, yet he knew. *How extraordinary!*

"I have half a mind to join you in there!" Mary shouted.

"You wouldn't dare! That would be a scandal of epic proportions."

Mary didn't disrobe, but kicked off her boots, then ran and cannonballed next to Sam, causing a huge wave that swamped him.

A few seconds later, he and Mary surfaced at the same time, both laughing too hard to tread water properly.

Sam drifted toward Mary and she drifted toward him as if drawn by magnets. He caught her in his arms, and with no preliminary words, kissed her.

Mary had not only expected the kiss, she was almost demanding it as she kissed him back.

They both stopped treading water as they slowly sank under the surface. When Sam's feet hit the bottom, he kicked back, and they rose out of the water into the bright Texas sun.

"That was one memorable first kiss, Mary," Sam said softly.

"I imagine the second won't be much different."

Sam continued to tread water but put his hands on her face and kissed her softly.

Mary put her arms around his neck and pressed her lips tighter against him as they again sank under the surface.

After Sam kicked them back to the air again, he let Mary go.

"Mary, I think it'll be safer if you get back on shore and dry off."

"Can't manage to control yourself, Sam?" she asked as she smiled.

"No. I'll admit it that it is getting more difficult by the second, as I'm sure you noticed it too. I'm very close to losing control, Mary."

"Oh, I definitely noticed, and I'm happy about it, too. I needed to make sure that you understood that you weren't going to be deprived in the same way that Frank was."

Sam smiled and was tempted to pull her back to him again, and do more than just kiss her, but knew that it was too soon, although he wasn't sure of that, either.

Mary took two strong strokes, reached the shore and stepped out.

Sam watched as her wet clothes clung to her body already aware when he had held her just how well-formed she really was under that loose shirt. He had felt her softness and swells against him under the water and it was what made it so difficult for him to let her go. But as he saw her in the bright sunlight with the wet cloth plastered to that well-formed young body, he knew that he wouldn't be able to leave the protection of the muddy water anytime soon.

Mary sat down on the patio rocks, wrung out her hair, then asked, "Sam, can I stay here tonight?", as if it was a normal question.

"Mary, you can't be serious. Staying here with Julia is one thing, but alone with me is something totally different. I've known you for two days, and you'd never be able to go back home again."

"Sam, I'm not asking you to make love to me, although I'm not asking you not to, either. I'm asking if I can stay here now. My mother doesn't want me to stay in the house any longer. She's worried that my father might lose his last bit of control and lash out. He was murderously furious with me last night. I don't have many things, so I'm almost asking for asylum, just like what you are offering Julia."

"In that case, Mary, yes, you can stay here. Do you still have the derringer?"

"I do. I put it in the saddlebags. I also have all my things, just in case. I was hoping I'd get a chance to ask you if I could stay. That's why I came to the swimming hole. That and I really wanted to use it. Everything that happened since you returned is just a very welcome bonus."

Mary paused, then continued, saying, "Sam, I'm not some wanton woman that throws herself at men. That kiss in the pool was my first, believe it or not. I'm just so comfortable with you. I don't worry about what you'll do or say, because I can already predict what you'll do or say.

"I would have been surprised if you had done or said anything different than what just happened because I wanted them to happen as well. I feel safe with you, Sam, and believe I could have stepped out of that pool stark naked in front of you, and you'd just have turned around."

Sam smiled and replied, "Probably, but I wouldn't guarantee it, either. Mary, I never once considered you a wanton woman.

To me you're the perfect innocent. You've done nothing but impress me from the first time I talked to you because you are so incredibly honest. I feel like there are no barriers between us.

"You and I can say what we think without worrying about how the other may react. Maybe that's what Joe saw in both of us, Mary. He would tell me how pretty you were, but he also talked about your openness and that you always said what was on your mind. That's when he kept telling me how well-matched we were."

"Well, now that we're agreeing that I'm moving into your house, did you want to get out of the water and get dressed so we can get me moved in?" she asked as she smiled.

"Alright. But I want you turn around and face the other way again."

"Okay," she replied before she turned around.

Sam kept his eyes on Mary as he slipped out of the water and quickly pulled on his pants. He had just pulled started buttoning the fly when Mary quickly turned back around and smiled at him.

"I thought you were going to turn the other way until I was dressed," he said, noting her mischievous smile.

"I said no such thing. You said to turn around and face the other way. You placed no time restrictions on how long I had to keep my eyes in that direction."

"Lord, you'd make a hell of a lawyer," Sam said as he grinned.

Mary walked up to him and touched his shoulder.

"Joe said you'd been shot twice. Is that one of them?" she asked quietly.

"It is. He didn't tell you where the other one was, did he?"

"Can I see that one, too?" she asked with a slight smile, knowing where the scar was.

"Not yet, wanton woman. Only my wedded wife can see that one."

"Are you telling me that you've never been with a woman?"

"Not since that wound."

"Oh. I was worried I was getting some inexperienced newcomer."

"When I honor you with my lovemaking, Miss Farrell, I will show you how experienced I am."

Mary slid her arms around Sam, and he responded by holding her close and kissing her again.

He then slid his lips down the side of her still-wet neck, and Mary felt a chill rip down her back and felt her toes curl.

Sam stopped, and she asked him to do it some more by putting her hand behind his head and pulling his lips to her neck again and tilting her head to the side as she moaned lightly, letting him know the impact he was having on her.

When he returned to kissing her lips, she pushed her hips against him and wanted so much more but knew it would have to be delayed.

When their lips parted, she leaned back slightly and softly said, "I guess I will be honored when we finally share our bed."

"No, Mary. I was just being funny. I'll be the one who is honored."

"Soon, Sam?" she asked as she looked into his eyes.

"Yes," he whispered before stepping back to prevent it from happening even sooner on those hard rocks under their feet.

C. J. PETIT

Once the sudden outbreak of lust had subsided slightly, Sam smiled and said, "You know it's going to be a tough ride for me going back to the house."

"Really? Why?"

"When men get excited and nothing happens, it's kind of uncomfortable. If they then have to ride a horse, it gets worse."

"We can walk back."

"Do you mind? I mean, it's almost a mile."

"We can talk while we stroll that way."

"That's a generous offer. I thank you, Miss Farrell."

Sam finished dressing while Mary watched, then pulled on her boots when Sam did, and they walked around the pool, took their horses' reins, and began to stroll back to the house, chatting comfortably as they stepped along, neither one thinking that what had occurred in the swimming hole was anything unusual at all. It was just the way they were and why each of them felt they belonged together.

———

Julia sat on her bed, wringing her hands. *How could she get away in the morning?* She needed as many of her things as she could squeeze into one travel bag: an extra dress and her riding outfit at the least. Maybe she could take two extra dresses, but she'd need her underthings, her hairbrush and toothbrush, and some other things, too. But it was that whole marriage thing that still bothered her.

She knew that she had no rights as a wife, and if Mike decided to come and take her back, he'd be within his rights as her husband. *Why had she ever consented to marry him?* She found out soon after they had wed that he had scared off any other potential suitors, but he had her in his control now. She hated it when she had to perform her wifely duties and

114

remembered how Joe had loved her in every way possible, and she had reciprocated.

Sam reminded her so much of Joe. Joe said in his letters that Sam was the best man he had ever met. She remembered how Joe had always written about him and knew that Sam would be every bit as attentive in bed as Joe had been. It had added to his mystique in her imagination and added weight to her decision to go with Sam tomorrow. She just had to find a way to get out of the house without attracting attention.

Mike was off on one of his secretive meetings, and didn't know if it was another woman, which she hoped for, or if he was arranging something violent. It was probably the latter. She knew of his protection game and knew it was hurting people, but there was something else, too. She didn't know what it was and had only caught snippets. It was something that involved scalawags.

———

Mike was indeed arranging something violent. He was meeting with his boys at the Slash D and had brought a bucket of coal oil and some torches from his lumber mill. They were sitting on the kitchen floor as they went over their plans.

"Pat and me will fire the house, Mike, while Paul and Reggie set the barn on fire. We're gonna stand at the doors to make sure nobody comes out. If they do, we start shootin'. It'll drive 'em back in. After the house is good and burnin', then we'll go and take out the bunkhouse."

Mike leaned forward and put his elbows on the table.

"Nah. Leave the bunkhouse. Let everybody think it was an accident. We'll put it out that the White Knights are riding to rid Texas of scalawags and carpetbaggers after a few days."

"Good thinkin', boss," replied butt-kissing Pat Toomey.

"I'm gonna head back to the house, so I can have an alibi. I'll give you all alibis, too. The wife will see me, and then I'll tell her we were playin' poker."

"Okay, boss. We'll do 'er right," said Reggie.

"This is only the first one, boys. There'll be others."

Mike Malarkey stood, left the room, then the boys started up a penny ante poker game to kill the time until the light was gone, and mischief could begin; mischief that would reach the level of murder.

———

"Sam, where did you get so many horses?" Mary asked as she was putting her things away.

Sam was sitting on the bed as he answered, "Well, I bought two more today for the buggy, and I bought two others when I bought Venus for the wagon. Rusty was my horse in Iowa."

"Where did you get the other three?"

"I was waylaid in Arkansas by three men, then fought them off and killed them. That's where the others came from, including Fire."

"Is it hard, killing men?"

"I've never killed a man who wasn't trying to kill me. That makes a difference, a big difference. But even then, after the fight with the three outlaws, I threw up. That had never happened in battle. Maybe because it was so unnecessary, Mary. Those guys could have asked for some money and I would have given it to them, but they didn't. They wanted everything I had, including my life."

"When a man gets desperate, he'll do anything, I guess."

"It depends on the man, I believe, Mary. None of those three men were short of weight. They look liked they'd been eating regularly. They had those nice horses, saddles, and pistols, too.

They could have done something else. They had no idea what desperation really is. When you have nothing, no food, no good water, and no hope, then you see truly desperate men. We had some men who would beat other prisoners for what little food they had. They even murdered some.

"Joe and I sat back-to-back for the heat, but also for the protection, so no one could sneak up behind us. We had just as little food as they did, but we didn't take from the other men. Most of those desperate men in the camp didn't steal from other men. There were times we shared what we had with those that had been robbed. We were all desperate men, but the true nature of a man is revealed when he's desperate.

"Those three that I killed had a lot of other things they could do besides murder and rob unsuspecting travelers. If they had been in the camp with us, they would have been the ones with the clubs."

"I know that you killed one of the prisoners, Sam. Joe wrote about it. I guess the Confederate censors thought it was okay to show how Yankees killed their own."

Sam looked at her in surprise and said, "I didn't know he wrote about that, Mary."

"You saved his life, didn't you, Sam?" she asked in a whisper.

Sam nodded before she asked, "Can you tell me what happened? Joe just wrote about it in one line."

"Only to you, Mary. No one else has ever heard this before."

Then he exhaled softly and said, "Joe had been snoozing and I was almost asleep, when I heard a noise from my left and glanced that way. There was a prisoner about to club Joe for his boots. I could tell because he was barefoot, and Joe's feet were the same size. I can still see him in my mind, raising that club high over his head. I didn't know where I found the strength, but from a sitting position, I whipped my right fist into the man's stomach and watched as he bent over with madness in his eyes.

"He was going to use that same club on me, but I didn't give him that chance. I grasped both of my hands together and slammed my left elbow into his nose. I don't know what I hit, but the big man fell flat onto his face and didn't rise. I just called the guard and the body was taken away.

"Joe saw the whole thing, but never said a word. I didn't think he realized how close he had been to having his head crushed, but I couldn't sleep for two days after that. Not because I was upset about killing him, but because I was worried that someone else would try to hurt Joe. He was already weaker than I was, and those bullies always looked for the weak ones. Especially if they had something worth stealing, like Joe's boots."

Mary stopped putting away her things and sat down next to Sam, but neither spoke. Mary knew that telling the story had brought back horrible memories that Sam must have been trying to keep away and regretted having asked for an explanation.

"I'm sorry I asked, Sam."

"No, Mary. It's alright. I suppose it's good to tell someone. I never talked about that year in the prison camp, not even to Anna. That surprised her, too. I didn't want to burden her with it, I suppose. It would have made her too upset to hear of the horrors. But I know how strong you are, Mary. I know you'll understand."

"I do understand, Sam. You can tell me anything, anything at all."

"Thank you, Mary. You're very special."

"No, Sam, I'm just a woman who understands you. You're the one who's special. You do things that most men don't do, just to help those that need help."

THE SCALAWAGS

Sam smiled at her and said, "I do have one more story for you that's less traumatic. It's how I came into possession of that derringer in your pocket. It's quite funny, really."

Mary smiled at the change and asked, "Is it off-color at all?"

"Only if I choose to make it so. I can clean up the details if you'd like."

"Don't you dare. I want all the lurid details," she said with a grin.

Sam smiled back at Mary and began the tale, saying, "Alright. It started on my trip down to Arkansas on the riverboat. There was this couple…"

As Sam told the story of the scam and the scammer's leap from the boat, followed by the 'coupling' of the victim and the temptress, Mary found herself laughing almost uncontrollably. Sam enjoyed every second of telling the story, just to have Mary laugh beside him. She was so perfect for him, and he hoped he could be just as perfect for her.

After he finished the admittedly ribald story, she said, "Well, Sam, it's time I paid for my sanctuary."

"Really, Mary, you don't need to do anything. You're a guest."

"I'm only interested in self-preservation, Sam. I'd rather eat my own cooking."

Sam laughed and said, "In that case, preserve away. It'll probably save me as well."

Mary stood and waltzed into the kitchen, leaving a smiling Sam behind.

After she left, he rose, walked to his room and thought of what he should take out to the bunkhouse.

The sun was setting when Sam and Mary sat down to eat their first shared meal, and both believed it was the first of thousands that they would have together.

———

Mike Malarkey was in his house making sure that Julia saw him while Julia had her travel bag stuffed and hidden in the linen closet. Each of them expectantly waiting for tomorrow for totally different reasons.

———

At the Slash D ranch house, Jimmy and Pat Toomey, Reggie Anderson, and Paul Hooper were still playing poker, Pat was winning.

At the Bar F, just south of the Slash D, Max Farrell was in the bunkhouse reading, while his mother, Sophie, was cleaning up after dinner. Earl Farrell was in the main room, smoking his pipe.

Everything remained peaceful for another hour and a half. The sun was gone, and there was no moon yet and Max was getting ready for bed as his parents were turning off lamps to prepare for sleep.

Mike was still annoying Julia with meaningless chatter while a few miles south of town, the boys had just quit their card game and walked out to saddle their horses.

Sam and Mary were sitting on the porch steps and had already extinguished all the lamps except one. They were engaged in a mild argument, if it even approached that level.

"I think it's just better this way, Mary."

"Sam, you're being a prude. I know you won't sneak into my room and ravage me. Besides, I would feel more secure with you in the next room."

"How do I know you won't slip into my bed while I'm sleeping and ravage me?" he asked as he smiled.

"You don't, do you? Or is that wishful thinking?" she asked as she grinned back.

"Maybe. But there is one real reason, Mary. I have nightmares that can be very disturbing. They show up often enough that I know they would ruin your sleep."

"Even if I'm in another room?"

"I'm not sure, but sometimes I think that I, um, get loud."

"Do you scream, Sam?"

"I think so. That's the best reason for me to sleep in the bunkhouse. They stopped for a while when I was traveling to Texas, but then they started again after I arrived. I keep hoping that they'll go away."

"Sam, maybe they won't go away until you're at peace with yourself."

"How can I do that, Mary? What do I need to do? I was in a peaceful place in Iowa on our farm, but they showed up almost every night. Here, I can at least go two or three nights without one sometimes. How can I ever find peace?"

"With me, Sam," she said quietly, "Sleep in the next room and remember that I'm right next door."

Sam thought about it and wondered if she may be right. Mary had been a soothing influence since they'd started talking.

"Let me think about it, Mary."

"Alright. I'm going to go inside and get ready for sleep. If you decide to sleep in the house, I'll know."

"Thank you, Mary," he said as she stood.

She leaned over and kissed him gently before walking across the porch and entering the house.

Sam sat and thought about the nightmares and Mary, but mostly about Mary. It had been such an amazing day, beginning with his discovery of Julia and then spending most of the day with Mary.

———

Max was already asleep. He liked sleeping on his own in the bunkhouse when it was warm because he liked to think of himself as a regular cowhand.

His parents were in bed and drifting off after a tense day. Earl had asked where Mary was, but Sophie had simply told him not to worry about it and he let it go. He really didn't care where she was anyway.

———

Julia was knitting, wondering why Mike was so chatty, despite her saying nothing in return. He rarely spent this much time with her, even when he yanked her into his bed. There was something going on and not knowing was making her nervous.

———

The boys took their soaked torches and started their horses walking toward the Bar F, almost giggling in anticipation of watching the house and barn go up in a hell-like inferno.

———

Mary was lying in bed with her boots off but was still wearing her britches and shirt. She was thinking as much as Sam was, but was thinking of very different things. Mary never wanted to leave his ranch and already wished that Sam was lying beside her. Surprisingly, it was more because of her firm belief that she could help him with his deep wounds that kept those nightmares from destroying his sleep. She admitted that she wanted the other things that sleeping with him would give her, but she wanted to help him even more.

Just thirty feet from where Mary lay awake, Sam rose, then walked to the barn. He figured as long as he was awake, he may as well make himself useful. He left the big doors wide open to let in what little light was available, then entered, picked up a brush and began to rub down Fire while he figured out where he would spend the rest of the night. Sleeping with Mary in the next room might bring peace to his mind, but not to anything else. He might not even get to sleep knowing she was there, so he kept thinking about it as he massaged Fire's flanks, unaware of the other fire that soon would be set ablaze just a mile northeast.

———

The boys had crossed onto Bar F land in the dark night after cutting the three barbed wires.

"We're almost there, fellas. Paul, when you and Reggie see my torch fired up, get that barn goin'."

Paul was grinning as he replied, "Okay, Jimmy. This'll be somethin' to see. I ain't seen no big fire before."

"Me neither. It'll be somethin' all right."

They reached the back yard of the ranch house and dismounted about a hundred feet behind the house.

Jimmy made sure they each had plenty of matches in their shirt pockets before they began walking to the house and barn.

———

Sam finished with Fire and finally decided that he'd sleep in the house. He wanted to know if it really could help with the nightmares and secretly hoped that Mary would join him but wouldn't even admit it to himself.

———

The boys were all in position, so Jimmy struck a match and set his torch ablaze. Reggie and Paul did the same and tossed their torches into the barn. One was thrown into a pile of hay just inside the big doors, and the second landed against the back wall, the flames crawling up the side of the dry wood. The hay ignited instantly and soon stretched back to ignite back wall.

But less than a minute after tossing the torches, the barn was already engulfed in flame.

Jimmy saw the barn starting to go and got excited at the sight, then tossed his torch onto the house's roof, thinking it would burn and drop inside, but hadn't bothered to notice that the house had a tin roof. When the hard wood handle of the torch struck the roof, it made a clanging noise and slid back down to his feet. He swore, picked it back up, and put it against the wall.

Pat had placed his flaming torch well, just under the back porch where it met the house. The wood almost sucked the flame from the torch and was soon blazing.

Inside, Sophie heard the loud clang and was still sleep heavy, so she wasn't sure she had heard anything. She lay there for another thirty seconds until she suddenly smelled smoke.

"Earl! Earl! Wake up! There's a fire!" she shouted as she jostled her husband.

"What? Fire?" he mumbled.

Sophie rolled out of bed and shouted again as she pulled him from the bed, "A fire! The house is on fire! We need to get out!"

Earl finally comprehended the danger and hurriedly got out of bed but insisted on putting on his boots.

Sophie waited until he had them on and followed him toward the kitchen, not realizing that the blaze was the strongest at the back of the house. They soon discovered that they had gone the wrong way, and Sophie turned, then hurried back down the hallway with Earl right behind her.

Jimmy had moved to the front of the house and had his pistol ready for anyone to try to escape the blaze. Pat was in back and both the house and barn infernos were still building, although the barn fire was much more advanced.

———

Sam was walking back to the house and saw the bright light from the direction of the Bar F. It took about ten seconds for him to realize that there was a fire, then he quickly ran into the house.

"Mary! There's a fire at the Bar F! Get up!" he shouted as he ran to his gun room.

Mary went from reverie to startled alertness immediately and sat up, pulling on her boots as Sam ran past.

Sam was still wearing his gunbelt as he ran into the gun room and grabbed his Winchester. He was quickly walking back to the front of the house as Mary shot out of her room.

"What can I bring?" she asked.

"Just bring yourself. We don't have time to saddle the horses, I'll just toss on some bridles. We need to help your family. I don't think this was an accident," he said loudly as they hustled out of the house, across the porch and raced toward the barn.

———

Sophie and Earl were gagging in the ever-thickening smoke as they made their way to the front of the house. Sophie saw the doorway and ran toward it when a shot cracked nearby, shattering the right side of the door jamb.

"Earl! Someone's out there shooting at us!"

Earl was behind Sophie and looked desperately for a way out, but there wasn't one, so he sank to his knees and started praying.

Sophie wasn't ready to give up yet. She ran to the left side of the door and stood there as two more shots were fired. She continued to cough and wondered how long she could last before she became desperate enough to face the gunman.

———

Sam and Mary were on their horses and charging out of the Circle W. Just seconds later, they reached the main roadway and headed north at full speed while Sam gripped his Winchester tightly. Both hoped they weren't too late.

Max was terrified. The barn and house were burning, and when he stuck his head out, he was met with gunfire from Reggie and Paul, who had been walking to the house to help Jimmy and Pat when they saw the boy emerge from the bunkhouse in bare feet. They had both started firing, but Reggie told Paul to get some burning wood and set the bunkhouse on fire while he kept the boy inside.

Max had dropped to the floor and buried his face in his arms still with no idea what to do.

Pat was the only one not to have expended any ammunition. He still had all six rounds in his Colt. They had all made sure all six cylinders were full before they had started. Jimmy had already used five rounds, Reggie had used five, and Paul had fired four. They hadn't brought any extra ammunition or pistols, and reloading wasn't an option.

Sam had heard the pistol shots over the loud drumming of the horses and the noise from the fires; the unmistakable crack of pistols separating itself from the other sounds.

"They're shooting, Mary! Stay back about a hundred yards until I drive them off!" he shouted.

Mary knew she was no good trying to help her family if those men were still there, so she yelled back, "Alright!"

They rounded onto the entrance road at a slowed speed and picked up the pace as soon as they were riding straight again. It was an awesome, but horrifying, sight that greeted their eyes. Sam could pick up Jimmy's shadow right away but wasn't sure if it was one of the bad men or Max, so he'd have to depend on scaring them off, or waiting until he saw muzzle flares.

None of the arsonists were aware of Sam's approach as they continued their work and the fire roared nearby.

Sophie was on her knees as well, but not in prayer, she was succumbing to the smoke. But by dropping down, she found cleaner air where the outside air was being sucked through the open door to feed the flames that were consuming the back of the house.

Earl had fallen face down to the floor in the center of the main room.

Paul had found a flaming board and was trotting toward the bunkhouse to use it in lieu of a real torch.

Pat had walked around the front of the house because the back was burning so intensely that he knew no one was coming out back there. He began firing into the house just to get some shots off, firing three rounds quickly.

Sam was within sixty yards when he slowed Fire down to a walk and began to fire his Winchester. He fired at Jimmy's feet first, the .44-caliber round exploding the ground just inches from his right boot.

For a second, Jimmy didn't know what to make of it, but then whirled around and saw a flame-lit Sam firing a rifle.

"Shooter!" Jimmy screamed at Pat, who had just fired his fourth round at the house.

Sam glanced toward the bunkhouse and saw one of the arsonists carrying a flaming board, was sure he wasn't Max, so he aimed and fired.

Paul took the round in the left arm after the bullet had creased the left side of his chest. He screamed and dropped the board.

Reggie panicked, then turned and ran away from the scene, heading toward his horse.

Jimmy turned toward Sam, aimed and pulled the trigger. The hammer fell onto a used percussion cap and just made a sickening click. Out of ammunition, he followed Reggie's lead and scrambled away toward the horses.

Pat snap fired his last two shots in Sam's direction before chasing after his older brother. Even the wounded Paul managed to get to his feet and join the full retreat.

Sam didn't chase after them because there was no time. He slid down from Fire, and raced to the front porch, which was still clear of flames, and entered the smoke-filled main room. He immediately saw Sophie on the floor, then turned, slid his Winchester back across the porch onto the dirt in front of the house, then crouched down in the heavy smoke, pulled Sophie into his arms, and carried her from the house.

Mary had seen everything and urged Venus forward. She arrived as Sam was carrying her mother down the porch steps as flames began pouring out of the front windows and soon the roof above the porch was ablaze and threatening to collapse.

Sam laid Sophie down on the ground, and she soon began to cough heavily, so he lifted her into a sitting position to let her breathe.

"Mama! Mama!" Mary shouted as she neared her mother.

Sam still was holding Sophie as she continued to cough, then looked at Mary and said, "Mary, can you help your mother? I've got to get those horses out of the corral."

"Go ahead, Sam. I'll help her."

Mary knelt by her mother as Sam lowered her gently to the ground before sprinting toward the horses.

He ran quickly past the intensely hot barn using his left arm to shield his face from the intense heat and reached the corral where the six horses were panicking as the barn's flames licked nearby.

When Sam knocked down the railings of the corral on the fence farthest from the fire, the six horses all raced past the opening into the nearby pasture. Sam used the rope that had been looped around one of the posts and began making a crude trail rope for the horses. The horses had all calmed down once they were a hundred yards from the flames, and they were soon just grazing as Sam looped his trail rope around each one. When it was done, he led the six horses around the far side of the house as far from the flames as practical and soon approached the front of the house.

Mary and Sophie were standing looking at the house. Sophie was still coughing, just not as severely.

"He's still in there, Mary. He stopped and began to pray. The last I saw of him he was lying face down on the floor."

"It was his time, Mama."

"I know, dear. He had changed so much since that blasted war. He seemed to hate everything and everyone. What do we do now, Mary?"

"Tonight, we'll go to Sam's place. He's got plenty of room."

"Mary, what can we do? Your father is gone. Where is Max?"

"Wasn't he in the house?"

"No, he was in the bunkhouse. He was camping out."

Sam walked the horses to Mary and Sophie and glanced back at the two infernos.

"We'd better get back from the house, Mary. It's ready to collapse. The barn will go first, though."

"Alright. But, Sam, we need to find Max. Mama says he was in the bunkhouse when this started."

Sam picked up his Winchester and handed it to Mary.

"I'll go and find Max. Take the horses out to Venus and Fire.

Mary nodded and took the trail rope.

She and her mother began slowly walking to where Fire and Venus stood grazing off to the north of the access road. Sophie kept looking back as Sam raced to the bunkhouse and feared for her only surviving son.

They had just reached Venus when the barn collapsed in a roar, sending heat waves and flaming debris rolling across the yard.

Venus jerked her head up, but Mary had already reached her and calmed her down. Fire never stopped eating the lush grass.

Sam jogged toward the bunkhouse and hoped that he'd find Max hiding under a bunk. He reached the door, saw Max lying face down on the floor and felt his stomach turn.

Max heard him approach and expected to be shot at any second.

Sam stepped forward and knelt next to Max, then rolled him over, expecting to have to close his eyes, but was greeted with a loud sigh followed by, "You're Sam Walker, aren't you?"

Sam blew out his breath and replied, "Yes, I'm Sam Walker. Max, you scared me to death. Let's go and see your mother and Mary."

Sam stood and waited while Max scrambled to his feet.

"How's my father?" he asked.

"He never made it out of the house, Max. I'm sorry."

Max didn't reply, but they headed out of the bunkhouse and walked down the access road, leaving the heaven-groping flames behind them.

Sophie saw Max with Sam and began to cry. She had feared the worst from the horror of the night. Losing her husband of twenty-seven years was bad enough, but if her remaining son had died, it would have been devastating.

Max saw his mother and trotted faster, leaving Sam behind. He reached her and was smothered in a motherly hug and kisses.

Sam approached Mary and asked, "Can your mother ride with you? I think Max can handle sitting on a horse by himself."

"I think so. I'll ask her."

Five minutes later, Mary and her mother were sitting on Venus, and Max was sitting on one of the Bar F horses as they plodded south to the Circle W, arriving at the house seven minutes later.

Sam slid from Fire's back, walked to Venus and helped Sophie down before Mary slid to the ground.

"Mary, could you take Max and your mother into the house? I'll get the horses taken care of and join you in a few minutes."

"Okay."

After the Farrells had gone into the house, Sam led the six new horses, Venus, and Fire toward the barn. He just let the lead rope drop and put Venus and Fire in their stalls and removed the bridles, tossed in some hay, then moved the six horses around behind the smokehouse, put them in their own corral and removed the rope. He wrapped the rope into a coil and hung it on a corral post before closing the gate and walking to the house.

He stepped up on the front porch and entered the main room finding it eerily quiet. Sam took a seat and looked at Sophie, who was still covered in soot.

"Sophie, what do you want to do about this? It's in the county's jurisdiction, so we can go down there tomorrow and have them charged with murder and arson."

"Did you see who they were?" she asked.

"I know one of them. Jimmy Toomey was out front of the house shooting his pistol. I'd have to guess that the other three were Paul Hooper, Reggie Anderson, and Jimmy's brother, Pat."

"But can you prove it?"

"I hit one of them. I saw some blood on the ground near the bunkhouse. I knew it wasn't a leg wound because he ran so fast to get out of there. If we check to see who took a shot to the arm, we could find him."

"Sam, the sheriff, won't do anything. He might even throw you in jail for shooting one of them."

"That's what I was afraid of. I already heard that Mulberry's sheriff is owned by Mike Malarkey, but it sounded to me like the rest of the town was just plain scared of Malarkey's crew. Sophie, what will you do with the ranch? Will you rebuild the house and barn?"

"I can't afford either. I may have to sell."

"Well, hold off until things are over."

Sam then looked at Mary and asked, "Mary, I realized tonight that you need to be better armed. Do you think you'll be able to handle a pistol?"

"I think so. My hands are pretty large for a woman."

"Max, how about you? You're going to have to grow up awfully fast."

"I will. I'll learn how to shoot, too."

"Now, I'll be arming you both just for defensive purposes. I'm not going to have you do anything beyond that."

"What about me?" asked Sophie, "I'd like a pistol myself."

"Alright. I have three gunbelts with Colt New Army pistols. Tomorrow, when I come back from getting Julia, we'll spend some time getting you familiar with the guns. Right now, I think we all could use some sleep. I don't think Malarkey is going to be very happy with his boys when he sees them tomorrow. He may send them back for another attempt."

"Okay, Sam," replied Mary.

"You and Sophie have the house now. I'll be in the bunkhouse with Max. Hopefully, Julia will be in the third bedroom tomorrow."

Sam knew they all needed some time to recover from the disaster. Earl Farrell may have been a bitter man his last few years, but he was still Sophie's husband and Mary and Max's father. Sam didn't say anything more before he quietly left the house and walked to the bunkhouse.

————

Jimmy had wrapped Paul's wound in a towel, but knew he needed to see the doctor and have it sewn up.

"Who was that bastard?" he whined.

"That musta been the new guy, the one who bought the old pig farm. Seems like an all right fella. He musta come over there because of the fire and saw us shootin'. But our problem now is what do we tell Mike? I say we ignore the whole shootin' part and tell him it worked great."

"How are you gonna explain this?" Paul shouted, holding up his arm.

"We say you caught a ricochet. No problem. Unless you guys wanna get Mike all pissed off, I say we don't tell him."

Reggie and Pat readily agreed and eventually, Paul reluctantly approved the deception.

"Alright, I'll take Paul to the doc. You two can stay here until the morning."

Paul was anxious to get his arm repaired, so he stood, and Jimmy went with him to the horses. They departed the Slash D an hour before midnight.

———

Mike Malarkey was still downstairs waiting for news about the fire. Julia had retired at nine thirty, not because she was tired, but because Malarkey usually let her be after she'd gone to sleep. Usually, but not always and Julia hoped this wasn't going to be an exception. It was unusual for him to be just pacing as he'd been doing for a while tonight. It was his habit to go to the saloon if he was still awake after ten o'clock, so she was certain that something was happening.

Around midnight, Jimmy Toomey finally arrived. He only had to tap on the door to get Malarkey's attention, then strode in with a big grin on his face.

Mike looked at his number two and said, "It looks like everything worked."

"You bet, boss. You shoulda seen those things burn!"

"Anybody get out of the house?"

"No, sir. Didn't see nobody. If they was in there, they're burned up now."

"Good. Here. Get all the boys some drinks on me," he said, tossing Jimmy a five-dollar gold piece.

"Thanks, boss. We appreciate it. Oh, I had to drop Paul off at the doc. He caught a ricochet."

"Bad luck for him. He probably won't get any whiskey."

"Probably not. Well, I'll go and tell the boys," he said, slipping the coin into his pocket.

"Y'all have fun," replied a smiling Mike Malarkey.

Jimmy gave a short wave and left the house.

Mike Malarkey was in a good mood and returned to his office where he took a decanter of bourbon and a crystal cut glass from his private bar, poured himself two fingers of the whiskey and slammed it home. It could have been moonshine for all he cared. He'd wiped out those scalawags and nobody would be the wiser.

———

Sam's eyes were shifting rapidly behind his closed eyelids. He had never seen it so crowded. There were so many of them that no one could sit down. Sam felt so tired. He needed to sleep, but he was being held on his feet by the jostling men. Where was Joe? He should be here somewhere. Sam began to turn, looking for his friend, but all the other prisoners weren't even Union men. They were all wearing butternut. This wasn't right and he knew that he shouldn't even be here. This is a Union prison. Sam had to be let out of this place, so he hurriedly began looking for a guard in a blue uniform. Where were the guards?

He finally spotted one right near the main gate. He began to shove the others away, swimming though men. They all grinned at him, as if they knew a secret he didn't know.

"Guard! Guard! I'm a Federal sergeant! Guard!" he screamed.

But the guard didn't even turn around.

"Guard! Let me out of here! I don't belong here!" he shouted even louder.

Finally, the guard turned to acknowledge Sam's screams and Sam almost vomited. It was Mike Malarkey. He looked at Sam and began to laugh.

Sam's eyes snapped open as he jerked into a sitting position, breathing heavily, with sweat dripping from his forehead.

"Sam, are you all right?" asked Max from across the bunkhouse.

Sam tried to calm himself and after a few seconds, replied, "I'm all right, Max. Sorry I woke you up."

"You were yelling for a guard to let you out. Were you having a nightmare about prison camp?"

"Yeah. I'll be all right now."

"Good night, Sam."

"Good night, Max."

Sam lay on back down on the bunk. The nightmare, in addition to triggering bad memories, had slipped him into a mild depression. Earl Farrell was dead. The Bar F had no house or barn. Beth had died, and Julia was in the hands of the hated Mike Malarkey. It was like God was playing with him. *What could he do to rectify these wrongs? Was it even possible?*

Sam felt so useless. He had no help and would have to do everything on his own. The more he thought about it, the worse it all became. His mood became as dark as the night as he faded back into sleep.

CHAPTER 5

Sam had set his pocket watch alarm for six o'clock, just in case he had a bad night. It went off and started his day as it was designed to do. His mood hadn't improved since last night.

He pulled on his clothes and gunbelt, grabbed his Winchester, and headed for the privy. He needed to move fast because he knew that it was going to be a busy day. With his luck, Julia wouldn't be there, and he'd have to figure out how to deal with that problem all over again.

Max watched Sam leave and rolled over.

After he had washed and shaved, Sam walked to the barn and prepared the buggy for the trip to Mulberry. He saddled Fire, too. He wanted to leave at eight o'clock, so he could take a detour to the Bar F and see if he could find where the arsonists had gone when they ran.

He saw smoke coming from the cookstove pipe and headed for the back door, stepped onto the porch and knocked, not wanting to intrude on Mary or Sophie.

Mary opened the door and smiled at Sam. When he didn't smile back, Mary knew something was wrong.

"Come in, Sam. You don't have to knock, you know."

"I don't want to walk in and surprise you or your mother."

"We expected to see you, Sam. It wouldn't have been a surprise."

"I'll be leaving early, Mary. I figured I'd take Fire with me to the Bar F and go track those house burners, just to see where they went. I'll leave him at the ranch and pick him up on the way back."

"Sam, why don't I ride with you in the buggy and trail Venus and Fire? I'll just bring him back when you leave the ranch to go to Mulberry."

"That's a good idea. I'll go out and saddle Venus for you and be back in a few minutes."

"I'll have breakfast ready. Mama's sleeping late. I don't think she got much sleep last night."

"I can understand why. I'll see you shortly."

He gave Mary a short wave and headed back to the barn, but still without a smile, nor were there any of the expected little comments that were already normal between them.

Sophie walked into the kitchen as Sam left and Mary turned to her mother, noting her almost normal expression.

"How are you, Mama?"

"I think I'll be all right now, Mary. It was just such a shock. I'll be honest, Mary. I don't know how much longer your father could have lasted. He was getting more out of touch every day. Ever since Joe died, it's been getting worse. You know that. What he did to Julia was inexcusable. I know he never cared for Julia, but to just throw her out like that was monstrous. Then his reaction to Sam's arrival showed just how far he'd slipped. Maybe it was best this way. I think he could have caused much more tragedy if he'd lived. That's why I asked if you could move here. I knew Sam would protect you, Mary."

"He already has, Mama. He's upset about something right now. I think he feels as if he's failing. I told him about Beth's death, and he was crushed, Mama. It was like he had lost his own child. Now Papa's gone, the house and barn are gone, and Julia's in the home of that Malarkey. Sam doesn't see what positive things he's done. He only sees the bad things that have happened, as if they're his fault for not stopping them."

"He saved my life, Mary. He probably saved Max too, by showing up when he did. If he had been another minute later, I would have died, and Max probably would have either been shot or burned to death when they set fire to the bunkhouse. You saw all that, Mary."

"I know, Mama. I just hope he can bring Julia back. Maybe that will be something that will help him."

"I hope so, Mary. I hope so."

Sam had both horses saddled and tied to the back rails of the buggy before returning to the house. He stepped up on the porch loudly and waited for a few seconds, then opened the door and walked into the kitchen.

"Good morning, Sophie. How are you?"

"I'm much better, Sam. I never did thank you for saving me and Max. You arrived just in time."

"You're welcome, Sophie."

Mary then said, "Mama, Sam and I are going to the Bar F and track the arsonists. I'll be back in about an hour, and Sam will head to Mulberry."

"Alright. Is Max still sleeping?"

"Yes, ma'am. I kept him awake too late, I'm afraid," said Sam.

"I think Max is happy to have you around, Sam."

"He's a good boy and I'm sure that he'll be a good man like his brother."

Mary set the breakfast plates on the table while Sam poured himself a cup of coffee, then took a seat and waited for Mary and Sophie to sit down before eating. He was still thinking about his nightmares. They had been getting more frequent, not less.

He mixed his thoughts of the nightmares with those of trying to get Julia away from Malarkey. *Would that blow up, too?* He'd be ready if Malarkey tried to stop him and hoped that he tried. He knew that he wouldn't be throwing up if he put a lead ball between his eyes.

His real concerns were if Julia decided to stay, or if Malarkey found out she was planning to leave. If he did find out, Julia would never make it out of the house. After last night's tragedy that, admittedly, could have been worse, he hoped that Julia would make it to the rendezvous.

Mary and Sophie glanced at each other a few times while they ate in silence. Mary was especially concerned. This was so unlike the Sam she had seen the last two days and felt it was up to her to help him return to the other Sam…the real Sam.

Sam finished eating and took his plate and fork to the sink, then finished his coffee and said, "I'll be outside whenever you're ready, Mary."

"I'll be there in a few minutes, Sam."

"Alright," he said as he smiled weakly and headed for the door.

When he got outside, he stopped and looked at the early-morning sun and tried to appreciate the wonder. It was going to be a beautiful day and he knew that he had to stop this morose behavior. The nightmares were just dreams. They were annoying and yes, they were disrupting his sleep, but they were only in his mind.

He couldn't have prevented Beth's early death, and he couldn't have predicted the arson attempt. But now he'd do what he could to keep the nightmares from getting worse. He finally told his mind to go hell with all this childish behavior. He had Mary now and she was worth everything.

He took in a deep breath and stepped down to the ground, then walked up to Venus and rubbed her neck.

"Venus, we're both lucky," he said quietly.

Mary popped out of the kitchen, saw Sam with Venus and smiled.

Sam heard her footsteps, turned and smiled at her, a real, genuine Sam smile that spoke volumes to Mary.

"I was just telling Venus how lucky we both were."

Mary laughed and said, "I've just spent more time in close contact with her."

"That can change, you know."

Mary didn't know what had happened in those last few minutes, but she was extremely grateful.

"I hope so. Are you going to assist me into the buggy as a true gentleman should?"

"Sure will, ma'am. I've been kinda hankerin' to show you how right polite I am."

Mary laughed as Sam bowed and offered his hand with the palm facing upward.

Mary took his hand and stepped into the buggy, still smiling from the inside out. This was the good Sam.

Sam hustled around the back of the buggy and climbed inside.

Once he took the reins, Mary slid over against Sam as he started the buggy forward and turned to the access road.

"Mary, I apologize for my bad mood this morning. I shouldn't have let things get to me. I'll be all right now."

"I understand, Sam. But I think the reason it all got to you was because you're alone."

"But I'm not alone, Mary. You're here, and now your mother and brother are here."

"I didn't mean alone physically, I meant alone in your mind. When you and Joe were in the war, and even in the camp, you shared everything. When we first started talking, you did the same with me, but you need to share more. Talk to me about everything, Sam. I'm your best friend."

"Yes, Mary, you are that. That and so much more."

"So, best friend, what's eating at you?"

"Aside from all the mayhem, my nightmares are more prevalent. They had dropped off to two or three a week, now they show up every night."

"Do they have Malarkey in them?"

"Funny you should ask. Before I got here, he never showed up in any of them. Now he's in every blasted one."

"Do you think it's because he's behind all this?"

"It could be. But the odd thing was that they started showing up before I even knew he was here. I thought it was because the old prison camp was so close."

"Sam, don't take this the wrong way, but would it be better if I slept with you? And I mean sleep, not the other use of the term."

"No, Mary, I don't think so. Having you so close would keep me from sleeping entirely."

"Even if I wore my heavy jacket?" she asked as she smiled.

"Even then."

"Well, I'll have to admit, I'd have a hard time myself."

———

They reached the Bar F and turned onto the access road where the barn and house were still smoldering piles of ashes and half-burnt wood.

"Sam, what should we do about the house and, you know, my father's body?"

"I think we'll contact the mortician in Bonham and ask him. I'm sure they've dealt with it before."

"Thank you. I was worried about that."

"I wonder how much it would cost to rebuild the house and the barn?"

"I don't know. I'm guessing around a thousand dollars."

"That's what I was thinking, too. Mary, before I left Iowa, my father said if I needed more money to wire him."

"Sam, that's a lot of money."

"I wouldn't ask him for all of it. I still have more than a thousand dollars in the bank."

"Sam, let's see what happens. A lot of things can change."

"That's an understatement, Mary. But you're right, I just wanted to let you know that your home isn't gone."

"My home will be wherever you are, Sam."

Sam took Mary's hand and kissed it softly.

"Thank you, Mary."

Mary just nodded. For some reason, the kiss on her hand touched her soul.

They arrived at the remains of the ranch house, and Sam stopped the buggy, then he and Mary stepped out of the buggy and mounted their horses.

"Now, those men took off behind the house. I don't think they'd be too far, just enough to avoid the flames."

When they reached the back of the burned porch, Sam kept the horses at a walk until he spotted the hoofmarks. They followed them northward across the pasture and arrived at the cut wires ten minutes later.

Sam looked at the distant ranch house and said, "It looks like they rode straight for the Slash D's ranch house. I wonder if Malarkey bought it."

"I don't think so. I think it's still on the market. Papa was thinking of buying it at one time but didn't have the money."

"How much were they asking for it?"

"When he asked two years ago, it was twenty-four hundred dollars."

"It's not much more than rebuilding your house and barn, and you'd double the size of the ranch. I don't they'd get that much for it anyway."

"There you go dreaming again. That's more than double the amount, Sam."

"I know. I never was great in arithmetic."

When they were a hundred yards out from the Slash D house, Sam had them stop.

"Mary, I'm going to go in and check around. I don't think they're in there, but I'd feel better if you'd stay here."

"Alright, Sam. I'll be waiting."

"I'll be right back."

Sam set Fire to a trot and was soon stepping down at the back of the house. There was a good amount of horse droppings near the back door hitching post, so they must have been there for a while, but none were fresh, so he thought they must have been long gone.

Just to play it safe, Sam pulled his Colt and cocked the hammer but didn't try to be stealthy. He wanted to let anyone inside know he was there so he could hear them moving.

He stepped up onto the porch and just walked in as if he lived there. The kitchen was a mess and Sam noticed large spots of blood on the floor and table. He spotted a deck of playing cards on the table and had an inspiration. He slid his big knife from its sheath and began cutting one card after another, arranging them on the table, before doing some quick carving in the wooden surface. When he finished, he slipped his knife back home and walked through the rest of the house. All three beds had been slept in recently and, like the kitchen, the rooms were housekeeping disasters.

He left the house and mounted Fire, wheeled him back to the south and rode back to Mary.

When he pulled up beside her, he said, "They were all in there for a while. There was blood splattered on the floor probably from the one I hit last night."

"Are we heading back now?"

"Yes, ma'am. I need to get to Mulberry. It's already getting late."

"Then let's get back to the buggy," Mary said loudly before she set Venus off at a fast trot.

Sam followed her lead, and they soon passed the broken wire and crossed back onto Bar F land. They reached the buggy just eight minutes later and quickly dismounted. Once on the ground, Sam handed Fire's reins to Mary and gave her a quick kiss before climbing into the buggy.

He waved at a smiling Mary and was heading down the access road as Mary stepped up on Venus and followed his path, trailing Fire behind in the dust left by the buggy.

She watched Sam turn north and hoped that he would be returning soon with Julia. What spoke volumes about how much she believed that she and Sam were meant for each other, Mary didn't have a twinge of jealousy knowing that he might be returning with her beautiful sister-in-law.

———

In Mulberry, Julia had run into some good luck for a change. She thought she'd have to use some subterfuge to get out of the house with her travel bag, but Mike Malarkey had been summoned to the lumber mill because the steam engine had stopped, and they couldn't get it running again.

He left the house leaving a trail of extraordinary expletives, so now all she just needed was to wait and hope he didn't return too soon. It was still early, but after waiting what seemed like an eon, which in reality was only five minutes, Julia walked out of the house carrying her overstuffed travel bag.

She reached the main street and was crossing to the other side's boardwalk when she spied a buggy coming up from the south but continued walking and was soon sure it was Sam Walker. She lifted her skirt and began to take livelier steps toward the approaching buggy but didn't wave or do anything else to call attention to herself.

There was no need for either as Sam had seen her as she was stepping down to the street and had begun to slow down and veer in her direction. He stopped the buggy, and Julia just handed him the travel bag then climbed in, propriety be damned.

"Can we leave quickly, please?" she asked.

"Yes, ma'am," Sam replied as he drove the buggy into the intersection, executed a U-turn and then headed back south.

As Sam was maneuvering the buggy, a very hungover Jimmy Toomey, having spent the five-dollar gold coin on whiskey and a woman, chose that moment to step out of the saloon and witnessed Julia getting into the buggy. His head was still pounding, despite the two additional whiskeys he had drunk to calm it down and wondered why Mrs. Malarkey would be getting into a buggy with some man who looked like that new feller. He shrugged, decided maybe one more drink would help, and swerved back into the saloon.

"Did anyone notice you, Julia?" Sam asked.

"I thought I saw Jimmy Toomey coming out of the saloon a minute ago. He looked at me, too."

"Well, it doesn't matter. It's all going to blow up soon anyway."

"Why? What's happened?"

Sam explained about the previous night's events and the new living arrangements for the Farrells before Julia continued.

"I suppose I'm expected to express some kind of remorse for Earl Farrell, but I can't. He threw me out and I had to marry Mike Malarkey to stay alive. Either that or go to work as a working girl. I hated that bastard. He blamed me for Joe leaving."

"Joe wouldn't have gone if he knew you were pregnant, Julia."

Julia sighed and replied, "I know," then asked, "Sam, now that I have you alone, can you tell me what it was like?"

"In the war or the prison camp?"

"Both."

Sam told the same stories he had told Mary earlier and received almost the same reaction.

"Sam, you skipped two important episodes. You saved his life twice. Once in the battle at Shiloh and once in the prison camp."

"He would have done the same for me, Julia."

"You took a bullet for him at Shiloh. You were fighting some Confederate soldier and saw an officer getting ready to shoot Joe with his pistol, and you jumped in front of him and took the shot in your shoulder."

"He didn't have a chance, Julia. I figured I could deflect the bullet."

"Sam, you could have died. Just like you're risking your life now by having come down to Texas. Why did you do it, Sam? You had a comfortable life up in Iowa, didn't you? Why'd you leave all that to come down here where Northerners are run out of towns on rails? Didn't you marry that girl of yours?"

"Because I promised Joe, Julia. Besides, I didn't fit in at home anymore. My girlfriend married my brother, so I wasn't tied down. But it was more than that, Julia. I felt like a misfit. All the time we were in the army, and even more so in the camp, we all talked about how great it would be to go home. We'd get married and have kids, eat as much as we wanted, and sleep late, too. It was all going to be so perfect.

"But there isn't any perfection, Julia. It was boring. I was grateful that my brother married my girlfriend, too. It turned out she was a real prude and treated their private time almost as punishment. Besides, I had come to realize that she wasn't right for me anyway. But that all aside, I left because I had made a promise to my best friend, my brother-in-arms, to come to Texas and look after you, Beth, and the rest of his family. He knew it would be a mess after the war."

"I was heartbroken when Beth died, and I'll admit that I resented Joe for not being there when I lost her. I took me a while to get past that and knew that even if he'd been there, he couldn't have done anything. But those feelings resurfaced when his father threw me out of the house. It was really only after I married that bastard I live with now that I understood just how much I missed Joe. I really did love him."

Then, after a pause, she asked, "But you didn't love your girlfriend back in Iowa?"

"No, ma'am. I really never did. I was almost relieved when I discovered she married my brother, Frank."

"That must have been a surprise, your brother marrying your girlfriend."

"It was when I received my mother's letter in the camp. The more I thought about it, though, the more I realized I had been rescued by my brother."

"Don't you miss anything about your home?"

"I miss my parents, of course, but I really miss my younger sister, Anna. I wrote to her a while ago but haven't received a reply yet and that's surprises me. She was always good about writing to me during the war. Of course, postal service must be pretty bad now, especially going north."

Julia changed the subject when she asked, "What are the Farrells going to do now?"

"I don't know, Julia."

They soon passed the Bar F, and Julia could see the large piles of charcoal where there used to be a house and a barn and knew that her hated husband had done this.

"I was wondering what he was up to, Sam. Last night he stayed up late and I had already gone to bed but heard Jimmy Toomey arrive late and tell him how well everything had gone. I wondered who they had burned out."

"He told Malarkey that everything had gone well? That's going to be a problem for him when Malarkey finds out that I shot one of his boys and drove them off."

Julia turned, looked at Sam and said, "That must have been Paul Hooper you shot. He told Malarkey that Paul had been hit with a ricochet."

"That lie will be easy to figure out when he gets wind of how bad Hooper's arm is."

"How'd you know you hit him in the arm?"

"Because he scrambled out of there as fast as the others. If I'd hit him anywhere else, he wouldn't have been able to move so fast."

149

"Thank you for getting me away from there, Sam. He was getting tired of me anyway. He was beating me more often lately, too."

"Why would he get tired of you, Julia? I'm sure you know that you're a striking woman."

"Thank you for noticing. Let's just say I wasn't enthusiastic about performing my wifely duties. The more he visited prostitutes, the more he would take it out on me. It was only a matter of time before he eventually had to get rid of me altogether. I think he saw me as more of a prize than a woman. I have to get over the whole idea of being married to him and hope I never have to return. I know what rights he has over me. I'm little more than a slave."

"You're free from all that now, Julia."

"I'll be forever grateful, Sam," she said as she smiled and rested her hand on his for a few seconds.

Sam was uncomfortable with the gesture and hoped it was just an innocent token of appreciation, but at the same time, he began to suspect that it was much more. He just hoped that Mary wouldn't worry. He was close to telling Julia of his instant affection for Mary but decided to let Mary handle that revelation.

They pulled into the Circle W just five minutes later, and halfway down the access road, Sam smiled as he saw Mary waving from the front porch and waved back.

"Looks like Mary is glad to see you back, Sam."

"We get along," Sam replied as he grinned.

He stopped the buggy in front of the house, picked up Julia's bag and expected Julia to get out at the same time, but she didn't. Sam walked around and assisted Julia out of the buggy.

"Thank you, Sam," she said, giving him a disarming smile.

"I'll put this in the house," Sam replied as he began heading toward the stairs.

He began to wonder if Mary and Julia really got along as well as Joe had described. Mary was embracing Julia as Sam entered the house, hoping that he'd get a chance to talk to Mary privately and the sooner the better.

After leaving Julia's travel bag in the last empty bedroom, Sam noticed that Sophie was still in the kitchen preparing lunch rather than going to meet Julia. He wondered about that as he headed back to the main room and out the front door.

Mary and Julia were climbing the porch steps when Sam exited and were engaged in animated chatter.

"Mary, I'm going to unharness the buggy, then I'll join everyone when I'm done."

"Okay."

"Thank you again, Sam," Julia added with another over-the-top smile.

"You're welcome, Julia," Sam replied, keeping his smile to a cordial level.

He never thought he'd have to scale back a smile before. Julia had been back for just a few minutes, and he was already wondering if he had done the right thing to bring her to his ranch, but he had promised Joe, so there was no need to doubt his decision. Besides, he had other things to worry about and Mike Malarkey was chief among them.

———

Mike Malarkey was in a foul mood. He had returned home from the steam engine problem without resolution, which meant that he'd have to pay someone to repair the damned thing. When he did get back, his damned wife was off somewhere and hadn't fixed him lunch, but he'd make her pay for her neglect the next time he saw her. He was heading for the door on his way to the café when there was a knock at the front door.

Malarkey whipped open the door and found Dr. Whitfield standing on the door.

"Mister Malarkey, Paul Hooper said you'd pay for fixing his bullet wound."

"Yeah, I suppose. How much?"

"Five dollars," he replied, inflating his fee because it was that bastard standing before him. He never collected his fees from his patients like this, but he relished this opportunity.

"What? Five dollars to sew up a quick ricochet?"

"It wasn't a ricochet, Mister Malarkey. It was a .44-caliber bullet wound that went clean through his left biceps after creasing his left pectoral muscle. No ricochet I've ever seen had that much energy left. He was shot, pure and simple."

Malarkey's rage intensified as he pulled out the five dollars and handed it to the doctor.

Doctor Whitfield didn't say thank you. He could see the boiling anger, so he just took his money and left with his level of satisfaction inflated beyond what he'd anticipated.

"That damned Jimmy Toomey lied to me!" Malarkey snarled.

He slammed his door and walked down the porch steps to the road. He knew where he could find Jimmy Toomey. He'd still be at the saloon where he probably drank and whored away the money that he'd given to him and would still be there finishing it off.

His boots made small dust clouds in the Texas street as he stomped his way toward the saloon.

As he had expected, Jimmy Toomey was still in the saloon. He'd moved on to beer as his funds had dwindled. He made use of the free bar food to keep his stomach from rebelling and felt

152

better now, so he figured he'd head back to his room and sleep it off. He tossed a nickel on the bar and finished off his beer with one long swallow, then waved at Lonnie, the barkeep, and started heading for the batwing doors. He was a happy man.

He remained a happy man until the doors slammed open, banging against the walls, and he was greeted with the terrifying sight of an enraged Mike Malarkey. He knew he was in trouble and had to deflect Mike's anger somehow.

"Mike! Come lookin' for the wife?" he asked, managing to avoid slurring any words.

"You lied to me, you little bastard! Paul was shot!"

"I thought he caught a ricochet, Mike. I made a mistake. I thought you were mad 'cause your wife ran out on ya."

Jimmy's strategy worked as Mike glared at him and asked, "What are you talkin' about? My wife wouldn't dare run off on me!"

"I seen her gettin' in a buggy a little while ago. I was just comin' to see you to let you know."

"Gettin' in a buggy? Who'd she get into the buggy with?"

"I reckon it mighta been that new feller. The one who bought the pig farm."

Mike's anger skyrocketed to new heights as he realized that Jimmy may be telling the truth. He didn't really care much about the woman, but he had been insulted. Everyone would know that she'd run off, and they'd all laugh at him behind his back, and he'd become the subject of jokes and suggestions that he couldn't satisfy her and he couldn't allow any of that could happen. He'd have to take care of it and take care of it soon.

"Get those other three nitwits and get over to my house as soon as you can. I'm gonna get some lunch, and then we'll figure out what to do about that faithless bitch I married."

153

"Yes, sir. I'll go and do that."

Malarkey would have slammed the doors again, but batwing doors don't provide the same satisfaction as a regular door, so he just charged out of the bar and headed for the café.

Paul stood staring at the swinging doors and let out a long, stinking breath knowing he'd escaped serious punishment. He'd get the boys and hopefully, he could work his way into Mike's good graces again and do whatever he asked. He suspected that it would eventually end with the death of that handsome young wife of his and was already thinking of how he could make use of her as he walked out of the saloon.

––––––

Lunch turned out to be more pleasant than Sam had expected as the ladies all seemed amicable toward each other, and Max seemed chatty as well.

"After lunch, are we going to get to shoot the Colts, Sam?"

"That's the plan, Max. I have a target already set up on the western pasture. The pistols are loaded and ready to go."

"You're going to show Max how to shoot?" asked Julia.

"Max, Mary, and Sophie all want to try, too."

"Can I come along? I might want to try it myself."

"Sure. I've got an extra Colt."

"I'd feel safer having a gun. You can't be around to protect me all the time, Sam," she said, looking at Sam with wide eyes.

"I do what I can, Julia."

Mary noticed and didn't like it one bit. She and Sam had gotten along so perfectly. and she knew that they were so right for each other. *What was Julia doing?* Mary had noticed the big smiles when they had arrived and Julia's need to be assisted when she got out of the carriage. *What had happened on the ride from Mulberry?* She needed to talk to Sam privately and soon, too. She wasn't worried about Sam so much as she was concerned about Julia.

Sam could almost read Mary's thoughts, but said, "I'm going to be lazy and not saddle the horses. It's only about a half mile north. I'll get the gunbelts, and we'll get ready to go."

"I'll clean up," said Sophie.

"I'll help," added Mary.

"I'm going to get changed into my riding clothes. I don't think a dress is appropriate for shooting. I see you're already wearing britches, Mary, so you're ready to go. Sophie, what will you wear?" said Julia.

"I can wear the dress. It'll work," she replied as she continued to gather the dishes from the table.

Ten minutes later they were gathered in the main room. Julia looked spectacular in her riding skirt and blouse and Mary suddenly felt inadequate. It was a new sensation for her. She had never worried about her appearance before and always had dressed to be comfortable in what she was doing. Now, being a tomboy didn't seem to be a satisfactory dress code at all. Suddenly her confidence in how Sam thought of her began to erode.

Sam began his instructions by saying, "Alright, I'll take the extra revolver myself. Max, come over here, and I'll get you ready."

Max jumped over and stood in front of Sam as Sam handed him an empty gunbelt.

"Try this on. Don't make it too tight. Just tight enough so it falls onto your hips. The pistol's weight will keep it there."

Max put the belt on, having to use the last hole because of his slim waist, but it stayed in place as he shoved the belt down.

Sam slid the Colt New Army into the holster and put the hammer loop in place.

"That little loop of leather will make sure the pistol stays in the holster until you need it."

Mary was next and Sam handed her the gunbelt.

Mary put it around her waist and snugged it down onto her hips. Sam smiled at her as he slid the pistol into her holster, and the warmth of his eyes and his smile made her feel better.

Sophie had no problem with hers and that left Julia. Julia walked in front of Sam, and he handed her the gunbelt.

Mary noticed that Julia stood a lot closer to Sam than she had and far too close in her estimation.

Julia put on the gunbelt and pushed it firmly against her hips. She smiled at Sam as he put the Colt into her holster and slipped the hammer loop in place.

Sam returned her smile and stood, but Julia hadn't stepped back, so they were very close.

"Thank you, Sam. This feels good."

"You're welcome, Julia," he replied, waiting for her to step back.

She did after another ten uncomfortable seconds, uncomfortable at least for Sam and Mary, but seemingly not for Julia. Even Sophie noticed, but Max was too busy admiring his new gun rig.

After she had finally stepped back, Sam led them out of the house, and they began walking west.

Mary managed to slip in next to Sam on his right side, but Julia beat Max to his left as they walked. Sam would have taken Mary's hand to let her know, but he needed both hands as he talked.

"Each of the pistols is loaded with five rounds. Most of the time, the last chamber is kept unloaded to reduce the risk of accidentally shooting yourself. When you think you're going to have to use it, you load the sixth chamber. These pistols take a lot longer to reload than the Winchester because they don't use cartridges. To get them ready to fire, you have to pour in gunpowder and add the lead ball or use a paper cartridge. I have a lot of the paper cartridges to save time. Then the pistol uses a lever to push the bullet into place. After that, you need to add percussion caps to the back of the cylinders. It's why I always keep an extra pistol."

"Why do you have so many?" asked Julia.

"I was attacked in Arkansas on my way here by three men. After I dropped their bodies off at the army post nearby, I kept my attackers' pistols and their horses."

"You shot three men?"

"They were bad men, Julia. They should have left me alone."

Sam then spent the rest of the walk explaining the shooting process with the Colt pistols. He wondered if Sophie's, Max's, and Julia's hands were big enough, but Mary had strong, large hands and should have no problems. He didn't realize that even as they walked, Mary was wishing she had smaller hands and was a bit larger elsewhere.

"You can see the target over there. It's about fifty feet away. Now I've already told you how to shoot, so I'm going to dry fire on my empty cylinder to show you how it's done."

Sam pulled his Colt from his waist and demonstrated in slow motion how to pull the pistol, cock the hammer with the left thumb, slide the left hand under the grip for support, then aim and squeeze the trigger. As he went through the motions, he described them in detail.

He didn't tell them that's not how he shot, but his hands were huge and made it easier for him to cock with his right thumb as

157

the pistol was coming up and didn't need his left hand for added support, although he did use it when he needed the extra accuracy.

"Max, do you want to go first?"

Max grinned and replied, "Yes, sir."

"Why am I not surprised? Now take it slow, Max."

Max nodded and did as Sam had demonstrated. He unhooked his hammer loop, pulled the pistol, cocked it, slid his left hand down to the grip and aimed the muzzle at the target. He held his breath and squeezed the trigger, then was surprised by the volume, smoke, and kick of the Colt.

"Not bad, Max. You were too low. Your shot hit the dirt just to the left of the target. Now try again, and don't spend so much time aiming. Just point the pistol's barrel like it was your index finger. Go ahead."

Max repeated the exercise and was pleased when he hit the target. It was about a foot low and eight inches off to the left of center.

"Excellent, Max. Now, go ahead and empty the pistol. Take your time to hit the target. Don't worry about going too fast."

Max nodded and began to fire. He fired all three rounds in less than ten seconds with two hits on the target and one miss. None were within a foot of the center.

"Really good for your first time, Max. You'll get better with more practice."

Sophie went second and never managed to hit the target but was in line with two of them.

Mary did better than both Max and Sophie, hitting the target with three shots, one within six inches of center. She stepped away grinning at Sam, who grinned right back at her.

Julia hit the target once, it was centered but about a foot low.

"You all did very well for first-time shooters. I'll clean and reload the pistols when we get back."

"Are we gonna get to see you shoot, Sam?" asked Max.

"Sure. Why not?"

Sam pulled his Colt and fired all five shots within ten seconds. All five were within four inches of the center and two were within an inch.

"Wow!" exclaimed Max. "Can you do that every time?"

"Pretty much. The key is taking your time. I know some shooters that can empty a pistol in four or five seconds, but their shots tend to be a bit wild. Shall we head back to the house? I'll burn your names into the gunbelts, so you'll get used to having the same pistol every time."

"What will you wear, Sam?" asked Max.

"I'll pick one up in Bonham later. We need to see the mortician anyway."

"Oh, that's right," said Sophie.

"Sophie, where do you want Earl buried?"

"I think right there on the ranch. There are some folks in Bonham that might raise a fuss about him being buried in their cemetery."

"Alright. Do you want me to take care of it, or do you want to?"

"If you could take care of it, I'd be grateful, Sam."

"After we get back to the house, I'll get the pistols cleaned and reloaded then I'll saddle Fire and head into Bonham. I should be back before sunset."

They walked back toward the house and because Sam had moved his weapons and ammunition out of what was now

Julia's room, the women headed to the house, and Sam and Max walked to the bunkhouse.

"Sam, want me to burn the names into the gunbelts?"

"Sure, have you ever done it before?"

"Sure. Lotsa times."

"Good. Now, let's get these five guns cleaned and loaded."

It took almost an hour before the guns were all cleaned and reloaded. Sam lined them up with their gunbelts on one of the spare beds alphabetically: Julia, Mary, Max, and Sophie. He left Max to do the naming and left his Colt as well. He'd have the Winchester and his derringer with him.

He walked to the barn, saddled one of the many geldings with a pack saddle and was saddling Fire when he heard someone enter. He turned and relaxed when he saw Mary.

"Mary, are you coming along?"

"I was hoping you wouldn't mind."

"Oh, I'd hate it terribly, having the best woman in Texas riding alongside of me."

"Am I still the best, Sam?" she asked.

"We'll talk on the way, Mary. I wanted to talk to you since I got back from Mulberry."

"I needed to talk to you, too."

Sam had just about finished saddling Fire, so he helped Mary saddle Venus.

Fifteen minutes later they were mounted and riding on the access road with Fire trailing the pack horse. After they had turned south toward Bonham, Mary began the conversation.

"Sam, what is going on with Julia?"

"I was going to ask you that very question. I have no idea. We were just conversing all the way back from Mulberry, and then something changed. I don't know what, but I became uncomfortable riding in the buggy with her, and then when we stopped, it was like she had suddenly decided that we were courting or something."

"That's what it looked like to me. I'll admit I was jealous, Sam. She's much more beautiful than I am."

"Mary, remember when we first talked, and I told you that the packaging was second? I'll tell you right now that Barbara Jean was every bit as beautiful as Julia, just not as dark. Have I been mooning over Barbara Jean?"

"No." she replied as she laughed.

"Mary, no other woman on this planet means more to me than you. I know we've only known each other for a short time, at least face-to-face knowing each other. But there isn't a shred of doubt in my mind that I love you deeply, Mary Farrell. Nothing can shake that. I'm yours until the day I die."

Mary hadn't expected the full-blown expression of love that she was so gratifyingly hearing, having only hoped for a denial of any infatuation with Julia, but this was incredibly better.

"Sam, I'm sorry for being so possessive. I just was afraid of losing you before I could even tell you that I loved you."

"Being possessive is all right if it's supposed to be that way, Mary. Joe had it right. He knew because he knew both of us so well. Now I feel as if I know you so well after such a short time. I knew when I was in that buggy that you would feel badly and that's why I wanted to talk to you privately."

"Thank you for being so understanding, Sam. I felt petty thinking the things I did."

"Mary, never worry about me, at least as far as how I feel about you."

"Meaning I should worry about the other things."

"Maybe."

There was a long pause before she asked, "So, are we going swimming later?" hoping to lighten the mood.

"I had planned on asking Max to come along. I think he needs to talk, Mary."

"Well, I'm not going swimming with my brother. I'll wait until I can get you alone."

"You are getting fresh now, aren't you, Miss Farrell?"

"Just admitting to my secret desires, Mister Walker."

They reached Bonham in fine fettle twenty minutes later and headed to the mortician, who expressed concern over the fire and said that he would send two men to comb through the fire and put the remains into a small casket. When he asked about a headstone, Mary provided the information. He said the burial would take place tomorrow at four to give them time to find the remains, but the headstone would take another week or so. Sam paid for the burial, and they left the mortuary in a more somber mood.

Sam and Mary went to Parson's Dry Goods with two panniers, and once inside, he handed John Parson his list for the heavier items and Sam and Mary began adding the rest of the order.

"John, do you have any of the Colt New Army pistols?"

"Nope. Got a couple of Remington New Army pistols that seem to be in good shape."

Sam followed John to the back, and John pulled out the pistols and handed them to Sam.

"They look a lot like the Colts. Fire the same ammunition, too. Some differences, though. Personally, I think they're a better gun."

Sam had been examining the revolvers and found that John was right. They were both in excellent condition. The rifling in the barrels was still prominent and showed little sign of wear. The actions were smoother than his Colt, too.

"How much?"

"Well, they're used, so how does ten dollars apiece sound?"

"I can do that. Need a rig, though."

"All I've got is the setup they came in. It's a two-gun rig, though. Might be a bother."

John reached behind him and pulled out the gunbelt and holsters. Sam strapped it on and was pleased that it gave him more balance.

"How much for the whole setup?"

"Twenty-five dollars. Comes with a cleaning kit and an ammunition pouch, too."

"All right, put it on my tab, John."

"You look like a regular gunfighter, Sam," he said as he grinned.

"Hardly that, John."

He slipped the two empty Remingtons into the holsters and then flipped the hammer loops into position. The biggest adjustment would be where to put his knife sheath, although it might not be so critical now that he had the large pocketknife.

Sam took the cleaning kit and heavy ammunition pouch and put them into one of the panniers, right next to the eggs, he noticed with a grin.

Sam paid for the order, then he and John loaded them onto the packhorse.

Mary and Sam rode out of Bonham late in the afternoon.

"Two guns, Sam?"

"If he had a Colt New Army, I would have only bought one. But these Remingtons feel a bit different. I didn't want to have two different guns. The gun rig was the only one he had. It doesn't feel bad, though. I'll load the Remingtons when we get back and use my Colt as a backup."

"We sure have a lot of guns, Sam."

"Yes, ma'am. Two Spencers, the Winchester, five Colt New Army revolvers, the two Remingtons, a shotgun, and the two derringers."

"Two derringers?"

"I bought a second one when I was in Mulberry. I got used to carrying it."

"So, I have the Elizabeth derringer, and you have, what, the Julia derringer?" she asked with a smile.

"If calling it that makes you happy, then you go right ahead. I'll just call it the Remington derringer."

Mary laughed as they rode on.

————

Mike Malarkey's mood hadn't improved over the day. He had his boys sitting in his parlor and knew he'd have to eat out again. *Damned woman!* They had fessed up about the shootout with that new guy at the Circle W and Jimmy thought it was just a neighbor helping a neighbor kind of thing. Mike would have bought it if it wasn't for Jimmy telling him that the same man had taken Julia away, which meant he was probably having his way with her right now at his ranch. *Bastard!*

"Alright, you four lying weasels, now we're gonna make that bastard pay for what he did, screwin' up the burnin' and then stealin' my wife. Jimmy, you're sure that no one got out of that house? Not a single one?"

"Positive, boss. We were shooting, and I saw one tryin' to come out. I think it was the old woman, but she ran back in."

Paul almost mentioned the kid but figured the kid must have died when they peppered the bunkhouse with bullets. Besides, he rationalized, it was only a kid and wasn't a problem.

Reggie was thinking along the same lines. He's probably dead, but he's only a kid.

"So, do you want us to go down there right now, boss?" Jimmy asked.

"No. You're still hung over, and Paul still has that arm in a sling. We'll wait two days. Jimmy, you stay away from the saloon unless you're just paying a visit to the ladies. Paul, what did the doc say about your arm?"

"He said the stitches need to come out in ten days, but I could use it for easy things."

"Well, you're right-handed, so you should be all right. So, I figure in two days, you all go in there at night. Just after sunset, so he'll have some lamps lit. Go in there and shoot up the place. Make sure he's dead when you leave."

"What about your wife, boss?"

"You can each have a go at her and then shoot the adulterous bitch."

The thought of having a go at Julia outweighed Paul's squeamishness about killing a woman but rekindled his previous fantasies about finding her.

Jimmy actually licked his upper lip and still wished that the Farrell girl hadn't been roasted in the fire, but having Julia was a better deal.

"Alright, boss. Tomorrow, we'll move into the Slash D, and we'll hit that pig farm right after sunset."

"Now get outta here. I'm going to go and get some dinner and spend some time with the ladies."

"Have fun, boss," said Pat, ever looking for an opportunity to suck up.

Everyone, including Mike Malarkey, left the house.

———

Sam and Mary arrived at the Circle W before sundown, and they'd barely reached the end of the access road when Max came running out of the bunkhouse wearing his gun and holster and saw Sam wearing the two-gun rig. He stopped and waved as Sam and Mary waved back.

"I see Max has gotten into guns almost as much as you have, Sam."

"I'd say it was a man thing, but you have two guns yourself, if you include the derringer, and you certainly don't qualify anywhere close to reaching the level of being called a man."

"You forget I was a tomboy."

"And maybe you've forgotten how close we were in the pool."

"Trust me, Sam, I'll never forget how close we were in the pool."

They reached the back of the house and stepped down.

Sam said, "I'll unload the pack horse if you want to take care of Venus. I'll bring Fire and the gelding in shortly."

"I'll be waiting, Mister Walker."

Mary led Venus away, and Sam lifted off one of the panniers and lugged it up the steps and into the kitchen.

Julia had opened the door and smiled at Sam as he passed.

"I see you've rearmed yourself."

"I felt naked without a pistol."

166

"Well, you're well equipped now," she answered with a wink.

Sam didn't know what to make of the comment or the wink, so he just smiled and walked the pannier to the center of the floor.

"Is the other matter taken care of, Sam?" asked Sophie.

"Yes, ma'am. They'll take care of everything. They'll bury him at four o'clock tomorrow afternoon. You'll need to pick out a spot for the burial, though."

"Can you do that?"

"I can."

"We'll start putting the food away," said Julia.

"Good. I'll be right back."

After Sam had lugged the second pannier into the house, he left to take care of Fire. When he led Fire into the barn, Mary was waiting, sitting on a stack of hay. Venus had already been unsaddled.

Sam began to unsaddle Fire, waiting for Mary to start the conversation.

"Any excitement in the house?" she asked with a hint of a smile.

"More Julia oddities. She commented on my two-gun rig saying that I was well equipped and winked at me."

"She winked at you? Really?"

"Uh-huh. I'm going to have to squash this soon."

"How do you intend to do that?"

"By kissing you in front of her."

"Sam," she replied seriously, "as long as it doesn't amount to more than mild flirtation, I wish you wouldn't. She's been through a lot in the last year and a half. We didn't find out about

Joe's death until July of '65. My father threw her out in September, and she lasted on her own for three months before she married Malarkey in January. She's had to deal with that bastard for more than a year now. Let her indulge in her fantasies. I can live with it if you can. I'd rather not take that away from her so quickly."

"Alright, Mary. I'll put up with it as long as you know that you're the only one for me."

"I wouldn't have made the suggestion before we rode to Bonham. I was ready to have a go at her myself, but you made it unnecessary. As we rode along, I began to see how she thought about you. You saved her, Sam. Joe had written to her about you constantly, and after Joe died, she was put in that predicament with Malarkey, so she probably saw you as a white knight."

"Does she know what Joe said about us?"

"She does. I just think she doesn't believe I could ever compete with her if she made up her mind."

"That's kind of frightening, Mary."

"Not really. It's just Julia. You should have seen her before she and Joe were married. I swear every male in the county at one time or another vied for the right to visit her. There were offers of ranches and large sums of cash to her parents just to get on their good side. Her parents got fed up with the barrage of suitors. They were Union supporters, too, and were uncomfortable with the situation in Mulberry. They told Julia they were going to leave and go to Colorado, but Julia refused because she had met Joe. So, they married her off to Joe, packed up, and left. Where they went, Julia never knew. It only became important when Joe died, but by then it was too late."

"Most parents would have at least taken the money."

"Oh, they did. They accepted the offers from three different gentlemen before they quickly married Julia off and disappeared. Her father was the barber, so they simply packed up his things and off they went."

"That's a strange story, Mary."

"It seems like everything around here is strange. But that's why she thinks she can get any man she wants, including you."

"Well, at least I'm better armed now, and I don't mean my well-equipped holsters."

Mary laughed, stood and said, "You know I'm going to find out just how well equipped you are sooner or later."

"Lord! Is there no end to your lasciviousness, woman?"

"What was that, a five-syllable word? You could have just said 'lust' and saved yourself some letters."

Sam just laughed and hugged Mary. She put her arms around his neck and kissed him deeply before he pulled her closer and kissed her harder. She finally turned her head to let him know how much she enjoyed it the last time, and he began kissing her neck. She felt the same thrill she had before as her toes curled inside her riding boots.

Sam finally released her, and she stood back and fanned herself.

"And you talk about my lasciviousness, Mister Walker."

"You are an inspiration, Miss Farrell."

"I've got to get back into the house before anyone suspects that there's something going on in here."

"We can't have that, now can we?"

Mary smiled and waved before she left the barn as Sam watched her stride away. There was no intentional sashaying, but at the same time there was no tomboy in that walk, either.

Sam turned and finished taking care of Fire before unsaddled the gelding, brushing him down and returning him to the corral.

Sam stopped at the cistern and cleaned up before returning to the house.

Max saw him enter and started asking about the new pistols. Sam explained the differences and took the cleaning kit and ammunition pouch from the empty panniers. Then he and Max left the house to return to the bunkhouse after leaving the panniers in the barn.

Sam cleaned and loaded the new pistols while Max showed him how he had put the names on all the gunbelts.

"Good job, Max."

"Do you want me to put your name on your new gunbelt?"

"I think we can tell these apart, don't you, Max?" he asked as he grinned.

"They look mighty mean, Sam."

"That's not their purpose, Max. If they start putting cartridges in the pistols like they have with the rifles, then I'll only need one. It takes too long to reload, even with paper cartridges. If they made metallic cartridges that didn't need a percussion cap, you could reload in just a few seconds. That's why I always like to have two pistols. It's at least ten shots, twelve if you're ready."

"That makes sense. Where are you going to put your knife?"

"Good question. I may not be able to carry the knife while I'm wearing the gunbelt. I could remove the left-hand holster, but I'm kind of fond of the idea of keeping both pistols handy. I think I'll just keep the knife on the saddle. Besides, I have my pocketknife."

"This knife is the best I've ever owned, Sam." Max said as he pulled the eight-inch knife from its sheath.

"I thought of taking the knives off the other gunbelts that the women wear but then figured it was an extra bit of protection for them."

"Aunt Julia really likes you, Sam."

"She's a nice lady, Max."

"Mary really likes you, too."

"I really like Mary, too."

"Joe always said that you two should get married. How would he know that?"

Sam studied Max before he replied, "I spent a lot of time with Joe. Probably more than I even spent with my own brother. He knew me well, and he knew your sister, Mary. He always told me that he thought we were well suited for each other."

"Was he right, Sam?"

"Yup, he was right, Max. As right as he could be."

Max smiled and watched as Sam put the freshly cleaned, oiled and loaded pistols into their holsters.

"Max, tomorrow we're going to bury your father on the Bar F at four. Do you know of any special place on the ranch that he liked?"

"There was a spot about two hundred yards along the south pasture that he used to go to smoke his pipe sometimes."

"I'm going to ride over there in the morning. Can you come along and show me the spot?"

"Alright."

"Then later, just after sunset, I'm going to go to the barn, and we need to get some of the fencing wire that's in there."

"I know where it is. The fence tool was on top of the reel, too. Are you going to make some fences?"

"Nope. I'm going to use it to make a booby trap."

Max laughed and asked, "A booby trap? What's that?"

Sam smiled as he answered, "A booby trap is a simple trick to catch people off guard. We used them a lot during the war when we set up camp in hostile territory to keep enemy soldiers from sneaking in."

"Why do they call them booby traps?"

"Some folks think it's because any boob can make one, because they're so simple. Others think it's the other way and only real boobs would get tricked by them. Now as we're going to be the ones making them, I vote for the second reason. We're going to trip up some boobies."

Max laughed and replied, "I'm with you, Sam. Let's trap some boobies."

After an uneventful dinner, they all sat in the main room where Sam made a point of sitting on the couch with Mary. Nothing as obvious as a kiss or anything, just a subtle message. He didn't know if Julia would take it as an indication of Sam's affection for Mary or as a challenge.

"Tomorrow morning, Max and I are going to ride to the Bar F. We won't be gone long. Then after the burial, we'll be doing some things at the Circle W to make it safer should Malarkey's crowd come around. Julia, can we guess that Malarkey knows not only you're gone but where you are?"

"I'm sure he does."

"Then they'll come either tonight or tomorrow night. Max and I are going to go out and do some work near the access road in case they come tonight. Tomorrow we'll be better off, but Max and I will be out there with the shotgun and the Winchester. If they haven't arrived by eleven, we'll return to the bunkhouse."

"What if they come later?" asked Sophie.

"Then we'll have to depend on some of the defenses we put out there to alert us."

"Alright."

172

"So, we'll get out there and get our work done, then we'll stay out there. We should hear them coming long before they reach the access road."

"Stay safe, Sam," Mary said softly.

"I will," he said as he stood. He wanted to give her a kiss but held back.

"Be careful, Sam," added Julia.

"Count on it."

He and Max left the main room and walked to the barn.

Once they were inside, he asked, "What are we going to do, Sam?"

"Make some more booby traps, Max."

Sam grabbed a shovel and handed it to Max, then took another for himself, and they walked down the access road. When they were thirty feet from the roadway, Sam laid his Winchester down on the access road and told Max to lay down the shotgun.

"Follow me, Max, and watch what I'm going to do."

Sam wandered to a spot in the tall grass and quickly dug a hole about two feet across and a foot deep, which only took a couple of minutes. Then he walked ten feet away and grabbed a bunch of grass and arranged it across the top of the hole.

"See that, Max. Anyone walking or riding who steps into that hole will go down. They usually curse or yell when they do. It will let us know where they are. Now, we'll dig a bunch of these and spread the soil out, so it doesn't make a hill, and don't put them in line, either. Did them in random spots."

Max grinned again before he said, "Okay, Sam. I can do this."

"Let's go."

They began to dig and pull grass. Sam had fifteen dug in an hour and then walked to the other side and helped Max. When they had finished, there were almost forty of the booby traps and two sweaty hole diggers.

"Let's head back to the cistern and get cleaned up, Max. The sun's almost down."

"Okay."

Sam grabbed his Winchester and shovel, and Max did the same with the shotgun. They left the shovels in the barn and headed for the cistern where Sam took off his Stetson and his shirt. Max took off his shirt and they both began washing off the Texas grime.

"Sam, is that where you got shot?" Max asked as he pointed to Sam's shoulder wound.

"Yup. I got that one in Shiloh. The other one I got in some skirmish that didn't even have a name."

"Where is that one? I don't see it."

"I caught that one in my butt."

Max started laughing before he stopped and asked, "Does it hurt to get shot?"

"At first it feels like someone hit you with a hammer. Then it burns for a second, and then you feel the pain and the blood. It's not a pleasant thing to happen to you."

"I'm afraid of being shot, Sam. It scares me."

"It should scare you, Max. Being afraid keeps you on your toes."

"You and Joe were never afraid, were you?"

"Max, we were always afraid. The man who says he isn't is either lying or he's not right in the head."

"But you never told anyone you were afraid, did you?"

174

Sam stood up and ran his fingers through his shortened hair to straighten it out.

"Do you know what Joe and I used to do?"

Max shook his head.

"Now, I was a sergeant, and Joe was a corporal. If we were getting ready to go into a battle, there would be some replacements that just had this look of fear in their eyes. You could see it. They were almost shaking, but they were afraid to admit how scared they were because they didn't want to be called cowards.

"So, I would turn to Joe and say in a loud voice, 'Joe, if I get any more scared, I'm gonna pee in my pants.' Joe would laugh and say just as loudly, 'Hell, Sam, I'll dry out your pants if you'll clean the crap outta mine.' Then we'd both laugh about it.

"Max, you could see the change in those men's eyes. If two old veterans like us didn't mind admitting we were afraid, we knew they would feel better about themselves."

"So, you were always afraid before fights?"

"That was the odd thing, Max. Everybody was afraid before the fight, but once we started, we were so busy fighting that we didn't have time to be afraid."

"Why did you and Joe go off to war?"

"A lot of folks had different reasons on both sides. Joe and I had the same reason. We didn't think it was right to split up the country. We thought this country's greatness will only come if we all stick together. Once we began serious fighting, the reason we fought changed, then we fought for each other."

"Mama said that Joe wrote in his letter that you got shot trying to save him."

"That's why I always thought of Joe as my brother. Now you're my brother."

175

Max smiled and said, "Thank you, Sam. I'm glad to have you for my brother, too."

Sam smiled, then they put on their shirts, and Sam put on his Stetson.

"We'll have to get you a Stetson next time we're in Bonham, Max."

"Really? That would be great!"

They returned to the front of the ranch and took their positions near the access road. They talked until eleven o'clock about things that Max wanted to know, mainly about the war, before returning to the bunkhouse.

In the ranch house, the three women were talking as well, but mostly about what would happen over the next few days, rather than what had happened in the war. To each of them, this was their war and it had to be won, hopefully with no casualties on their side.

CHAPTER 6

Early the next morning, Sam and Max rode out of the Circle W and headed for the Bar F, entering the access road minutes later and past the burned-out barn before riding to the south pasture.

"Right there, Sam," Max said, pointing at a small grove of cottonwoods.

"Alright. We've got to pick out a spot far enough away, so they don't run into any roots."

They walked their horses to a good location, Sam stepped down, walked to the cottonwoods, and found a four-foot long fallen branch. He walked to the spot for the gravediggers, and stuck it into the ground, mounted Fire, then he and Max rode past the barn and out the access road.

After they had returned to the Circle W and unsaddled their horses, Sam and Max walked to the back corner of the barn, just behind the wagon, and found the spool of fence wire. Sam began unraveling about a hundred feet of the steel wire, then cut it with the fence tool and wound it into a smaller coil.

"Okay, Max. We have the makings of our second booby trap."

"When do we make it?"

"After sunset tonight. I'm holding off making it earlier because we need to use the access road ourselves later today. So, right after the sun goes down, we string the booby trap. We don't want anyone seeing us build it. It's got to be a surprise, or we don't catch any boobies."

Max smiled, and they returned to the house.

––––––

As Sam and Max were planning on building booby traps, Jimmy, Pat, Reggie, and Paul were getting their final directions from Mike Malarkey.

"Now, don't wait until it's too late. Just an hour after sunset should be right. You should see the light from the house. The only ones in there should be him and that thankless wife of mine. Shoot him first. Load him down with lead. She won't be able to stop you from doing whatever you want to do with her. When you're finished, if you don't want to shoot her, just strip her naked and leave her there. Then burn the house down."

Even Jimmy was disturbed by Malarkey's vehemence.

"We'll head over to the Slash D to get ready, boss" Jimmy said, already disregarding Malarkey's instructions in his mind.

He was making other plans for Julia. She may not burn, but she would be naked.

"Go ahead. Get back here when you're done. All of you."

"Yes, sir," Jimmy said before they left the room to ride to the Slash D.

––––––

After Sam and Max had departed from the Bar F, the mortician's men arrived and began sifting through the charred house. It wasn't hard to find Earl's remains, and as expected, there wasn't much left. They just lifted what they could, put them into a box and sealed it, loaded it onto a wagon, drove it around the barn and stepped out. They were told to look for a marker, and spotted the tall branch sticking out of the ground. They drove to the branch and started digging. An hour later, they drove back to Bonham for the mortician to put the remains in a proper casket. It wouldn't be a full-sized casket, but one that was used for children or, in this case, the charred remains of an adult.

———

Sam and Max walked back into the house and found all three women in the main room, standing in a group, seemingly waiting for them.

"Sam, while you were gone, you received a telegram," said Mary.

"A telegram? Who sent it?"

"I don't know. We didn't read it, Sam. It was for you," she said as she handed Sam the yellow sheet.

Sam was worried as he opened it. This can't be good news.

He read:

SAM WALKER CIRCLE W RANCH BONHAM TEXAS

WILL BE ARRIVING ON STAGECOACH JUNE 12
MUCH TO TELL YOU

ANNA WALKER CLARKSVILLE TEXAS

Sam must have looked ill, because Mary asked, "Sam, are you all right? Do you want to sit down?"

Sam shook his head and said, "No, Mary. I'm fine. I'm just surprised. It's from my sister, Anna. She's coming here the day after tomorrow on the stage. I guess she took the train to Clarksville, that's the end of the line right now."

"Sam, why is she coming to Texas?"

"I don't know. She just said that she had a lot to tell me. I really will be happy to see her, but her timing is terrible."

"Did you want me to go and get her with the buggy, Sam?" asked Mary.

"Let me think about it. A lot depends on what happens tonight and tomorrow."

"We'll do what we can, Sam."

"Thank you, Mary. I'm still a bit stunned. I have no idea why Anna would leave Iowa."

"How old is she?" asked Julia.

"We had her eighteenth birthday party just before I left Iowa."

"Do you think she's running away from home?" asked Sophie.

"No. She was happy there. I'm trying to think if there was anything that I put in my letter that would give her any concern. I specifically avoided all the problems so she wouldn't worry. Why would she undertake such a long and dangerous journey, especially alone?"

"Maybe she's not alone," suggested Mary.

"I guess we'll just have to wait and see what happens."

"Where will she sleep?" asked Julia.

"That's a good question. I have no idea. I'll think of something."

"If you have some bedrolls. She can share my room," offered Mary.

"That should work. I'm just nervous about the 'much to tell you' line in her telegram."

"Did you find a nice spot for Earl, Sam?" asked Sophie.

Max answered, "Yes, Mama. That stand of cottonwoods on the south pasture where he used to go and smoke his pipe sometimes."

"Wonderful. Thank you both."

"I'll harness the buggy at three o'clock. Max and I will ride. Who can drive the buggy?"

"I'll drive," said Mary.

"Alright. We're all set then."

"We're going to get lunch ready," said Sophie.

"We'll be out in the bunkhouse. I need to arrange things with Max."

"Okay," Mary replied, almost as curious as Sam was about his sister's surprise visit.

Sam and Max left the house and headed toward the bunkhouse, and as they strode along Sam said, "Max, after lunch we need to take a bath."

"Aw, Sam, I had one just a week ago."

"Max, I take baths four or five times a week. It's only when I'm busy that I can't have one."

"But Mary and Julia will probably be using the bathtub anyway."

"Who said anything about a bathtub? I haven't used the tub since I've been here."

"Where do you take a bath? In the cistern?"

"No, sir. In my swimming hole."

Max's attitude about having a bath changed dramatically as he asked, "You've got a swimming hole?"

"Made it myself. It even has a flat-rock patio to stretch out in the sun. The only danger is if any women try to use it."

"You mean Mary."

"I mean Mary. She likes it, too. So, if we get there first, we get the swimming hole."

"What if she comes while we're there?"

"We get out of the water really fast if we see anyone coming."

"This will be fun!"

They reached the bunkhouse and Sam set aside some clean clothes, a bar of soap and even two towels. Then he and Max talked of booby traps as they headed out to the swimming hole.

———

The intended victims of the booby traps were pulling up in the back of the Slash D ranch house. They dismounted, tied their horses to the hitchrail and stepped up to the porch.

"You know," Jimmy was saying, "I was kinda partial to that new feller. He seemed like a decent sort, and I kinda hate to fill him full of lead, but if he run off with the boss's wife, we've got to pull the trigger."

"I'm just lookin' forward to havin' my way with her," Pat said before he giggled.

Jimmy shook his head and opened the door to the kitchen. He may have shaken his head, but the same thought was on his mind. In fact, Jimmy had thought of little else since the meeting with Mike Malarkey. *They had been given permission to take his wife! Talk about a bonus!*

They all walked into the dark kitchen and were in a good mood, until they saw the kitchen table.

"What happened to the cards?" asked Reggie as he stepped over to the table.

"Looks like someone messed with 'em," said Paul.

"Wait a minute. Look at this. There's the king of spades on top and then the four jacks underneath in a line. They've all been cut with a big X in the middle. There's words carved in the table too. I can't read 'em in this light. Give me a match."

Reggie produced a match and handed it to Jimmy. He ripped it across the rough cookstove, and it blazed to life.

Their eyes all took in the short message and felt a deathly chill.

Cut out across the table were the words: *YOU WILL ALL DIE.*

Jimmy blew out the match and scattered the cards across the floor.

"What bastard did this?" he shouted, his voice shaking.

"I think it was that nice feller from the Circle W," suggested Paul, "The same one who shot me."

"Then the hell with him. We go over there tonight, and I'll show him who's gonna die, and it ain't gonna be any of us!"

"What'll we do now that we ain't got any cards, Jimmy?"

"We can always play pitch-a-penny," Pat answered.

"I didn't bring no change," said Jimmy.

When they checked, only Pat had any change, and he only had two cents.

"Looks like we're gonna have a few boring hours," said Paul, "I think I'll go and take a nap."

It then became a race to see who got the beds and who got stuck on the too-short couch and Pat lost.

All four were dozing in less than thirty minutes.

———

Sam and Max were sunning themselves after a glorious bath in the swimming hole.

"Sam, I think I could learn to like taking baths."

"You get used to them after a while, Max."

"When do we have to go back?"

"Oh, not sooner than an hour from now, I think."

"Are you watching out to make sure that Mary isn't coming?"

"Sometimes. If she shows up, she shows up."

"I don't want Mary seeing me naked!"

"Then put on your britches. It's getting kind of warm anyway."

"Nah. I'll wait."

An hour later they were clean, and so were their clothes. Sam had Fire saddled and the buggy harnessed, then he led the buggy to the front of the house and left it standing.

Sam and Max then brought their horses out of the barn and hitched them to the front hitching post.

"Let's go and see if the ladies are ready to go, Max."

"Yes, sir."

They walked up the steps onto the porch. Sam knocked on the door which was quickly opened by Mary, and he was surprised at her appearance because he had never seen Mary in a dress.

"Mary, you look very nice."

She smiled and replied, "Don't get used to seeing me in a dress, Mister Walker."

"There are so many comments I could make in response to that, Miss Farrell, but I'll let this one go. Is everyone ready?"

"We are."

Mary turned and called, "Mama, Julia, the buggy is out front."

Julia floated out from her room looking truly amazing. Her hair was brushed, and she was wearing a dress that showed her figure to her advantage. It wasn't exactly funeral attire, but they didn't have unlimited wardrobes.

Sophie exited her room wearing a blue dress that was probably the closest anyone was wearing to mourning clothes.

It was mid-afternoon when they boarded the buggy, and Sam and Max escorted them out of the Circle W. As they passed under the wide sign fifty feet from the road, Sam gave it a quick look. Those tall posts would work well for the wire booby trap.

They entered the Bar F a few minutes later, and found that the hearse was already waiting. The hearse followed them as they turned toward the south pasture where everyone stopped short of the freshly dug hole.

Sam and Max quickly dismounted, hitched their horses to the back of the buggy and helped the ladies exit.

They all stood by the hole while the mortician's men carried the light coffin to the hole. There was no formal ceremony. Sophie had told Sam that as soon as everyone was there, they should lower the coffin. They did as she had requested and were soon shoveling the dirt back into the hole. They put up a temporary simple wooden cross marker, and then the men left quietly.

Sophie walked close to the grave and said something quietly that no one could hear, and then she walked back to the buggy. Mary just looked at the grave, turned and followed her mother. Julia walked back with Max and soon everyone was returning to the Circle W without a word having been said aloud.

After they returned, and Sam had taken care of the buggy and the horses, they adjourned to the main room.

"One of these days, Max, we'd better go and check on your cattle. They've been neglected."

"They'll be all right for a while, Sam."

"They might solve your problem of rebuilding your house, Sophie."

"Sam, I'm not sure I want to rebuild anymore."

"You're always welcome here, Sophie."

185

"I know, and I'm grateful, Sam. I'm just floating downstream without a paddle."

"I know the feeling, Sophie. I think you'll find direction soon."

Sophie looked over at Mary and then back at Sam before she said, "You may be right, Sam. We'd better get dinner going now. You and Max have things to do."

"We do. Let's get the guns ready. After dinner, everyone will be armed. Max and I will be out by the access road again tonight. Again, if nothing happens, we'll return to the bunkhouse at eleven. We'll be back in a little while."

Sam and Max left the house to go the bunkhouse and make sure all the pistols were loaded.

"Sam, are you going to use the Winchester again tonight?"

"I think so, but I may grab the shotgun if I think it'll be more effective, depending on the situation. Which weapon I use will depend on how they're aligned when they arrive. It they're close together, then I'll use the shotgun. If I do, leave the Winchester where it is. Once I fire the shotgun, I'll want the Winchester available. If the shooting starts, they'll see where I'm firing from because of the flare from my gun. I'll move quickly to get the Winchester. If you fire your pistol, immediately move at least six feet either way before you fire again. I'll open up with the Winchester after I get it, then I'll fire and move. The only thing that will get you shot is if you stay put but be careful of your own holes that we already dug. They'll be firing at your Colt's flare. You understand all that?"

"I understand. Leave the Winchester. Don't fire until you've fired. When I fire, I should move six feet before firing again."

"Right. This whole thing will be over very quickly. Stay low until I tell you it's clear."

"Okay."

They reached the bunkhouse and began to check the pistols. Sam felt as armed as he ever had, ten pistol shots, fifteen in the Winchester, two shells in the shotgun, and then the two .41-caliber backstop shots in the derringer. Hopefully, he wouldn't need anything past the Winchester and Max shouldn't have to fire at all.

Max and Sam brought the women their gunbelts when they returned forty minutes later. The sun was low in the west by then, and Sam felt that this wasn't going to be a quiet night as it had been the night before.

———

Paul was the first one to wake up from his extended nap, then sat up in the bed and shook his head. He noticed the dying light and knew that it was almost time to make their run at the ranch.

"Jimmy! It's almost time. It'll be sunset in another half an hour!" Paul shouted.

The others either yawned or scratched as they awakened. After five minutes, they were all in the kitchen having a cup of cold coffee.

"Alright, here's how we do it," began Jimmy, "He won't be expecting us because we didn't show up last night. Besides, there's only one of him, and he'd probably prefer being in bed with Julia than out in the front waiting on us."

"So, would I," Pat said as he grinned.

"You'll be last in line, brother," Jimmy snarled.

"I don't care. As long as I get some," Pat mumbled.

"Anyway, we ride down the access road pretty as you please. Keep it slow so the horses don't make a lot of noise. Don't cock your pistols until we're at the house. I don't want any noise."

"You don't want to go around from the side?" asked Reggie.

"Nope. Too much chance of steppin' in some gopher or snake hole."

"Okay. When do we leave?" asked Paul.

"It's almost sunset, so it'll be in another hour or so. We need to wait until it's good and dark, but not too late that he's gone to sleep. We should be able to get a few shots at him through the window."

"What if he's like huggin' her or something?" asked Pat.

"If you've got a good shot at him, take it. If it kills her too, well, Mike will owe us."

"Alright."

"We still got some cards left. Wanna play poker?"

"Okay."

So, the four men played a jack-less, king-of-spades-less game of poker while they waited for the sun to set.

––––––

"Sam, it's almost dark. Are we ready to go?" asked Max.

"Yup. Let's head out."

The women were all armed and in the main room, talking about everything except what Sam and Max were doing.

Sam had the fence tool and his coil of steel wire while Max carried the shotgun and the Winchester as they walked down the access road toward the ranch's sign. When they reached the sign, Sam set down the coil.

"Alright, Max, here's what this booby trap is for. I'm going to string a wire across the access road about a foot and a half above the ground. That'll trip any man or horse that tries to come down that road. Now, if I had wanted to kill them, I'd string it about seven feet above the ground. The horses would pass underneath, but the men would catch the wire in their chests if they were lucky, or in their throats if they weren't.

"I want to give them a chance, Max. They can either fight it out or run away. If they run, I don't think that they would go back to Malarkey. They'd be too afraid to admit that they had failed. I intend to shout at them to drop their guns and leave. If they do that, I'll let them go. If they don't, it's going to get messy. Either way as soon as I shout, I'm going to move ten feet away, so I don't let them know where to fire. Follow all that?"

"Yes, sir."

"Good. Let's get this booby trap set up."

It didn't take Sam long to build their tripwire booby trap. He started by making three loops around one of the poles and wrapping the end tightly around the wire with the fence tool. He stretched it across to the other post and pulled it taut before tightly looping the wire around the post and wrapping it around the stretched wire. He clipped off the loose wire and tossed it aside. Just to test it, he pulled the wire up and released it to a satisfying twang.

"There you go, Max. You're only ten feet away and know where it is, but can you see it?"

Max smiled even though Sam couldn't see him and replied, "No, sir. Not a bit."

"Alright, let's get into position."

Sam picked up both long guns and headed back down the road another thirty feet where he knew they'd be almost invisible in the dark night with their equally dark clothes.

"Max, make sure when you're moving that you don't step in any of our other booby traps."

Max giggled and replied, "No, sir. I've already found where they are."

"Good man."

Sam was impressed with Max. For a twelve-year-old, he was proving to be an able companion and he hadn't been just trying to make him feel better when he'd told Max that he was a friend. He saw a lot of Joe in him which added to his confidence in the young man.

Sam laid the Winchester on the berm at the edge of the access road so it wouldn't reflect any light and walked eight or ten feet into the grass. As Max had done, he searched for any of the hole booby traps, found one nearby and marked the position in his mind before he sat and waited.

"You ready, Max?"

"Yes, sir. I'm ready."

Sam didn't doubt it as he and Max waited silently under the stars for any approaching boobies for their trap.

––––––––

"Alright, boys. Let's mount up and get this game started," Jimmy said loudly to cover his nervousness.

He'd never let on, but the cards had him spooked. It was such an eerie way to make a threat.

None of them were unaffected from the ominous message that Sam had left with the cards, but none would admit to their deep-seated feeling of dread as they walked out into the night to mount their horses.

They left the Slash D cloaked in the black night to make the short ride to the Circle W.

Jimmy had them all moving at a medium trot on the road as there was no sense in being quiet way out here.

Sam heard them coming when they were a half mile off, but didn't say anything to Max. He had to assume that Max had heard them as well and was right in that assumption.

Sam cocked both hammers of the shotgun and knelt in the tall grass knowing it wouldn't be long now. He noticed the lack of any fear as he waited for the oncoming riders and hoped he wasn't getting overconfident.

Jimmy slowed them all down to a walk when they were within a hundred yards of the access road.

"See! His lights are on!" Jimmy whispered loudly.

"This is gonna work!" Pat replied too loudly to suit Jimmy.

Sam and Max heard both men but barely breathed.

The four riders rounded the turn into the yard, pulled their pistols and were two abreast as they approached the sign.

Jimmy's horse was the first to find the wire and screamed as his forelegs buckled, throwing Jimmy headfirst to the ground.

Pat's horse hit the wire just a fraction of a second later and repeated the same pattern of a screaming horse and a thrown rider. Both Toomeys hit the hard Texas dirt almost simultaneously, but Jimmy had extended his arms to soften the fall and his left forearm snapped as it struck the ground, both radius and ulna broken like a wishbone on Thanksgiving.

Pat Toomey fared marginally better when he landed on his right shoulder, dislocating it at the same time that he fractured the adjoining clavicle. Both men's screams joined that of their horses.

Paul and Reggie avoided the booby trap and cocked the hammers of their revolvers.

Sam shouted, "Drop the guns now! I've got two barrels of buckshot aimed at your heads!"

Then he shifted rapidly toward the left, avoiding his booby trap holes.

Neither Paul nor Reggie seemed to believe Sam, because both fired toward the sound of Sam's voice and Sam soon made believers out of them when he pulled the trigger of the shotgun. The mammoth blast of the two barrels momentarily lit up the scene before Sam dropped the weapon and didn't wait to see the results as he moved away from the spot and reached for his Winchester.

There was no need for the repeater as both Paul and Reggie paid for their decision, as did their horses. The blast of dozens of large lead pellets at only thirty feet was horrendous. Which of the pellets were the fatal ones was simply irrelevant as both were thrown off the backs of their horses. The horses took multiple pellet wounds as well and screamed in shock and pain but raced away. Neither of their riders did more than grunt after they hit the ground and then each moaned for a few seconds as their life's blood drained onto the Texas soil under the ranch sign.

Sam had the Winchester cocked as he approached the sobbing Toomey brothers, found their Colts on the ground nearby and tossed them toward Max. He stepped past them and the shaken horses and found the two dead men, then pulled their guns, carried them back past the Toomeys and set them on the ground near the first two pistols.

Convinced that there was no more threat, he shouted, "Max, you can come out. It's clear."

Max walked slowly up the berm of the access road and was surprised how well he could see without a moon. He still couldn't see the booby trap wire, though.

Sam knelt near Jimmy Toomey and said, "Now, Jimmy, I should by all that's good and holy execute you and your brother for murder and arson, but I'm not an overly vindictive man. I'm going to load those two bodies on their wounded horses. Your horses were startled, but they're okay. I'm going to make trail ropes for you and your brother, so you both can ride back to Mike Malarkey and get to see a doctor. Now, you may not want to see Mike, but if you do, tell him I will kill him. He's going to get no mercy from me. He sent you boys here to kill me and he cost those two their lives. You remember that, Jimmy. He's the one who cost you your arm and your friends their lives."

Jimmy, despite his agony, just looked at Sam and said, "You don't sound right. You sound different."

"I'm from Iowa. I was a sergeant in the Union army, and I was held in a prison camp over near Tyler. That merciless bastard you call your boss was a guard that everyone, including his own men, hated. You feel free to tell him that. You tell him that Sergeant Sam Walker of Company C of the Fourteenth Iowa Volunteer Infantry Regiment is here to make things right."

Sam helped Jimmy to his feet and put him on his horse, then walked over to Jimmy's brother and did the same. He thought about putting his shoulder back into place, but figured he was already letting them off with their lives, so he just let it go. He didn't know about the broken clavicle, and probably would have made Jimmy's injuries worse if he'd tried.

It took him a few more minutes to track down the two injured horses, then get the two dead men thrown over their saddles, before he tied their reins to the saddles of the two Toomey brothers.

"You boys better start riding."

Jimmy had nothing to say, so they started north for the four-mile ride.

After they had gone a half mile, Sam turned to Max and said, "Let's clean up this mess and go talk to the women."

Back in the house, the women had heard the initial screams of the Toomeys' horses, then the pistol shots, followed immediately by the shotgun. Then there had been silence…a terrible, unknowing silence.

"Should we do anything, Mary?" asked Julia.

"No. If Sam or Max had been hurt, I think we would have heard more pistols being fired. I wonder if Malarkey was there."

"I don't think so. He never went out on those raids. He'd always send his boys."

"The suspense is driving me mad," said Sophie.

"I believe that Sam and Max will walk through the door in two minutes," said Mary, unsure of why she made the prediction.

Her mother looked at the doorway and said, "I hope so."

———

As Mary made her prediction, Sam and Max were heading their way.

"Sam, why did you let them go?" asked Max.

"They weren't a threat anymore, Max. They'll be out of commission for weeks and I wanted Malarkey to know that he was alone now. That's only if they go and see him, and if I were in their shoes, I wouldn't. But they may have no other choice."

"But they murdered my father, Sam."

"I know that Max, but around here the law wouldn't have done anything to either of them. If I had killed them, I would have been a murderer, Max. They had no guns. They were defenseless. Could you have lived with that?"

"No. I guess not."

"When you shoot at a man, he's got to be a threat. If you shoot one who isn't, you're a murderer. You've got to understand the difference. All killing isn't murder. If we lived in a normal time or even back in Iowa, where I'm from, if they had done what they did to your ranch and your father, I'd have simply brought them to the sheriff, where they'd have been tried and hanged. Out here, we have to be our own law, but I refuse to kill a defenseless man."

"I understand, Sam."

"Good. It's an important thing to know."

They stopped at the bunkhouse and left the four pistols, the shotgun, and the Winchester before heading for the house. As soon as their feet hit the porch, the door slammed open, and Mary shot out of the house and jumped onto Sam, wrapping him in a hug.

Sam held her suspended above the porch and said, "Hello, Mary. Glad to see me?"

"Of course, I'm glad to see you, Mister Walker. Glad to see you without any new bullet holes."

As Julia and Sophie stepped through the door, he set her down and said, "They walked their horses right into the booby trap. The Toomeys took a nosedive into the ground and broke some bones. I told the other two to drop their guns, but they fired instead, so I fired the shotgun, which killed them both. I got the Toomeys on their horses, threw the two dead ones on theirs, and sent them back to Malarkey."

"Won't they come back?" asked Julia.

"Not those two. They have too many injuries. The only one left now is Malarkey. He's alone and I don't think he knows how to work by himself."

"Let's go inside," said Sophie.

They all entered the main room and took seats, Sam ensuring that he and Mary shared the couch, although it wasn't necessary as Mary had her arm wrapped around his.

"Sam, what do we do about Malarkey?" asked Sophie.

"We have to wait for him to come here," answered Sam, "I can't hunt him down. They'd hang me for sure."

"Won't they go to the sheriff with those two bodies and say that you killed them?" asked Julia.

"They can do that, but it would be hard to explain why they were here late at night and why they were shot in the front and not the back. I think they'll go and see Malarkey despite their failure because they need to see the doctor. I just have no idea what Malarkey's reaction will be. Could I get some coffee?"

––––––

Two and a half hours later, Pat Toomey, his shoulder relocated and wearing a heavy wrap for his broken collarbone, sat across from Mike Malarkey. Jimmy was still at the doctor's office but had argued against seeing Malarkey. Pat figured that he wasn't in charge, so it would be a chance to show his loyalty and maybe get a nice reward. So, against his brother's almost-violent objection, he had gone to see Mike Malarkey.

"Reggie and Paul are dead, so where are the bodies?" asked a surprisingly calm Mike Malarkey.

"We left them at the mortuary. Nobody was there, though."

"And you four idiots all fell right into his trap."

"Mike, it wasn't like anyone could see anything. I still don't know what happened."

"Why didn't he shoot you and that idiot brother of yours?"

"He wanted us to give you a message."

Malarkey was glaring at him as he snapped, "Well? Let's have it."

"He said he was a Yankee sergeant from Iowa. He was in a prison camp where you were a guard, and he said that Sgt. Sam Walker was going to make things right."

That news rocked Mike Malarkey. *A Yankee back here seeking revenge!* He didn't say anything to Pat Toomey for a few minutes as he tried to think of any advantage to knowing that Sam Walker was a Yankee. Maybe he could rally some support from the locals, but quickly tossed that idea aside. He knew that he was hated and feared by them. *Maybe the law could be used.* That weasel sheriff Ralph Morton could arrest Walker for murdering Reggie and Paul, but he knew that was a bust, too. Too much would come out in a trial and how could he trust the jurors? Besides, Malarkey wasn't sure how much power he had anymore, so he needed to keep that bit of information quiet, too.

"All right, Pat. I need you to go down to the mortician's and get those two bodies and walk 'em out west of town a few miles. Find a gully and take them a half mile off the road and dump 'em."

Pat was about to protest that it was night and he was wounded but didn't want to risk a show of disloyalty.

"Okay, boss."

"When you get back, just go to your room and relax. Tell Jimmy to do the same. I don't want either of you to come here for two days. I figure that Yankee will try to sneak into my house and shoot me. Well, I'm gonna be ready. Anybody comes through that door, knockin' or not, gets shot."

"Okay, boss. I'll tell him."

Pat was hoping for some financial reward for his confession of failure, but none seemed to be forthcoming.

He was about to ask about the doctor's bill but thought better of it. Mike wasn't in a killing mood, and he was better left that way. He turned and left the house, feeling better once he was out the door. For some reason, a calm Mike Malarkey seemed more dangerous than the screaming version.

———

Sam's eyes were closed as he laid on his bunk, but his mind was wide awake.

Sam was back in the prison camp, but he knew that the war was over. How he knew was never a question, he just knew.

The prison camp's gates were thrown open and he knew he could leave any time he wanted. He could go home and marry his Mary. *Mary? Why would he marry her instead of Barbara Jean?* It bothered him, but he'd figure it out after he got home. All he had to do was walk through the gates, and he'd be in Iowa. Iowa was right past those open gates, not Texas.

He began to walk and soon reached the gates and walked through, feeling exultant. *He was almost home!* Then he heard a loud, cruel cackle. It was Malarkey's laugh and Sam spun around, but Malarkey was nowhere in sight. The laugh grew louder, more vindictive but even if he couldn't see the bastard, it came from everywhere. He decided to ignore the laughter and just go home.

Sam kept walking, then passed through the gates and soon entered another fenced compound. *It was supposed to be Iowa! Where was the green grass? The rows of corn? Where was Anna?*

He whipped around as the laughter began to dominate everything. Behind him was the gate, which was still open, and beyond the gate was his home. He could see the farmhouse just in the distance and began to run as the hideous Malarkey laughter thundered across the camp. He passed through the gate and looked for the house and found another camp where the farmhouse had been just moments before as the laughter shook him to his soul.

He wheeled about and saw an open gate again, and just beyond it, he saw Mary smiling at him. *Mary? Where was Barbara Jean?* The ground was shimmering from the pervasive laughter, as Sam began plodding toward Mary, hoping she could explain all this to him. But as he drew closer, she morphed slowly into a grinning, hideous Mike Malarkey.

Sam exploded from his bed, screaming, *"No!"*

Sam's heart and breathing were sprinting as he sat with sweat dripping from everywhere.

"Sam, are you okay?" asked a sleepy Max.

"I'm sorry, Max. Get some sleep."

Sam stood and walked out of the bunkhouse, still shaking. It was still warm as he left the confines of the bunkhouse and stepped into the moonlit yard. He knew that he needed sleep…just one long, good night's sleep.

He'd had the nightmares every night for the past ten days and was waking up Max now. *Was there never going to be an end to it?* He was shirtless and shoeless as he walked toward the smokehouse. He hadn't used it for anything since he'd bought the place. Maybe he should set up a bunk inside for himself, so Max could sleep.

Then, as he began thinking about changing the sleeping arrangements, he suddenly remembered that Anna was coming tomorrow. *What would she think?*

He swerved back toward the house and soon sat on the back steps and shifted his thoughts to the necessary work ahead of him. He and Max would have to remove all the booby traps later. He didn't think Malarkey would fall for any of them and he wanted Malarkey to come but was now concerned for his sister's safety as well. She was coming into a hornet's nest.

CHAPTER 7

Sam never did return to sleep that night. He stayed awake but returned to the bunkhouse and put on his boots, shirt, Stetson, and gunbelt. The armory had grown significantly after the last attack. He knew they were almost superfluous now. He thought it would be much more personal with Malarkey. Malarkey would want to kill him with his hands, a knife, or maybe that hickory club he had used in the camp. The same one he had never used on him and began to wonder if he'd been saving it for this special occasion.

After dressing, Sam walked to the cistern and washed up, but would shave later when there was light. He walked to the smokehouse, opened the door, and went inside. It was too dark to see anything, so he returned to the barn and took a lamp from a hanger, lit it, then left the barn and reentered the smokehouse.

There was still the smoky, meaty scent in the wood and lots of hooks hanging from thick poles which could slide along the length of the smokehouse. He imagined hams and slabs of bacon hanging there. There were shelves lining the walls as well. It was a large smokehouse, the biggest he'd ever seen. He wondered if it could have any other uses as he left the building and closed the door behind him. He didn't want to tear it down, but the wood was too deeply saturated with smoke and meat juices to be useful for anything else. Sam came to the brilliant solution that its best use was as a smokehouse.

He blew out the lamp and returned it to the barn. All the horses were still sleeping. At least they didn't have nightmares, then began wondering if they did. He knew dogs did. They used to have a yellow dog on the farm back in Iowa named Penny. She'd be snoozing by the fire and would suddenly yelp and jerk awake, looking around for whatever dream enemy had caused the imaginary fear.

Sam returned to the back steps and sat down. He guessed it was after four o'clock in the morning and the predawn would arrive soon. It was almost the middle of June. June 11th now as midnight had long passed. Anna would be coming tomorrow and was probably going to be arriving in Paris tonight, and Sam thought briefly of going to Paris to greet her there. But his place was here. He had to stay here and wait for Malarkey. Mary could go and pick up Anna tomorrow in Bonham.

Sam smiled at the mental image. Anna would be a bit surprised to see Mary wearing britches and packing a Colt on her hip. Mary had been in his last nightmare, yet not as someone to fear, but as a symbol of hope. She had been the final goal that had been taken from him by Malarkey.

Sam suddenly had a horrible thought. *Was the dream a prediction? Was Malarkey going to take away his Mary?* He never believed in such things. Dreams were dreams, nothing more, but even the very idea itched at his soul. He'd have to protect Mary. She'd be armed going into Bonham, *but was it enough?*

He decided that he'd have Max ride with her. Between them they'd have three guns. Maybe he'd let Max take the shotgun, too. That idea seemed to quell his worries, Max as escort with the shotgun. Sam felt better, even though he didn't believe in dreams as predictors of the future.

Forty minutes later the predawn began to spread across the sky, driving the stars back into their own sleep. The late moon was still high in the western sky and wouldn't set for three more hours.

C. J. PETIT

Sam decided to shave now that there was some light, so by the time dawn officially arrived, Sam was clean-shaven and ready for the day. He knew he should be hungry but wasn't. He did want some coffee though and figured he could sneak into the kitchen and get the coffee started, so he stepped softly up the porch steps and across the back porch, opened the door quietly and entered the kitchen. So far, so good.

He put some kindling in the cookstove and set it ablaze before adding some heavier wood, then closed the cookstove's fire box door gently and held the coffee pot under the pump and began to pump water into the pot. The pump's lever wasn't as silent as he wished, but it only took three good pumps to fill the pot with water. He placed it on the stove and sat down, putting his Stetson on the table.

Less than a minute later, Mary stepped out of the hallway and saw Sam, smiled and held up a finger as she pranced past and out the back door. Three minutes later, Mary reentered the house and closed the door quietly behind her. She walked over to Sam in her nightdress and sat on his lap, putting her arms around his neck.

"Good morning, Sam," she whispered.

Sam didn't answer but just kissed her good morning.

Mary pulled herself closer and held on tightly, and Sam was too aware of just the single layer of flannel that separated him and Mary.

"Nightmare?" she asked in the necessary whisper.

Sam nodded and whispered back, "You showed up in this one."

She smiled and said, "I hope I don't scare you that much."

"You were my ultimate aspiration, Mary. You were my hope."

Mary sighed, looked into his tired eyes and said, "I still think you need me to be with you, Sam."

202

"Max might object, or your mother might think it's unacceptable."

"I think the only one who might object is Julia. She asked me later, after I had thrown myself at you, if you and I were a couple."

"What did you tell her?"

"That we hadn't coupled yet, but we were matched."

"You really are going to drag me down into perdition with such thoughts, aren't you, Mary."

"I hope so. I suppose I'd better get down before someone else comes out."

"Or I get carried away."

"I should be so lucky," she replied as she kissed him quickly and slid back to the floor.

She took the chair next to Sam, and two minutes later, Julia arrived, wearing her nightdress. She managed to look seductive in a flannel nightdress, with her hair all disheveled and hanging over her shoulders.

"Good morning, Sam and Mary," she said.

"Morning, Julia," replied Sam.

"Hello, Julia. I just got here. Did you hear Sam pumping water for coffee, too?" asked Mary.

"No, I heard movement, and I thought you were up. If I'd known Sam was here, I'd make myself more presentable," she said as she smiled.

Mary looked at Sam and rolled her eyes.

"You look fine, Julia," Sam said as the corners of Mary's mouth turned upward ever so slightly.

Julia's smile widened and she replied, "Why, thank you, Sam."

Sam guessed that Mary's "couple" response hadn't had any effect and wondered just how he could deflect her intentions without causing any damage.

The coffee water was boiling, so Sam rose, added coffee and poured three cups. Mary and Julia added sugar to theirs.

"Did either of you want some cream? I have some in the cold room that I need to use anyway."

They both nodded, and Sam retrieved the jar of cream from the cold room, then poured some into a small pitcher before returning it to its shelf and handing the pitcher to Mary.

"What's the plan for today, Sam?" asked Mary.

"Max and I have to go out and remove all the booby traps. That'll take a couple of hours. Then I'm going to build another bed for Anna. It won't be a proper bed, but it'll do until we find out what's happening. I don't know if she plans on staying permanently or if this is just an extended visit. If it's permanent, then I may have to add another bedroom or two to the house."

"Am I going to go to Bonham to pick her up, Sam?"

"I think so. I'm going to ask Max to ride along with the shotgun. I have to stay on the ranch until Malarkey decides to come here to kill me."

"I understand. I appreciate having Max along. I wonder if he'd ride with me in the buggy on the way down and trail the horse. It would be a boring drive otherwise."

"It's up to the two of you. If he's in the buggy, make sure the shotgun is, too."

"Okay. I'll start breakfast."

Sam nodded and watched as Mary stood and began fixing breakfast. Julia noticed him staring at Mary and decided she'd help with breakfast and add a little flair to the process. She stood and had to straighten her hair as she walked to the cookstove.

Sam couldn't help but notice. It was an alluring movement, showing Julia's figure to advantage. It was hard to take his eyes away, but he managed. Julia noticed the initial impact and thought she had made progress. She was pleased and thought it was the start of a shift away from Mary. Julia didn't see it as mean or underhanded, she just wanted to let Sam know that she was interested, nothing more.

Mary hadn't seen any of it as she was laying the sliced bacon into the frypan. She was under no illusion about being in Julia's league in physical beauty. She was counting on the deep and durable bond that she and Sam had discovered and continued to forge almost hourly. She wondered if Joe would have ever expected that Julia would look at Sam as his replacement.

The three were eating breakfast when Max arrived from the bunkhouse.

"Sam, did you ever go back to sleep last night?"

"No. It was too interesting outside."

Max poured himself a cup of coffee and added some sugar and cream.

"What was interesting?"

"The smokehouse. I was in there and wondered if it would have any other uses other than as a smokehouse."

"Well, you could cut out the doors wider and put the wagon in there."

Sam replied, "Maybe. That would free up barn space. All I would need to do is cut to the next beam on either side. That'll be wide enough for the wagon. We could store grease, a spare wheel, and a spare axle inside as well. I wonder what use we could make of all those hooks."

"Bring them to the smithy in Bonham. He'll buy them for the iron. Better yet, he'll trade you for a bunch of horseshoes. As many horses as we have now, it'll be good to have spares."

"Max, you're a real genius. I may leave a couple to use as pulleys to get heavy things out of the wagon."

Max was grinning at the praise as he sat down.

Mary finished her breakfast and stood to make Max his while Julia stayed seated next to Sam.

"Max, today we need to go and fill in the holes and remove the booby trap wire. Tomorrow you'll be escorting Mary into Bonham to pick up my sister. I want you to take the shotgun with you."

"How come you're not going?"

"Because I have to stay on the ranch if Malarkey comes."

"Oh. That's right."

"Something else, Max," Sam began as he reached into his pocket and pulled out twenty dollars then handed it to Max.

"Buy yourself a Stetson when you're there. Get one for that tomboy sister of yours, too. She needs to look more like a Texan."

Max laughed as he accepted the money and said, "This is a lot of money, Sam. They won't cost this much."

"Keep the rest, Max. A man needs to have some spending money."

"Thanks, Sam!"

Max was having a great day already.

"What was with the tomboy crack, Mister Walker?" asked Mary as she took the bacon out of the frypan and began cracking eggs.

"Just repeating what I was told, Miss Farrell, by the self-proclaimed tomboy herself."

"Well, maybe I'll buy myself a riding skirt and blouse when I'm in Bonham, Mister Walker."

"It wouldn't surprise me in the least, Miss Farrell," Sam replied.

Max wondered why they were arguing. Julia also missed the real thrust of the conversation and thought they might be having a falling out.

"You know, Mister Walker, perhaps you should try taking a bath sometime. Then you'd be able to see what a true lady I really am."

"A bath, Miss Farrell? Why, the thought repulses me. I haven't put a toe into that bathtub since I bought the place, and I doubt if I will use it until the days darken into winter."

Julia was stunned by the comment. Sam had smelled so very pleasant when she was near him and so masculine, too.

Max caught on with the bath comment. He knew how much fun they had using the swimming hole and realized that Sam and Mary were joshing each other.

"I don't doubt that, Mister Walker. Perhaps I should show you how to properly bathe."

"I doubt if you could teach me anything, Miss Farrell. You probably bathe fully clothed."

Mary almost lost it on that one, but she held on.

"Think of me as you will, Mister Walker, but I will accept your offer of a new Stetson and wear it proudly as a daughter of the great state of Texas."

"Excuse me, Miss Farrell, perhaps you would allow me to finance your purchase of some riding regalia as well. Max, here is another ten dollars to buy your sister some riding skirts and blouses so that she may cast aside her tomboy image," Sam said haughtily as he handed Max a ten-dollar bill.

"I'll see that she purchases the items, sir," Max answered.

Mary brought Max his breakfast and sat back down on Sam's left to finish her coffee.

Julia didn't know what to make of the whole conversation. Neither seemed to be angry, but the words were hurtful, bordering on mean.

"When are you and Max going to remove the booby traps?" Mary asked as if the whole previous war of words had never happened.

"As soon as he finishes breakfast. It should take about two hours. Then we'll head to the barn, and I'll build Anna's bed. What are you, Julia, and your mother planning on doing?"

"Household stuff, mainly. We need to get some laundry and cleaning done, and we need to organize a bit. How much is Anna going to be bringing with her, do you think?"

"I haven't got even a hint for a guess. She could show up with a single travel bag or three giant trunks. At least with the smokehouse, we have storage space."

"Does it smell in there?" Julia asked, "That could make her things smell bad."

"It does, but it's a very pleasant smell. It's like a gentle barbecue aroma. I'll probably put in a couple of windows to get some light and air inside, but right now, it's still a smokehouse."

———

Sam wasn't the only one who hadn't slept the night before. Mike Malarkey had spent most of the night with a pistol on his lap. He had moved an easy chair against the wall opposite the front door and sat there just waiting for Sergeant Sam Walker to burst through the door. He had drifted off a few times but never moved.

When he finally stood, he was more than just stiff, he was seething with pent up fury and disappointment. His planned attack on Walker had failed, he felt like a prisoner in his own house, and Walker had his wife, too. He didn't miss her a bit, but it still wounded his enormous pride.

He walked to the kitchen, keeping the loaded pistol in his hand. He had to make a run to the privy and suddenly wondered if Walker was out there waiting for him to do just that. There were few things in life more predictable than an early morning run to the privy.

He opened the back door slowly. The house had a wide-open yard in back, so there were only a few places he could hide, so he focused on the privy. That was where he'd be, right behind the privy. Walker would wait until he was inside the little house and then blast away.

"Well, Sergeant Sam Walker, Sergeant Michael J. Malarkey is smarter than you," he said as he grinned, then stepped down the stairs quietly and walked toward the privy.

He cocked the hammer of the Colt and approached warily, just in case Walker popped around either side of the privy at the last second. When he got within ten feet, he unloaded all five rounds through the front door of the privy. The bullets blasted holes in the front door and quickly made similar punctures in the back wall. He had spread the shots widely to be sure of hitting Walker. Walker was supposed to be a big man, so he couldn't miss. He laughed and ran quickly to the back of the privy expecting to see Walker spread-eagled on the ground in a pool of blood but found nothing.

"Son of a bitch!" he screamed as he threw the pistol at the wall of the privy. It hit the weakened boards and crashed right through, leaving a gaping hole. So much for privacy in the privy.

He entered the holey little house and used it anyway. He wouldn't be able to sit on the seat for a while, though. One of his .44s had demolished the seat, leaving large splinters. And Mike's mood sunk even lower.

When he finished his morning business, he returned to the house, leaving the empty pistol in the privy. He walked inside, started a fire in the cookstove and filled the coffee pot. After putting it on the cookstove, Malarkey returned to his office, went to the gun cabinet and pulled out his last revolver. It was a Cooper Pocket model. It had one big advantage over the Colt: it was a double action pistol, so there was no need to cock the hammer, all he had to do was just pull the trigger. A shooter could empty all five of its cylinders in just three seconds.

It had three disadvantages over the Colt, though. It only had five maximum shots versus the Colt's six. It had a shorter barrel, so it wasn't as accurate, and its biggest disadvantage was that it fired a .31-caliber round. But Mike didn't mind right now. He'd be able to put the gun in his jacket pocket and appear to be unarmed. If Walker came through the door, he'd throw up his hands as if he was surrendering, then when the bastard lowered his pistol, he'd let him discover the Cooper. After listening to Pat Toomey, this Yankee won't shoot an unarmed man. Mike smiled with his plan for deception and wanted the Yankee to show up soon.

He returned to the kitchen and had his coffee. He would wait. He sure wasn't going to go and find Walker on that ranch of his. It took the deaths of Reggie Anderson and Paul Hooper to show him that. He'd wait for Walker to come to him, and knew he'd come today.

—————

Sam had removed the wire booby trap easily by using a hatchet. One quick blow and the wires were cut from the right-hand post and twanged loudly as the tension was released. He walked to the other post and cut the other three loops, then coiled the wire and set it aside.

Max had already started filling in his holes while Sam took care of the wire, then once the wire was clear, Sam began to refill his holes. It was a lot faster than digging them, and Max was whistling while he filled in his holes. Sam's treatment of him like a man had made him feel grown up. He knew he was still twelve and would have to return to school in the last week of August, but the stories he'd be able to tell!

Sam had let him pick his own horse out of the group, and Max had picked one of the three geldings that Sam had brought from Arkansas. The horse was a tall boy, almost as tall as Sam's Fire. Like Fire he had four boots but was a lighter brown. He had a star on his forehead as well. When Sam had told him the story of how he had named Fire, Max thought he should name his horse a foreign word, too, but Sam didn't have any other ones that sounded right, so he named him Flame. Sam said that he liked the name, and Max did, too. Fire and Flame looked like brothers, just like him and Sam, although he wasn't nearly as big as Sam.

Sam noticed Max's cheerful demeanor and it helped him without realizing it. Despite his earlier self-admonishment about not letting the nightmares impact his moods, this one had. It took a lot of willpower to keep despair away and Max's still-boyish enthusiasm for getting Flame and filling in the booby trap holes was infectious.

Sam had almost covered up the blood from last night's incident and then decided against it. Let it stay in case any bought-and-paid-for sheriff arrived to 'investigate' the death of his town's outstanding citizens. The blood was on his property, so he had every right to defend himself and his land.

They finished filling the holes and walked side by side back to the barn, shovels on their shoulders like soldiers on the march.

"Sam, are we gonna use the swimming hole?"

"Well, Max, I don't know about you, but I feel pretty dirty after all that work."

Max looked up at Sam, grinned and replied, "So do I."

They dropped the shovels, the coil of wire and the fence tool in the barn and returned to the bunkhouse. They retrieved some clean clothes and a bar of soap then started walking east to the swimming hole, both still wearing their gunbelts.

"Sam, do you think Malarkey's gonna come today?"

"I don't know, Max. If he comes, it'll be late, I think. But I don't know him well enough to predict when he'll show up. We hurt him pretty bad last night, Max. He's got no more men now. He'll have to do this by himself. I don't know if he's ever been in combat or a fight before where he might lose. He used to beat the prisoners because they couldn't fight back."

"Did he beat you and Joe?"

"He beat Joe a few times, but he never hit me. I don't know why. I sure glared at him enough. Do you know what the other guards called him?"

"No, sir."

"That Miserable Mic Mike Malarkey."

Max laughed, then asked, "The guards didn't like him either?"

"No, sir. He used to take their food, and he'd beat some of them, too. He had a small group of toadies that followed him around and got some of his crumbs."

"Were they the same men that came last night?"

"Nope. I would have recognized them."

"Sam, was it alright that I didn't shoot last night?"

"Max, I am really proud of you for how you behaved last night. A lot of men would have just started shooting willy-nilly when those two yahoos started shooting, but you were disciplined. You did exactly as I told you. No commanding officer could be prouder of any of his men than I was with you last night."

Max beamed at the praise. He had been worried that Sam might have thought he was afraid. But it had been just like Sam had said it would be. He was scared to death as they waited, but when things started happening, he felt himself grow calm and knew what he had to do. He had held his gun ready to shoot if Sam needed it, but Sam's plan had worked perfectly.

They reached the swimming hole and stripped. Max took a look, saw Sam's other wound and started to laugh.

Sam turned and knew what the inspiration for the laughter was and said, "It's funny now, but when that Minié ball hit my ass, it sure wasn't funny."

Max stopped laughing and felt bad, but only for a second.

"It could've been worse though. Another inch or two and I would have become a steer. And I'd talk like this," he said with his last sentence spoken in an unmanly alto.

Max started laughing again, relieved that Sam really hadn't been offended at all.

While he was laughing, Sam cannonballed into the water, doing to Max what he had done to Mary earlier. Max laughed harder and cannonballed into the water as well.

Sam swam to the patio and grabbed the soap, lathered and then handed it to Max.

While the male side of the population was off cleaning themselves, the female side was conferring about the arrival of Anna.

"Mary, are you sure you want to give up part of your room to Anna? I'm in the biggest bedroom. She could stay with me," said Sophie.

"No, Mama. I really want Anna to stay with me. From what Sam tells me, she and I should bond as quickly as Sam and I did. He told me how much I remind him of her. Not in the way I look, but in how I think."

"Does that make a difference to Sam?" asked Julia.

"All the difference in the world. His brother Frank is different, I think."

"The one who married his girlfriend?"

"That's the one. Sam says he's about two inches shorter than he is but is good looking. Sam says he's better looking than he is, but I doubt that."

"That would be hard to believe, wouldn't it?" said Julia.

"But Frank seems to place greater stock in a woman's appearance. If he were here, Julia, I wouldn't stand a chance, provided I were interested in anyone other than Sam."

It was out in the open now, so Julia asked, "Do you believe that you and Sam are going to be married?"

"Absolutely."

"But you were both at odds this morning about bathing."

Mary laughed, then said, "We do that a lot. We accuse each other of being either too prudish or too lust-filled, for example."

"You've accused him of having too much lust?" Julia asked with wide eyes.

"No, he's accused me of that. I called him a prude. Of course, this was after we shared the swimming hole."

"But you weren't unclothed, were you?" she asked with a horrified expression on her face.

"No, I was still dressed. He was naked, though," Mary stated factually to get the startled reaction she expected.

"He was naked!"

Sophie sat off to the side with a slight smirk on her face.

"He was already in the water, though. I didn't get to see him totally undressed until he came out and then it was just with no shirt."

Julia was debating which question to ask and chose, "What did he look like?"

"My Sam is all man," she said with a sigh to accent the comment.

"You didn't do anything did you?" when she asked the other part of her question.

"While we were in the water, we kissed for the first time. We sunk to the bottom as we did, too. It was almost a religious experience."

Julia was getting excited by the conversation yet was still a bit shocked.

"How long had you known him? Didn't he think you were a loose woman?"

"I had spoken my first words to Sam the day before. I told him that I wasn't that way, and he told me that he never even thought of me as anything other than an innocent. In fact, he called me the perfect innocent."

"But you were so forward. How could he think that of you?" asked the flabbergasted Julia.

"Because he knew me, Julia, just like I knew him. I felt totally safe and comfortable with Sam from the moment we met. Maybe it was Joe's letters, I don't know. He felt the same way. It's hard to describe. He said that neither one of us has to worry about the other saying something that we didn't mean. He knows we have no secrets between us and never will."

Julia had a hard time believing that. People just can't tell someone everything.

"So, if he did something bad, he'd tell you about it?"

"I don't have a doubt in my mind, and I would do the same. He's told me things that he's never told anyone, not even Anna. Anna would be surprised because he had always told her everything."

"Maybe he'll do the same to you."

"No, I think when Anna arrives, Sam will now be able to tell her what he told me. He said that he didn't want to tell Anna because it would hurt her."

"But he told you. Wasn't he afraid of hurting you?"

"No. He said I was stronger, but I think Anna's willingness to travel to Texas to see him was proof enough that she was strong enough after all."

"Well, you two need to stop talking about poor Sam, and let's go and fix some lunch, so he and Max can eat," said Sophie.

Mary and Julia followed Sophie to the kitchen, Mary feeling more secure and Julia more confused.

———

Sam and Max were walking back from their enjoyable baths as Max asked, "Sam, are you going to build a bed for Anna this afternoon?"

"That's the plan. Want to help?"

"Sure. Have you built anything before?"

"Yup. That gun cabinet in Julia's bedroom was the last one."

"You built that? It looks really nice."

"The good news is that I still have a lot of boards left over from repair work that I had to do. I hope they didn't come from Malarkey's lumber mill. I'd hate to think that I gave that bastard some profit."

216

Max nodded, feeling grownup when Sam used words in front of him that women aren't supposed to hear, even though Sam told him that grownup women used them anyway.

They returned to the bunkhouse, tossed their dirty clothes onto their bunks, then headed to the house for lunch.

Even though the day was incredibly peaceful, Sam had a difficult time trying to maintain his focus, knowing that Mike Malarkey was out there and probably just biding his time before coming to his home to either try and take Julia back or kill him, but probably both. Having Anna added to the mix wasn't helping either. *What was wrong back in Iowa?*

———

Mike Malarkey was sitting at the café having his lunch when Sheriff Ralph Morton walked in and spotted him. Malarkey hoped he wasn't going to come over to his table, but that hope was dashed when Morton approached his table, pulled out a chair, then sat without asking.

"Mike, we got a couple of problems. Some of your neighbors complained about a bunch of gunfire at your place this morning."

"Sorry about that. Had to shoot this big rat over near the privy. Missed the bastard too, even with five shots."

"That's what I figured. The other one is a bit more serious. Seems that Pat Toomey was seen riding out of town this morning with a couple of bodies draped over his horses."

Malarkey figured he'd see if he could get his money's worth out of the sheriff but knew that there was a chance he might rebel now that he only had two wounded strongarms.

"Those bodies used to be Reggie Anderson and Paul Hooper. They got killed last night by that Sam Walker down at the Circle W. I didn't want to bother you with it because it's out of your jurisdiction."

217

"Well, maybe. Where did they get it?"

"Like I just told you, down at the Circle W. That's why I didn't let you know."

"Oh. I figured you was just sayin' that he was down there. Was it on his property?"

"I don't know. If you're interested, you could ask Pat, but it's still the county's problem, not yours."

"Yeah, I suppose. Why'd he shoot 'em?"

"Because he stole my wife. I sent 'em down there to bring her back."

"Well, now that's different. I'll head down there and arrest him for kidnappin' 'cause it happened here, and I'll bring your wife back. You shoulda come to me rather than waste your boys. How are Jimmy and Pat Toomey?"

Malarkey was a bit surprised that the sheriff hadn't hesitated and had actually volunteered to go down there. It wasn't his normal behavior. Normally, he'd just look the other way as he was paid to do.

"They're laid up. Jimmy has a broken arm, and Pat has a broken collar bone."

"Damn! That's bad. This feller did all that?"

"Yeah. Turns out he's a Yankee from Iowa. Can you believe that?"

"A damned Yankee comes down here, buys a ranch, steals your wife, and then guns down your boys? Well, I sure ain't gonna put up with that. No, sir!"

"If you go down to the Circle W, Sheriff, I'd make it worth your while, too."

"Well, I sure do appreciate it, Mike. I'm gonna head down there and take care of this feller and see about gettin' your wife back."

Mike shook his hand and said, "Thanks, Ralph."

The sheriff nodded, stood, then hiked up his gunbelt, turned and marched away from the table.

Mike smiled to himself as he watched the puffed-up Ralph Morton exit the diner and mount his horse. *Who knows?* Maybe the sheriff would get something done. His only concern was that if Morton returned his wife to him and did nothing else. That would be worse than nothing at all. But after hearing about what that Yankee bastard had done to his four boys, he doubted if Ralph would return at all.

Even as the sheriff was riding away, Mike Malarkey began to plan to use the sheriff's death as a way to get to Walker.

————

Sam and Max entered the kitchen to find all three women preparing lunch, which was a bit different.

"I thought too many cooks spoiled the broth," said Sam to no one in particular.

"Only if the cooks are men," replied Mary.

"She wounds me yet again. Will nothing curtail your sharp tongue, woman?"

Mary answered, "No, kind sir. For alas, I am but a woman of ill breeding."

"Well, be that as it may, my fellow hard-working partner, Max, and I will simply take our seats at the table and await our luncheon to be served quietly by you subservient women. Which is the proper position for the gentle, yet inescapably inferior sex."

Mary curtsied, then said, "Why, of course, my lord. We will endeavor to make your dining experience as pleasurable as possible, and perhaps, you may allow us to thank you for your mere presence."

"Now, that's the proper attitude that all women should take to their sexual superiors."

"I bow to your greatness, oh king of all that is masculine."

Sam began to scan the room as he said, "Wait! I seem to have misplaced my crown. Where is that damned thing?"

"Ah! Here it is, my lord," Mary said, picking up his Stetson and placing it carefully on his head.

"Thank you, cooking wench. I shall reward you with a shilling," Sam replied, taking a dime out of his pocket and handing it to Mary.

While this was all going on, Julia had stopped cooking and watched as they played their parts as Sophie stirred the stew with a big grin on her face.

Mary stared at the coin on her palm and said, "But, Your Majesty, this is too much for a poor cooking wench to have. I could use your largesse to go to the tawdry part of town and purchase the services of a handsome lad, for I am a wanton and lecherous maid."

"Fear not, my dear woman, I will gladly serve in that capacity. For my days as a royal lecher are well known in these shires."

"I knew of such things but dared not hope for such glory. I will await Your Majesty at his pleasure."

"Alas, poor wench, I am ill of late and cannot fulfill your desires. I seek the healing baths of yon pool of soothing waters."

"I thought you and Max just took a bath?" Mary asked, dropping the drama.

"We did. As Max and I will be working in the barn this afternoon, I thought it would be generous of us to leave it for your use."

"That does sound good."

Mary turned to Julia and Sophie and asked, "Do either of you want to go for a swim this afternoon?"

"What will you wear?" asked Julia.

"The same outfit that Sam wore when he took his bath."

"You're going to be naked outside?" Julia asked in astonishment.

"There is no one within miles. It's a lot more private than having a bath in the tub with people in the house. Besides, the water's cool, and Sam made the pool a good size, too."

"I'll come along, but I may not go in the water."

"Mama?" Mary asked, knowing her answer.

"Not on your life."

"After lunch, we'll walk out there."

Sam looked over at Max and wiggled his eyebrows but was trying not to picture Mary when she dove into the pool.

"I saw that Sam Walker. You'd better not come out there and spy on me."

"Mary, I would never do that. Well, mostly I wouldn't do that. All right, I probably would normally, but not with Malarkey around. We could see the house and a good mile of the road while we were at the pool and the road, and I kept an eye out. But while you're out there, we'll be busy building Anna's bed, anyway."

"I want your promise that you won't bother us."

"I promise I won't even look your way. We really will be too busy."

"If it was only me, I wouldn't mind at all, but Julia might decide to join me."

"I wouldn't mind, either," said a grinning Julia.

"Wait a minute. Mary, you get me to promise and now it doesn't matter?"

"Just proving a point, Your Highness," Mary said with another curtsy and a smile.

Sam smiled back and said, "Point taken, Your Royal Majesty."

"As long as you know who really reigns supreme."

"I bow to your superior intellect."

Mary laughed, and they began serving lunch.

————

After they finished eating, Mary and Julia grabbed two towels, a bar of soap and started walking east as Max and Sam left Sophie to clean up while they went to the barn to begin working on that bed.

As they were walking to the barn, Sam notice a dust cloud coming down the road from Mulberry but wasn't overly worried.

"That wouldn't be Mike Malarkey. I can't see him being so obvious. Anyway, Max, let's go and grab the Winchester and shotgun and head out to the access road and see if they are coming here or riding past. He's moving too quickly to ride all the way to Bonham, I believe."

Max nodded, then they jogged to the bunkhouse where Max grabbed the shotgun, and Sam took the Winchester. They were both wearing their pistols as they left the bunkhouse and walked calmly toward the access road. Sam glanced behind him at the disappearing women. They were already four hundred yards away, so they were safe.

Sam and Max walked side by side until Sam felt it was a good spot, about a hundred feet from the roadway.

"Right here, Max."

"Okay, Sam."

They stood, Sam with his Winchester's butt on his hip and Max with the shotgun held in his hands, but neither weapon was cocked.

Sheriff Morton saw them as he neared the access road and began to get a bit nervous. All he had was a pistol, but he was the law, by God, and that man had broken the law.

He slowed his horse down to a slow trot and turned the corner onto the access road before pulling to a stop about ten yards away.

"You Sam Walker?"

"I am. I'm guessing you're Mike Malarkey's sheriff."

Ralph bristled and replied, "I am the elected sheriff of Mulberry and you are under arrest for kidnapping Julia Malarkey."

"I didn't kidnap anyone, Sheriff. I simply asked Julia if she wanted to leave and she escaped from that bastard who had married her. Julia's out back with Mary Farrell at the moment, and if you want to talk to her, you can, but it will take a while. She was afraid of Malarkey, Sheriff. He was beating her, but that's never going to happen again. She's under my protection now and you can tell Malarkey that. He knows what really happened and I told that to Jimmy Toomey last night when those four rode in here trying to kill me."

"Mister Malarkey sent them here to retrieve his wife. You bushwhacked them."

"Does that make any sense to you at all? Go back and check their bodies, Sheriff. They were all hit in the front. Jimmy and

Pat's horses hit my wire booby trap that I had stretched across the access road. If they had come to get his wife, why did they wait until it was dark? If you'll look down, you'll see the blood stains from Reggie Anderson and Paul Hooper. I told them to drop their pistols because I had two barrels of a twelve-gauge pointed at them. They must not have believed me, because they opened fire. I fired once and that shot killed them both, but I let the other two go, despite the fact that they were on my property and intended me harm.

"If that wasn't enough to justify what happened to them, they had also burned down the Bar F house and barn last week at the direction of Mike Malarkey. Didn't you even notice that when you rode past? They murdered Earl Farrell in that fire, and it was only by the barest of margins that Mary Farrell and I arrived in time to save Max and her mother. Max can give you the facts about that, if you don't believe me.

"Now, if you want to argue any of these points, feel free. But I don't lie, Sheriff. Julia Farrell, I'll never give her that other name, is here of her own free will to be safe from that murdering bastard. I want him to come and try to kill me again, and I'll kill him. I'll kill him legally because he'll be on my property while he's trying to kill me."

The sheriff had indeed noticed the charred remains of the Farrell ranch house and barn and was pretty sure that Mike's boys had done the job. Having Max Farrell standing alongside Walker pretty much confirmed his assumption. He felt queasy knowing that they had tried to burn the place with the family inside, but there was that one other facet to his visit.

"Mike said you was from Iowa. You were a Yankee soldier."

"I was. I was imprisoned in Camp Ford outside of Tyler for more than a year. Malarkey was a mean bastard of a guard who beat his own men just as much as he beat the prisoners. He doesn't give a rat's ass about the Confederacy or his wife. All he cares about is himself. If getting something he wanted meant

224

throwing you to the wolves, he'd do it in a heartbeat, Sheriff, and that includes you. The man has no honor."

Sheriff Morton did look down and see the blood and was suddenly embarrassed to be sitting there defending Mike Malarkey. He knew how he was. He'd been taking Malarkey's money for years and wasn't proud of it. If Malarkey were gone, maybe he could start over with a clean slate.

The sheriff was still weighing his options as he studied Sam then asked, "How sure are you that you could take Malarkey?"

Sam was stunned by the question, but quickly replied, "Almost positive. I can outshoot him and beat him in a straight fight. The only problem I have is that he never fights fairly. He always looks for the unexpected angle. Now, Sheriff, he has no one to help him anymore. He's alone.

"If he's gone, you'll be able to run your town the way it should be run and follow the law. Malarkey will come for me, so it'll be out of your jurisdiction anyway. Maybe he won't come today or tomorrow, but he'll come. When he does, I'll finish him. But right now, your citizens won't have to worry about paying him protection money any longer. He doesn't have anyone left to collect it. Pass that word around, and you'll be the most popular man in Mulberry."

If Sam couldn't sway his mind with reasoned arguments, the idea that he would garner more votes in the next election seemed to have made its mark.

He sat back in the saddle, grinned and said, "Well, maybe I'll do just that. You Yankees mighty not be all bad after all."

"Shucks, Sheriff. I can't be a damned Yankee. I'm just a country feller what traveled a tad too far north."

Morton laughed, tipped his hat, then turned his horse northward, thinking, "There sure is something mighty friendly about that Walker feller, but I sure wouldn't want to tangle with him. No, sir."

While the men were discussing Mike Malarkey's future, Mary and Julia reached the swimming hole. Mary, without hesitation, pulled off her clothes and dove in.

Julia watched in embarrassment. No woman had seen her naked before, but the water was so tempting, so she finally shrugged, quickly stripped off her clothes and followed Mary into the water.

Once in the water, she suddenly felt like a young girl again, when she was free of fear and worry and free to be herself. She smiled and plunged under the surface feeling the refreshing water flow over her naked skin.

She surfaced and saw a grinning Mary just a few feet away.

"Wonderful, isn't it?" Mary asked.

"It is that and more. I feel like a girl again," replied Julia as she grinned.

"Did you see the rider down at the road?"

Julia spun around and saw two figures in the distance she assumed were Max and Sam.

"There was a rider?"

"There was. I could be wrong, but I think it was either the sheriff of Mulberry or Bonham. I saw a badge flash when he turned."

"I wonder what he wanted."

"You or Sam, maybe both. But he's gone, and you and Sam are still here. It'll be interesting talking to Sam about this."

"Mary, I have a confession to make. I was thinking of trying to take Sam away from you."

"I know. Sam did, too."

"He knew?"

"We talked about it."

"You talked about me trying to win Sam?" she asked in surprise.

"We talk about everything, Julia."

"That's why I am conceding defeat, Mary. You two are amazing. I've never seen anything like it. Joe and I got along famously, but the way you and Sam simply merge like that is incredible. I'm insanely jealous, Mary, but not for the old-fashioned reason. I wish I could find what you and Sam have."

"Thank you for the concession, Julia. It'll make things less stressful."

"So, now that I'm no longer a threat, what was it like having Sam naked in the pool?" Julia asked as she laughed.

Mary explained in uninhibited detail and continued at length with all of their other private times and her hope for much more intimate sharing in the near future.

As she listened to Mary while they treaded water, she could understand why they had connected so quickly. They were so much alike in their personalities and in the way that they looked at the world. Suddenly, Mary's lack of restraint about being naked out in the pastures made sense to Julia. Mary simply did what she wanted to do, and Sam loved her for being who she was.

It was that revelation that made Julia decide that she would be who she wanted to be, not what everyone else wanted her to be.

———

It was four in the afternoon, and Mike Malarkey still hadn't heard from the sheriff. He thought about going to visit his office but believed that it was beneath him. Morton should come to him, not the other way around.

But not knowing what had happened left him feeling decidedly out of touch. Without his boys to feed him information, he didn't know what was going on and he didn't like the feeling.

He walked out to the privy, retrieved his Colt, then returned to his office and cleaned it before reloading it with six rounds. He never believed that hogwash about shooting yourself in the first place. He wanted every bit of firepower that he could get out of his pistol now.

He was growing more confident that Walker wasn't going to come to his house today or anytime soon. He'd stay at his ranch and wait for him.

'Well, two can play at the waiting game," thought Mike, "I'll stay in Mulberry as long as I need to. I have money. I don't have to go down there at all. To hell with him."

———

As Sam finished drilling the holes in the boards for the bed, Max wondered why Sam had cut so much wood and in longer lengths than he had expected. *Was his sister as tall as he was?* He'd never asked what she looked like, but the thought of a woman over six feet tall almost made him giggle.

When Sam began reaching into his box of precut wooden pegs, he finally understood that Sam wasn't building one bed, he was building two.

"Sam, why are you building two beds?" he asked as Sam began pounding glued pegs into the boards.

"One is for Anna, and one is for me. I'm going to sleep in the smokehouse, Max. I've been disturbing your sleep too often."

"No, you haven't, Sam. I'm all right."

"Max, you know better than that. If it makes me tired, I know it's making you tired. At least one of us needs to be alert when Malarkey shows up."

Max didn't want to admit that Sam's nightly screams, shouts, or other loud noises kept him awake, but they did.

"Okay."

"Besides, Max, I'll get the honor of sleeping where bacon was created and lived before being fried. No man could ask for more."

Max laughed as he looked at his hard-working friend. Sam always found a way to make fun out of bad things.

"What are you going to do for a mattress?"

"Anna will get two bedrolls covered by a sheet. I'll get the last bedroll and put two of the bunk mattresses side by side underneath. Those bunkhouse beds are a little small for me anyway. This bed is a lot longer and wider, so when I have my nightmares, I won't fall off so often."

Max nodded as Sam began sanding the assembled bed frames. They weren't highly polished hardwood, just smooth, unfinished pine, but would serve the same purpose. Max took another sheet of sandpaper and began sanding the other side of Sam's bed and soon both of them were ready to support a sleeping human.

Sam and Max carried Sam's bed first, because it would be easier to get into place as the door to the smokehouse was wider than the house's doors. Sam had removed all the hooks and put them on the shelves, so he didn't walk into them at night.

Max noticed the change and said, "That was smart. It could have been pretty messy late at night."

"It would have been a lot worse for whoever found me the next morning."

Max shivered at the imaginary sight as they lowered the bed into the center of the floor so Sam could fall off either side.

Sam said, "It really was a violation of the man code to move those hooks, though."

"The man code?"

"Yup. Never do anything smart. In this case, I should have left them in place until I smacked my melon into one of those iron hooks at night, cursed, then told myself how stupid I was for not moving them first. I'm sure that I'll hear from the Real Man Council about my transgression."

Max laughed and asked, "When do I start having to do those things?"

"You grow up that way, but never notice. Men do stupid things all the time and women look at us and shake their heads wondering if we have one tiny bit of brain in our thick skulls. Think about it. Everything we do, from something simple like how we take off our boots when we insist on tossing them into the corner to see if we can get them to stand up to a full-blown war like the last one, is all just stupid, but we do them anyway. I've known men who think they're being smart by not going to see a doctor when they've almost had their foot cut off."

"I guess that's true, isn't it?"

"Yup, but the Golden Rule is that we can never admit it to the women. If you do, then the Real Men Council will send their gelding team out to find you and turn you into a woman, or at least a steer."

Max laughed before he asked, "Are you going to move all the guns in here?"

"Most of them. I'll leave the shotgun in the bunkhouse and you'll have your pistol, of course."

"Okay."

Sam popped his hand on the head bedpost, then said, "Let's get the second one into the house."

Max nodded, then they left the smokehouse/bedroom, walked to the barn and hefted the smaller bed frame from the floor, carried it across the yard and onto the back porch.

Getting it into the room wasn't difficult at all because it was smaller and only a frame.

After putting it in place in Mary's room, Sophie looked at the new bed with her hands on her hips as she asked, "Already done, boys? It looks very strong, Sam."

"Might as well do it right, Sophie."

The had to return to get the slats for the frame and once they were in place, the bed was ready for the soft parts.

She followed them back out of the room and when they returned a few minutes later with the two bunkhouse mattresses, blankets and pillows, then set the bed up as well as they could, she watched with approval. It wasn't perfect, but it would do until they could get some proper bedding.

"Sam, I'll make the bed."

"Thanks, Sophie."

"We've got to make Sam's bed now," said Max.

"Why did Sam need a bed?"

Sam replied, "I'm keeping Max awake at night, Sophie, so I'm moving into the smokehouse. The man needs his sleep."

"You're a very considerate man, Sam."

"Max is my brother and I have to take care of him."

Max smiled at his mother, then Sam slapped him on the back before they left the house to set up Sam's new bed.

Sophie watched them leave and smiled, pleased that her son had found the perfect role model. If Joe hadn't died, then he would have had two, his normal father and his healthy older brother, but now he had Sam Walker, and she knew that Max would become a good man.

———

As they walked back to the bunkhouse after putting his slats in place, Max asked, "Sam, why don't you use two sleeping bags? There are four left."

"Maybe I will, Max."

After entering the bunkhouse, they took Sam's mattress, pillow and blankets then, loaded down with bedding, left the almost stripped place and headed for Sam's Smokehouse Hotel.

They were just twenty feet out of the bunkhouse with their bedding treasures, when Sam noticed Mary and Julia sitting on the back porch watching them.

Mary said loudly "We saw you going into the bunkhouse and wondered what you were doing. Now we're really wondering what you're doing."

"Sam built himself a bed, so he could sleep in the smokehouse and not wake me up all the time," Max replied as he and Sam walked closer.

Julia glanced at Mary, who waved off her obvious question for the time being, before they stood and followed Sam and Max to the smokehouse.

"Do you mind if we see your construction, Mister Walker?" Mary asked.

"No, ma'am."

Sam and Max entered the aromatic room and Sam laid his mattress on one side, and Max laid the second one on the other half making one wide mattress with a gap at the end that Sam already planned on filling with one of the bedrolls.

"That's a large bed, Sam," Mary said with a bit of a smile.

Sam didn't reply, but simply spread his long arms and smiled.

"Yes, I know. You're a big man, but why so wide?"

"To keep me from falling out of bed so often."

Julia laughed, then asked, "You fall out of bed?"

"I must want to walk in my sleep or something," Sam quickly replied before Max could say anything.

"It's really well built, Sam. Is Anna's done, too?" Mary asked.

"Sophie was putting sheets and a quilt on it when we left."

Mary could tell that Sam didn't want to talk about his nightmares, so she turned to Julia and said, "Let's go and see Anna's bed, Julia."

"Okay. Bye, Sam. Bye, Max."

"Goodbye, Julia," they both said in unison.

Mary smiled at Sam and waved before she and Julie passed through the open doors.

A minute or so after the women left the smokehouse, Max and Sam followed them outside to retrieve two of the bedrolls.

As they walked, Max asked, "Sam, why didn't you tell Julia about the nightmares?"

"It's not the kind of thing I like to talk about, Max. You know about them because you had to put up with them. Mary knows about them because she guessed I was having them. Other than that, I'd rather not talk about them."

"Okay."

After they picked up three bedrolls rather than two, they returned to the smokehouse, which Sam christened his Bacon Boudoir, then after folding one and filling the gap, set the other two on top of the mattresses, and covered them with a blanket. It was actually a very comfortable sleeping arrangement when it was complete.

They then each bounced on it because it was the proper and stupid thing to do. Neither wanted to be ejected from the Real Man's Club.

Satisfied that his bed wouldn't collapse under him, Sam said, "Let's go and collect the guns and ammunition."

It took two trips to move all the pistols and ammunition from the bunkhouse which kind of surprised Sam. He simply hadn't realized just how many guns he'd accumulated since leaving *The Northern Swan*. When they finished it turned the smokehouse into an armory in addition to Sam's new bedroom.

When everything was in its proper place, they took a seat on Sam's new bed and Sam said, "Tomorrow, Max, Mary wants to have you ride with her in the buggy on the way to Bonham. I think it's a good idea. Keep the shotgun in the footwell. When you're returning, you'll be the man. The two most precious women to me in the world will be under your protection."

"I'll take care of them, Sam."

Sam smiled and said, "I know you will, Max."

He gave Max a manly pat on the shoulder, then they left the smokehouse to return to the house.

Mary and Julia were admiring Anna's new bed when Julia said, "That's better than the beds that were here already."

"It's simple yet seems to be sturdier."

"So, why is Sam moving into the smokehouse. Does he want the privacy?"

"In a fashion. Sam has horrible nightmares, Julia. They show up almost every night now and they're always about the prison camp, but not the battles that he fought. I've heard him screaming some nights, but I'm sure that he doesn't know that I can hear him."

"I must be a heavy sleeper because I've never heard him."

"He doesn't like to talk about them, but Max knows, of course."

"But he told you."

"I asked before I heard him wake up in terror. I suspected he was having them, and I offered to sleep with him to see if it would let him rest."

"You offered to let him bed you?" she asked incredulously.

"No. I told him it was just for sleeping. He understood that, but he still turned me down."

"Why?"

"Because he said he wasn't sure he could control himself."

"Wow! That's something else altogether."

"He's something else, Julia. Sam is everything to me now. I hope he never asks me how worried I am about what he needs to do. You lived with Malarkey. Am I wrong to worry?"

"No, you're not. I think Sam can beat him in any fashion as long as he expects something underhanded."

"He probably knows Malarkey better than you do and expects that he'll try something sneaky."

"Let's hope he stops him, and not just because I hate Mike Malarkey. I want him stopped so you and Sam can finally spend your time together without worrying about him."

Mary smiled at Julia and gave her a short hug, happy that Julia could be a true friend again, just as she had been when she married Joe.

———

Anna and Frank arrived in Paris, Texas, on the afternoon stage. It had been a long trip but staying the night in Clarksville had been a good break.

After having their luggage brought to the hotel, they were sitting in the lobby, discussing the end of their long journey.

"Anna, the stage for Bonham leaves at eight o'clock. We can have breakfast at seven and be ready to go after that."

"Frank, I'm so excited to see Sam again. I can't wait to meet Mary, either."

"I wonder how he'll react to the news?"

"Which news? There's so much to tell him."

"I just hope he doesn't bite my head off. I treated him pretty badly over the past few years."

"Frank, you worry too much. Sam will be happy to see you. Especially when you tell him about Barbara Jean."

"Don't remind me."

Anna laughed, then said, "I'm sorry, Frank. I'm just so happy."

"I've noticed," Frank replied, smiling at his young sister.

Anna was almost rapturous about seeing Sam again, but even after her reassurance, Frank was still unsure of how his younger brother would react when he saw him, especially after giving him all of the news that could change everything. He was most worried that Sam would decide to return to Iowa and that could be a bigger disaster. He even had a slight, but real concern that Sam might shoot him.

Mike Malarkey may have convinced himself that there was no need to go to the Circle W, but he still hated the monotony and tension of simply waiting. He had nothing to do, despite having hundreds of books in the house. He could barely read and had no friends or acquaintances who would drop by and pass the time. All he had was his two broken hooligans who he'd told to stay away. He was even beginning to miss having the woman around.

Mike decided that what he needed to do was to go to the saloon and throw down a few glasses of whiskey and spend some time with the ladies. That would take care of his boredom, and he doubted that if Walker would be there or even in Mulberry.

He walked to his office, grabbed his jacket and pulled it on. He liked the idea of carrying a hidden pistol rather than the heavy Colt, so he left the Colt at home and walked out of the house, locking the door just in case Walker showed up.

He walked quickly down to the main street and crossed over to the other side, then two minutes later, he was walking into the saloon. As soon as he entered the barroom, he spotted his two erstwhile employees sitting at a table drinking beer. After his initial irritation at seeing them, which only resurrected the memories of that failed assassination attempt, he stepped to the table and pulled out a chair.

After sitting down, he smiled and asked, "How are you boys doin'?"

"All right, boss. Pat's arm isn't doing as good as the doc said it should, though. He's wonderin' if he didn't break something when it popped out."

"I thought he broke his collarbone."

"Yeah, he did. But the doc thinks he mighta broke somethin' else too."

"How's your arm?"

"Really itchy. I can barely move my fingers. Doc says it'll be this way for two months."

"You up to doin' a job for me?"

"I don't know, boss. The sheriff has been kinda watchin' us."

"What do you mean that he's kinda watchin' you? That bastard was supposed to go down to the Circle W and arrest that damned Yankee."

"Well, he must not have done it. Some of the store owners have been stoppin' us and told us they was gonna have us strung up. I think they're serious, too."

Malarkey automatically fell into his crime boss function and snapped, "They have, have they? Who are they? Which ones?"

"All of 'em, boss," answered Pat meekly.

"What did they say you'd hang for?"

"They said extortion, whatever that is."

"Well, you boys better lay low until I need ya."

"We're both almost outta money, boss."

Mike dug through his pockets, found fifty-four dollars and handed each one twenty dollars.

"That should hold you for a while."

"Thanks, boss. If it's okay, we'll head back to our rooms."

"You go ahead. I'm gonna bend back a few and then visit upstairs."

"You have a good time, boss," said Pat as they each tossed their remaining beer down their gullets.

Malarkey waved to them as they walked through the batwing doors as he tried to come up with some way of reasserting his dominance over the town. He'd need more muscle, but that was harder to find than most folks realized. But the fact that the storeowners felt they could threaten his boys without fear did bother him, as did the sheriff's lack of action. He had a lot to think about and suspected he was running out of time to correct all of the problems that Sam Walker had created.

Once they were far enough away from the saloon, Pat turned to Jimmy and said, "Jimmy, I don't know about you, but I want to get outta here. I don't wanna be hung for extortion. It ain't a lotta money, but we can go to Bonham and stay there for a while."

"I don't know, Pat. That Walker feller goes there a lot. I'd rather head west to Sherman."

"That's better. Let's get our stuff together and get outta here."

With their decision to clear out of town, Mike Malarkey lost his only two supporters, and he wouldn't even notice their absence for two days.

———

Everyone was in the sitting room at the Circle W ranch house after a big supper and conversation was lively about Anna's arrival tomorrow and Sam's carpentry expertise.

Sam was glad to see everyone in such a good mood, but his very real concerns were still always in the background, even when he was thinking about something else.

Aside from the omni-present expectation of Mike Malarkey's arrival, there were those that revolved around Anna's decision to come to Texas. *What could have happened that would drive his younger sister to travel so far and especially if she was unaccompanied?* He thought if it had been bad, he would have received a telegram from someone in Iowa before the one from Anna after she'd already arrived in Texas. *Why hadn't she telegraphed earlier?*

It was almost as if she was worried that he might forbid her from coming in the first place. He smiled at that idea, though. Anna was a lot like Mary in her character, and he knew that she'd be coming to Texas no matter what he told her.

He was also dreading his first night sleeping in the smokehouse. He had found the lamp inside and filled it with kerosene, so he'd have light, but it was after the lamp was extinguished that worried him. *How bad would it be tonight?* With the aroma of smoked meat constantly flowing into his nostrils, *would it add another twist to his nightly horrors?*

Just when he thought he had exhausted every possible terror that could be brought down on him, his mind thought of a new way to torture him. *Would it take the death of Mike Malarkey to make them go away? What if he killed Malarkey and they still came?*

He had been listening to the chatter as he thought and didn't let it interfere with his responses when they asked him a question. When Mary looked at him, he was certain that she knew what he was thinking. She always knew, which is why she was his Mary and Joe had been so right from the first.

After two hours it was time to call it a night as there were a lot of things going on tomorrow. The sun had set, so Sam and Max made their farewells and walked outside.

"Max, make sure you close the door to the bunkhouse. I know it'll make it hotter, but you'll hear the door open if Malarkey decides to show up. You might even want to run some twine from the handle to something that will make a noise if it's opened."

"Okay, Sam."

"Good night, Max."

"Good night, Sam"

Sam turned, then walked to the smokehouse and opened both doors. He'd leave them open so he could hear anything outside. He, like other men who'd been in extended combat, had developed an almost sixth sense about encroaching dangers, even when asleep. He didn't bother with the lamp that night as he removed his Stetson, tossed it to one of the many shelves and wondered if it would pick up a bacon scent after a while. There were worse things that could happen to a hat. He kicked off his boots and pulled off his shirt, then rolled onto his bed, but didn't bother with the blanket.

Sam lay on his back, his hands behind his neck, staring at the overhead rafters in the dim light. There was just enough reflected moonlight leaking through the doors to give his eyes something to do. A smokehouse had to have no cracks to let out the smoke, and this one was still solid, even after years of disuse. He soon drifted asleep, despicable, unwanted sleep.

It wasn't very long when that sixth sense woke him instantly. His eyes popped open and he listened intently for the sound that had brought him back to the waking world. He must have heard something, but it wasn't much.

As he slowly sat up, he held his breath and then heard the sound again, only more clearly. They were footsteps of someone trying hard not to be heard. How he even heard the footsteps was beyond him, but then he knew whose footsteps they were, relaxed and laid back down.

A few seconds later, Mary stepped through the doors and without a word, climbed into bed with him. She just snuggled in close and put her arm around him. Sam put his arm around her waist and pulled her closer as he closed his eyes.

She sighed, and Sam was close to doing the same but just relaxed inside feeling her softness and warmth against him.

———

The next thing Sam knew, Mary was kissing him, so he opened his eyes and saw her smiling at him as sunlight streamed in through the open doors.

"Good morning, Sam. Sleep well?"

"I slept very well, Mary. Thank you."

"I've got to get back. I'm sure they know I was going to sneak out."

"I love you, Mary Farrell."

"I love you, too, Sam."

She leaned over the bed and kissed him again before trotting out of the smokehouse.

Sam laid in the bed just smiling; smiling because of the full night's dreamless sleep, but mostly because of Mary. He had no idea why just having Mary so close had kept the demons at bay, but she did. He got out of bed to begin the day, knowing that a lot of questions would be answered today.

CHAPTER 8

Sam suddenly realized that he had nothing to do. Mary and Max had gone in the buggy with Flame trailing, and Julia and Sophie were cleaning the house and getting things prepared for an arrival luncheon for Anna.

Sam thought he may as well take advantage of the situation to do some more practice shooting followed by an extended bath. He didn't want Anna to arrive and find a dirty big brother.

He went into the smokehouse and picked up a bar of soap. His clothes were clean, and he was wearing his two Remingtons, but when he left the smokehouse, he also brought the Winchester for some target practice. He had put in a new target a week earlier but hadn't used it yet.

He walked out to the firing range and made short work of emptying his two pistols. He tried a few shots with his left hand and, as he had expected, was terrible with it, and considered himself lucky that he didn't shoot his foot off. He did better than he usually did with his right hand as compensation.

Then he tried ten shots with the Winchester from a hundred yards. Again, it was better than he usually did, which was already outstanding. He left five shots in the Winchester just in case Malarkey chose this moment to arrive which was highly unlikely during the daytime.

He walked to the pool and scanned for prying eyes, namely Julia's. Mary had told him that Julia had conceded, but he didn't want to tempt fate. A naked Julia would tempt the saints themselves. Heck, a fully clothed Julia could do that. He wouldn't mind a bit if Mary decided to watch.

243

The coast was clear, so he dove in and enjoyed a good bath followed by an hour of sunbathing, then dressed, picked up the Winchester and returned to the ranch.

———

In Bonham, Mary and Max had already picked out their Stetsons and, true to her word, she bought three riding skirts and blouses. Mary then packed the clothes on the back of the buggy's shelf, wondering again how much Anna would be bringing and even more about Anna herself.

They drove the buggy to the stage depot, pulled it to a stop, then exited and Mary tied off the horse before they took seats on one of the depot's two benches. The stage should arrive in twenty minutes, but unlike trains, were rarely on time.

As they sat, Mary was suddenly concerned about her appearance. She felt like a tomboy again, even though she was wearing a dress. Her hair was long and just tied with a gold ribbon. She looked at her large, calloused hands. They weren't smooth like ladies' hands should be. They were slim and womanly, but they weren't soft and smooth.

It was too late to change how she looked now, when she could see the stage in the distance. It was a little earlier than scheduled.

"Here it comes, Mary," Max said.

"I see it."

The six horses pulling the stage rumbled into the depot at a slow trot, and as soon as the coach stopped rolling, the driver yanked back the parking brake, then he and the shotgun rider both stepped down. Mary noticed two large trunks on the top of the stage, and hoped they weren't Anna's. The buggy could handle one, but not two.

She and Max were both standing at the edge of the boardwalk when the stage's door opened, and a man stepped out. Mary recognized him immediately, even though she'd never met him before. He was a shorter, softer around the middle and not nearly as handsome, in her estimation, version of Sam. He had to be his older brother, Frank. Her guess was confirmed a few seconds later when he helped a very pretty young lady with dancing eyes from the coach. Mary couldn't help but smile at her first glimpse of Anna.

"Anna!" she exclaimed as she stepped forward still wearing her welcoming smile.

Anna saw Mary, immediately seeing the reason why Sam was smitten, then smiled and stepped away from the stagecoach.

Mary walked over, approached Frank, offered her hand and said, "And you must be Frank."

"I am. And you, no doubt, are the famous Mary," he said as he smiled at her and shook her hand.

"None other. Frank and Anna, this is my brother Max."

Anna dazzled Max with a smile and shook his hand, saying, "Sam is awfully proud of you, Max."

Max blushed at the praise and not because he was shaking hands with Anna.

Frank then shook his hand as well before Mary said, "We have a buggy. Are those your trunks?"

"They are, but the freight company associated with the stage line will bring them along behind us. Frank and I each have a travel bag."

"Good. Let's get those loaded, and we'll head back. It'll take just under an hour."

"Wonderful. It'll get us a chance to talk before I see Sam again. I'm sure you have loads to tell me, and we have a lot of news too, but it'll wait until we see Sam."

Mary smiled at her future sister-in-law and said, "That'll work. Let's get everyone into the buggy and go to see Sam."

Ten minutes later they were rolling north, and Anna asked, "So, Mary, how is Sam?"

"Sam is perfect," Mary replied with a smile.

"From what he wrote, he is yours, too."

"I've been his longer, I think, but not by much. Let me tell you some stories."

Mary began her tales of confrontation, death, fire, and shootings, but mixed them with other stories of humor, affection, and the deep bond between her and Sam.

Anna was astounded by what Mary was telling her because Sam hadn't mentioned a word of any of it in his letters. Sam had done so much good, but still had one lingering problem that needed to be removed. Mary had omitted any references to Julia because she wanted Julia to tell those stories.

As both had anticipated from what Sam had told each of them, they became sisters almost immediately, and even their voices and manner of speech were so close it made watching them necessary to tell them apart.

Frank just sat back, amazed by the pair of women while Mary drove. He still had misgivings about seeing Sam again, but listening to Mary talk about his brother still fascinated him. *How could Sam have done so many things in such a short time?* He had a ranch that Sam had described was a small ranch, yet it was two square miles. He had tangled with and defeated bad men in gun battles, rescued a woman from a burning fire, and found his future wife. *He hadn't even been gone a month!* Of course, Frank had to admit that he'd had a lot happen to him in the past month as well.

Surprisingly, all of those events in Iowa were created by Sam's departure. He continued to listen to Mary and Anna chat, laugh, and giggle as they rode along.

———

Sam sat on the front porch with Sophie as they waited for the buggy to roll onto the access road.

"You know, Sophie, I think I should get some rocking chairs."

"Can you make them?"

"I could, but they're not as easy as beds. Besides, good rocking chairs aren't very expensive. I think four or five would do it, don't you think?"

"As long as you make one of them a double for you and Mary," she said with a light laugh.

"You have an extraordinary daughter, Sophie."

"She told me about last night, Sam. What you two share is almost unheard of. She had told me of Julia's plans and how she was absolutely confident she wasn't going to lose you. There wasn't any chance, was there?"

"None whatsoever. If you are fortunate enough to find someone that fills your life as Mary has mine, that's something that is far too precious to squander."

Sophie just nodded.

"You know, Sophie. The one thing that I've never asked you about is something that I should have asked the first time I met you."

"And what was that?"

"Pecan pie. I've never had it, but Joe talked about it incessantly. He said I'd never have anything as good as your pecan pie, and I would tell him a pie made out of nuts was nuts."

Sophie laughed and said, "It does sound kind of nutty, doesn't it? But it's very good. I'll make one for you one of these days when everything has quieted down."

"I'm sure it'll be very good, Sophie."

Sophie nodded with the smile still on her face.

"Here they come, Sophie," Sam said as he saw the buggy turn the corner onto the access road, then squinted at the oncoming conveyance.

Without taking his eyes from the buggy, he said, "Sophie, that's Frank with them. My brother came along with Anna. Now there has to be a story behind that."

"I thought Anna's arrival was surprise enough. I'll go and get Julia. She wanted to look her best when Anna arrived."

"That'll be something to behold," Sam said as he stood and started walking toward the buggy.

"There's Sam!" shouted Anna, her excitement unleashed.

Mary and Anna waved simultaneously, then Sam waved and smiled back.

"I think he's gotten bigger since he left," said Frank.

"He has. He looks even heavier than when he left to go into the army," said Anna.

"No fat, either. Trust me, I know," said Mary.

Anna glanced at Mary, then laughed before looking back at Sam waiting by his ranch house.

Frank quickly rubbed his stomach and then took his hand away as the buggy rolled to a stop before Anna boiled out of the side of the buggy to greet her brother.

Sam picked up Anna in a bear hug and swung her in a circle before kissing her on the cheek.

He set her down, then turned to Frank. Frank offered his hand, and Sam bypassed his outstretched arm and embraced his older brother in another bear hug.

Frank was both astounded and relieved as he hugged his younger, bigger brother.

"I'm so glad to see you both!" said Sam as Julia made her grand entrance, for that was what it was.

It had been meant for Anna, but that changed when she saw Frank.

Sam turned and said, "Frank and Anna, I'd like you to meet Mary's mother, Sophie, and this is Julia."

Frank was speechless as he stared at Julia, so Anna made her introductions to Julia and Sophie, giving Frank time to adjust to Julia.

Frank eventually greeted Sophie and then spent a little longer saying hello to Julia.

Sam wondered what Barbara Jean would think, as Sophie ushered them all inside. Max took the reins of Flame, then led him and the buggy to the barn to take care of the animals.

When they were inside, they continued past the bedrooms to the kitchen for a welcoming lunch. It was almost a feast as Sophie and Julia had expected to be impressing Anna.

Max rejoined them ten minutes later as Mary and Julia put the food on the table. There was even fresh lemonade.

As they ate, there was just general chatter about Anna and Frank's trip. Sam took note of Max' and Mary's Stetsons, and Mary quietly assured Sam that she had bought some riding outfits as well that she would even share with Anna. Anna was two inches shorter and quite a bit slimmer than Mary, but the clothes would fit.

The freight wagon arrived with Anna's trunks, then the freighters set them on the porch and Sam gave each of the freighters a dollar tip before they rolled back down the access road.

"What do you have in there, sister?" Sam asked.

"One is mine. The other is all of your things that you left behind."

"Oh. Anything good?"

"You can go through them later."

Sam and Frank brought Anna's trunk into the house, and they moved the second into the smokehouse for storage before returning to the house.

After lunch, they put aside the dishes for cleaning later and adjourned to the main room to relax and get the real news.

Sam took the couch with Mary, then asked, "So, Anna and Frank, now that we've all eaten and are content, tell me the bad news. Why did you both leave Iowa?"

Frank replied, "I'm only here temporarily, Sam. I escorted Anna, who wants to stay with you, if you can put up with her. I just needed to talk to you, and maybe have you sign some things before I head back."

Sam began to feel a sense of dread as he looked at his older brother and quietly asked, "What happened, Frank?"

"Well, it was all because you left, Sam."

"It was my fault?"

"Indirectly. It started when Barbara Jean began moaning about how she should have waited and married you and saying that you wouldn't make her do those dirty things that I asked her to do."

Mary interrupted when she asked, "Oh, you mean like having sex with no clothes on?"

Frank was momentarily stunned until he looked over and saw Sam smiling and shrugging his shoulders as if to say, "It's just Mary."

"Well, yes, that. I guess she didn't know that I was the more prudish of the two Walker boys. I thought she understood that, Sam."

"Frank, you've got to realize that we never got past the kissing stage because she would swat my hands away when they got too busy. She never really got the message, I guess."

All the women laughed at the thought. Mary and Julia laughed because they wondered why any sane woman would do such a thing.

Frank continued, saying, "Anyway, she got pretty irate with me and stomped off. I thought she was just mad. The next day I went to work in the fields as I usually did, and when I returned for lunch, she was gone. I hunted around and talked to our parents, but they hadn't seen her either. We found the buggy gone, so I rode into Tipton and found she had run off with Mister Fletcher."

"Reverend Fletcher? The minister?" asked Sam with big eyes.

Anna grinned as Frank answered, "Yup. So, rather than go chasing after her, I filed for divorce the next day based on adultery. But to be honest, if it had come right down to it, I doubt if she did anything with Mister Fletcher. According to the note she left at his house, Mister Fletcher had promised her a 'loving, but chaste relationship worthy of a woman of her character.'"

His last sentence pushed all of the listeners into a state of uncontrolled laughter, especially Mary and Sam.

Frank smiled at Julia, and when she stopped laughing, said, "Continuing the story, after she had gone, and I had filed for divorce, which was granted by the way, papa was so mad at what had happened, he took his favorite horse for a hard ride. He tried to jump a three-wire fence and fell as the horse balked and the fall hurt his back badly. He can still walk, but that's about it. He can't ride or do any work. He and mama talked and decided that they wanted to retire."

"Retire? Papa is barely fifty."

"He told me that he wanted to enjoy life now. He said when the railroad reaches Bonham, he and mama may even come and visit. They took out about a third of their money from the bank and bought a house in Davenport. It's a beautiful house, Sam, and even has a big library with lots of books. Papa is very happy, and you know if papa is happy, mama is as well."

Sam sat back, astonished that all this could happen so quickly, but was relieved too when he learned that his parents were still both alive and happy.

He then said, "So, you own the farm now, Frank. That's great. You deserve it."

"That's just it, Sam. I don't own the farm, we do. Papa said that the remaining bank account and the farm belongs to the two of us. You can come back to Iowa if you'd like, or I can buy your half of the farm. That's how papa wanted it."

"What about Anna?" he asked as he looked at his sister, who wore a knowing smile.

Frank replied, "Once he found out that Anna was planning on coming here to be with you, he thought you'd take care of her rather well."

Anna looked at Sam and smiled as if to say *"Please?"*

Sam gave her a smile, a wink and a nod, then watched as Anna's smile blossomed into a grateful grin.

"So how can I help you, Frank? I have no intention of going back to Iowa. I belong here now."

"That's what I thought you'd say, and I'll admit that I was hoping that you would. I brought you a bank draft from home for your half of the bank account. It's six thousand four hundred and thirty-two dollars and twenty-two cents. Now, your half of the farm is worth another seven thousand two hundred dollars. I can't afford to buy you out directly, but I'd be willing to send you two hundred dollars a month for three years to pay off your half."

"Frank, I don't need the money. I'll just sign over the farm to you."

"I appreciate the offer, Sam, but papa insisted. Now, don't feel bad about it either. The farm is very productive, and our income is over four thousand dollars a year now. Even after costs, we net almost three thousand dollars. So, I'll have my six thousand four hundred and thirty-two dollars and twenty-two cents in the bank, and in three years I'll have the money coming in untouched and own the farm. What do you say? I've already got the papers filled out by the lawyers. We just need to have them notarized."

Sam sighed as he thought about it. It was a lot of money, but he could do a lot of good with the cash, too.

"Alright. We can go to Bonham tomorrow. That's where I have a bank account."

Frank grinned then said, "Great! This is fantastic. I thought you'd still be mad at me for the whole Barbara Jean thing."

"Frank, there are two people I am forever grateful to for the whole Barbara Jean fiasco, and they're both related to me and they're both in this room. Anna warned me before I left that she wasn't right for me, and you married her. Well, Anna, dear sister, you've met Mary. Is she right for me?"

Anna looked at Mary but didn't smile. She simply said, "Sam, she's a much prettier and softer version of you. Mary may become my sister-in-law, but she's already my sister."

Mary looked back at Anna and just smiled softly and nodded, unable to say a word.

Sam knew that there was nothing he could add either, so he looked at his older brother and asked, "So, Frank, you're unmarried again?"

"I am. It's kind of odd, really. Barbara Jean was a bit of a shrew and obviously no great amount of fun as a wife, but having a woman around takes the edge off. It makes us more civilized and I miss that."

Julia, who had absorbed every bit of the conversation but had said nothing, finally asked, "So, Frank, do you have a prospective replacement for Barbara Jean yet?"

Sam was almost surprised by the directness of the question, but after the past few days, he should have expected it.

"No one yet. Applying for the job, Julia?" Frank asked with a smile.

"Maybe. I'm still married, though."

"You are? Where is your husband?"

"He's in Mulberry. He's the one who ordered the burning of the Bar F ranch that killed Sophie's husband and then had his men come here two nights ago to try to kill Sam."

"Is he the one who is still trying to kill Sam?"

"We think so. It's just a matter of time."

Sam said, "Julia didn't realize it at the time, but her husband, Mike Malarkey, was a sergeant guard at my prison camp. He was in charge of the other guards and beat everyone he had control over, including the other guards. I had promised her husband, Joe, who was my best friend, that I would look out for her. I found out what her situation was and took her out of there. She lives here now and I'm hoping she's a widow in another few days."

Frank didn't know what to think. He surely admired Julia. *What man wouldn't?* But Sam talked so casually about killing her husband, and Julia didn't say a word. *How bad was this man?*

"Sam, you talk about killing him as if it were just milking a cow. Why haven't you just had the sheriff arrest him for murder?"

"I talked to the sheriff just yesterday. He's afraid of the man, Frank. I told him that I wouldn't go to Mulberry and hunt him down. That would be murder. But on the other hand, I do expect him to come here some night and try to murder me. When he does, I'll kill him in self-defense. There is a chance he'll kill me, but I have a lot of advantages. I know what he looks like, but he's never seen me. I'm sure I'm a much better shot than he is too, and I'll be fighting on my home ground. I know this place. I also have Max as my backup. Right, Max?" Sam asked as he smiled at Max.

Max smiled back and replied, "That's right, Sam."

Frank said, "I noticed that Max carries a pistol. How old are you, Max."

"I'll be thirteen in November."

"And you carry a Colt?"

"We have a lot of Colts. Eight Colt New Army pistols, and Sam has his two Remingtons. I usually carry the shotgun, and Sam has his Winchester. He has two Spencers, too."

Frank grinned and said, "Well, at least you don't arm the women."

255

Mary, Julia, and Sophie all laughed, before Frank's eyebrows shot up before he pointed at the laughing women and said, "No. Surely they don't…"

"They do," answered Sam before he finished, "They're all certified, pistol-packing ladies. They even have their names burned into their gunbelts, so they always get their own pistols back. I'm sure they'll be more than happy to demonstrate their prowess at the target range."

Frank threw up his hands in surrender.

"Frank, when do you have to go back?" Sam asked.

"Oh, I can afford to hang around a week or so."

Sam didn't have to wonder why his brother probably just amended his travel plans to include some extra time on the Circle W.

"Alright. Right now, we're hard up for room. I'll put you up with Max in the bunkhouse. I've already added a bed for Anna in Mary's room, so the house belongs to the ladies."

"Where do you sleep?"

"After last night, I sleep in the smokehouse."

"Why?"

"I'm a lousy sleeper. I keep folks awake. But last night, for some inexplicable reason, I slept like a baby."

Mary, Julia, and Sophie held back their laughs.

Anna looked over at Mary, who gave her a finger wiggle that said *later*. Anna smiled knowing that it would be an interesting story, not realizing that it wasn't at all what she expected.

Sam then said, "So, let's straighten out the transportation side now. We have a bunch of horses, but Anna, if you're staying with us, and you are, you'll need your own horse. If you don't like any of the horses you see, we'll find one that you do.

Mary has Venus, Max has Flame, and I have Fire. How many others do we have, Max? I've lost track."

"Um…I think it's twelve others."

"Anna, would you and Frank like to see the ranch?"

"I'd love to. Frank?"

"I'm going to stay here for a while."

"I'm staying too," added Julia.

Sophie stayed to chaperone without being asked.

The others all went out to the barn to saddle and meet the horses. As soon as she spotted Mary's Morgan, Anna loved Venus and asked Sam if he could find her a nice mare as well. He said he would, and after twenty minutes of preparation, Sam, Mary, Max, and Anna all rode west into the pastures. When Anna saw the swimming hole, she looked at Mary and began to laugh, and Sam had no doubt that Mary had already spilled the beans on their mutual bathing activity during the ride from Bonham, even though that was all it was.

It was a pleasant afternoon as they toured the ranch while Frank and Julia were getting better acquainted. Julia didn't consider herself married in any true meaning of the word, so she felt under no obligation to Malarkey and began to think about moving to Iowa. It would be a big change, but the more she thought about it, the more appealing it became.

———

After a smaller dinner that consisted mostly of leftovers from the enormous lunch, the large group spent a few hours expanding on news and stories already told.

They began shutting off lamps an hour before midnight, and Mary and Anna were the first to go to bed.

Sam expected a nightmare-filled night, as Mary would be with Anna. Besides, he wanted to see if Mary's one visit would ward off tonight's nightmares.

He was in bed for almost an hour when Mary padded into the smokehouse, slid under his blanket and wedged herself in close to Sam.

"I thought Anna would kind of act as a deterrent to another visit," he said softly.

"Hardly. She acted more like an advocate. I told her about your nightmares, and she asked if it would help if I slept with you. That's when I told her that I already had. You know, she didn't even ask if it meant if I had made love with you or just slept."

"She's a very special person, Anna. Just like you, Mary."

With that, Mary pulled Sam closer and kissed him, and let him know without saying a word that if he didn't want to just sleep, it would be alright.

Sam received her message and if it hadn't been for the possibility of Mike Malarkey arriving in the middle of the night, he would have given into his deep need to fulfill both of their fantasies. She was so close, and so...Mary. But he could almost imagine that in the middle of their night of passion, Mike Malarkey would arrive to kill him, and he wouldn't be able to protect anyone, so he managed to hold her close, and she seemed content as she slipped off to sleep.

Sam did as well, but it took a while because of Mary's presence and the threat that might arrive. When he did finally fall asleep, it was another restful night. He didn't get his chance to discover if Mary's absence would bring back the nightmares or not but didn't mind. Among all of the other things that she'd given him, Mary brought him peace.

THE SCALAWAGS

When his eyes had opened to find Mary close, Sam thought that with the coming of the sun, the threat of Mike Malarkey's arrival was gone for a little while and finally expressed his appreciation for her arrival when he kissed her gently and let his hand slide under the blankets and caress her left breast.

Mary smiled, but kept her eyes closed as she put her hand on his to let him know that she enjoyed his touch, then slid her hand where she wanted it to be.

For a few minutes, they enjoyed each other, but Sam finally whispered, "Soon, Mary."

"Soon," she whispered in return, acknowledging that it was time to get to work.

Mary kissed him again, then slipped out from under the blanket and smiled down at him before she tiptoed out of the smokehouse into the bright sun.

Sam waited for a minute before he awkwardly slid out of his new bed, dressed quickly and paid his morning visit to the privy. After washing and shaving, he finally made his way to the kitchen for breakfast with the crowd.

The increase in population also required that they eat breakfast in shifts. Sam and Frank had business in Bonham, so Sam saddled Fire for himself and saddled the third outlaw horse for Frank. As he saddled the horse, he told Frank the story of how they had come into his possession.

Once they were on the road, he told Frank the far more humorous story of the Mississippi riverboat scam.

They reached the bank by midmorning and were soon seated in front of Roger Summers, the same clerk that had opened Sam's account. They quickly added the large draft to Sam's account, and Roger told him that because it was a bank draft and not a personal draft, the money would be available immediately.

He notarized the transfer of the farm to Frank, and Frank obtained the bank's account information so he could wire the two-hundred-dollar monthly payment to Sam's account from Iowa.

After they left the bank, Sam turned to Frank and said, "We have one more stop to make."

"Okay."

Sam and Frank reached Parson's Dry Goods and as soon as they entered the store, John Parson caught sight of them and said, "Morning, Sam."

"Howdy, John. This is my brother, Frank. He's just visiting, but he sure looks out of place, doesn't he?"

"I wasn't going to say anything," John replied with a grin.

Sam walked down the aisle and picked up a nice tan Stetson and popped it on Frank's head.

"There. Now you blend in a little better."

Frank shook his head and smiled as Sam walked back up front and paid for the hat.

"Now we can head back to the ranch."

When they reached the horses, Frank asked, "Sam, before we go back can I ask you a question?"

"About Julia, I assume."

"Yes, about Julia. Do you think she'd come back to Iowa with me?"

"As a widow or as a still married woman?"

"That's a big problem, isn't it?"

"Not as big as you might think. I think she'd go if you asked her, regardless of whether she was a widow yet or not. What happens when you get to Iowa is something else. If she becomes a widow, then there's no problem at all."

"How long before that happens?"

"I don't think Malarkey can stand waiting much longer. I have family and friends with me to keep me from getting lonely or just plain ornery. Malarkey is all alone now and had no real friends to begin with. He sits in that big house of his and does nothing but stew in his own hate. He's got to come after me soon."

"Well, I'll stick around a week and see how things work out with me and Julia. She is a beautiful woman."

"She is that and more, Frank," Sam replied as he mounted Fire.

Frank was already appreciative of his new Stetson as he mounted the gelding with his eyes in the shade of its long brim.

"Hold on for a second, Frank. Look over there in the livery's corral."

Frank turned and smiled.

"Glad you caught that one, Sam."

They rode over and ten minutes later were trotting north, trailing a golden Morgan mare with a blonde mane and tail. She had a star on her forehead but no other markings. Just like Mary's Venus, the young mare had Anna's name on her the moment she was foaled.

———

As Sam and Frank began their ride north, Mike Malarkey had finally reached the conclusion that Sam Walker wasn't going to come after him at all. He could have let it go at that, but the thought of a Yankee thumbing his nose at him was too much to handle. He decided that after he ate dinner, he'd head down to the Bar F and end this once and for all. He'd kill Walker first, and then he'd take care of that faithless wife of his. He'd have his way with her and then shoot her for adultery.

But just like all plans, military or otherwise, going into action with either bad or a lack of intelligence almost guaranteed failure, and Malarkey's intelligence was incredibly inaccurate. He was still operating under the illusion that all the Farrells had perished in the Bar F holocaust because even after the shootout at the Circle W, no one had even noticed that Max was present. He still believed that the only ones on the ranch were Sam and Julia.

He was at the café eating an early lunch when Sam and Frank turned into the Circle W.

———

Anna, Mary and Julia were all out on the porch as they rode down the access road. Mary had seen the mare and waited for Anna's reaction, knowing that she wouldn't have long to wait.

"Mary! Look what's trailing behind Sam's horse!" Anna exclaimed, bouncing as she pointed at the riders and their trailing mare.

"Anna, I think Sam found your horse."

Her hands over her mouth, Anna was behaving very much like the teenaged girl that she still was as she continued to bounce on her toes.

Sam saw his sister and waved before Anna pulled one of her hands from her mouth momentarily, waved, and put it right back.

Sam rode close to Anna and handed her the reins to the Morgan.

"Anna, I believe this mare is yours. I found her in Bonham, and she asked me to take her to you."

"Sam, she's so precious! I can't believe you found her. I'm going to call her Aura. Is that all right?"

"She's your horse, sweetheart. We'll get a saddle picked out for you and adjusted. Then you and Aura can go for a ride around the ranch."

"I've got to get changed," she cried, then turned and rushed into the house, her light brown hair flying behind her.

Mary approached Fire and looked up as she said, "I think you've made another young woman very happy, Sam."

"You're easy to make happy, Mary."

"You wish," she said with a laugh as Sam stepped down.

Julia walked over to Frank, who had also dismounted, and said, "That Stetson becomes you, Frank."

"Then I guess I'll wear it every day, Julia."

Mary looked at Sam and rolled her eyes, acknowledging that it wasn't a conversation that they would ever come close to having.

Sam led Fire to the barn with Mary strolling beside him.

"Mary, I have a lot of money now. What do you want to do with it?"

"What do you mean, Sam? It's your money."

"Mary, what I have is yours: the ranch, the money, and my heart, soul and body. I only brought up the money part because there are a lot of things we can do. We could add onto this house for more room, we could rebuild the house and barn on the Bar F, or we could even buy the Slash D."

"Those are a lot of things to think about, Sam."

"They are. I just wanted you to start thinking about our future together, Mary."

"I don't worry about all those things, Sam. I just want to be able to be with you and not have to worry about other things."

"Soon, Mary."

Mary smiled at him, remembering the short session they'd had earlier that morning in the smokehouse and softly replied, "Soon."

Sam finished stripping down Fire when a riding-outfitted Anna floated into the barn towing her new Morgan friend.

"You look ready to ride, Anna."

"I'm more than ready."

Mary asked, "Sam, can we get Venus ready, too? I'll ride with her."

"Sure, Mary. You get ready, too. Your gunbelt is in the smokehouse now."

Mary left as Sam began saddling Venus as Anna stood nearby with Aura, stroking her gently on the neck. Sam had already selected and adjusted a good saddle for Anna, so after finishing Venus, he began to saddle Aura.

He almost had Aura ready when Mary returned in her Stetson and wearing her gunbelt.

"Sam..." began Anna.

"Yes, Anna. I'll fix you up with a pistol and a Stetson when we get the chance, but you need some training on the use of the gun first."

Anna laughed and said, "It's good to be back with you again, Sam."

Sam soon had Aura saddled, then both women mounted and headed west toward the swimming hole. Sam watched them fade into the pastures and couldn't help but notice how similar they were in appearance, at least at a distance. Mary was taller and fuller of figure, but their horses were close in shading and in height, and their dress and hair were alike. Anna was unarmed and bareheaded, but that would change when he had the time.

He walked to the house, leaving Frank and Julia still talking in the front yard, and decided to let Frank take care of the horse, assuming he remembered that he had the animal's reins in his hand.

Sam entered the kitchen and found Sophie giving cooking lessons to Max.

"Learning a new trade, Max?" he asked.

"Just trying to figure out the easy stuff like bacon and eggs and steaks."

"Sophie, I need to talk to you and Max anyway. I just deposited the money from my parents in the bank. I have a lot of money now and don't have any firm plans. I was thinking of a few things, like building a second house here, rebuilding the Bar F house and barn, or even buying the Slash D. What do you think?"

"Sam, if I were you, I'd snatch up the Slash D. You could pick it up for a bargain price right now, and with it adjoining the Bar F, it would make a large ranch."

"Replacing the house and barn on the Bar F wouldn't cost much, either."

Sophie put down her carving knife and said, "Sam, I don't want the ranch anymore. It means nothing to me. I'm just going to sign it over to Mary, and when you two get married, you can join the three ranches together. I just want to stay here with you, Mary, and Max. Is that all right?"

"What about Max?"

"I trust you'll take care of Max. Isn't that right, Max?" she asked, turning to her son.

Max smiled and replied, "Yes, Mama. I'm not sure I want to be a rancher, anyway."

"I'll either add on to this house or build a second house nearby once things all settle down."

"Sam, if you build a cottage nearby, I can live there with Max and Anna, and you and Mary can have your privacy."

"You've got it all figured out already, do you, Sophie?"

Sophie nodded and said, "I've been thinking about it since Frank arrived with the news."

"I'll talk to Mary when she and Anna return from their ride."

————

Mike Malarkey was sitting in an easy chair in his parlor, planning the final end to that Yankee's meddling. But what he considered a plan was more akin to fantasizing than planning.

He would watch the house an hour before sunset to make sure they were still there. Then, after the sun was down, he pictured himself sneaking quietly into the house, boots off, entering their bedroom, where Julia would be lying naked. She would see him and scream, then he would toss her aside and strangle the life out of that Yankee bastard. Then, with her quaking before him, he would take her, and she would squirm and fight him, but he would have her as he had always wanted her to behave, enjoying her terrified attempts to keep him back.

When he was finished and she realized what she had missed, she would beg him to take her back. She would be at his feet, in her glorious nakedness, pleading for his forgiveness.

But he would give her not an ounce of mercy. He had never given anyone mercy. After she had begged enough, he would slap her for a little while, then the more she begged and cried for him to stop, he'd tell her that he was sorry. She'd smile and thank him as he helped her to stand, then once she was on her feet, he'd smile at her and then start seriously beating her until she died. She would die in pain and knowing that she was going to die. There would be no merciful quick death for that woman, because he didn't believe in mercy.

With the two bodies lying beside each other, he'd simply give them a short salute, then leave the house and burn it to the ground. After that he would return to his house and when the Toomey's were back in shape, he would get his town back in order.

Yes, he thought, it would be a glorious night, and it would begin in just a few more hours. He closed his eyes and restarted his imaginary victory sequence from the beginning.

———

After lunch, attended by Julia and Frank at last, Sam and Mary walked to the pool. They weren't going into the water, but they just needed some time to be alone and talk. Sam brought a bedroll for a softer surface than the rock patio.

They held hands as they made the gradual climb through the grassy pastures to the pond but said little.

Only after Sam had spread the bedroll onto the rocks, doubled it over and they'd taken their seats beside each other did serious conversation begin.

"So, Mama thinks you should buy the Slash D?" Mary asked.

"That's what she said. We'd add the Slash D and the Bar F to the Circle W and have one large ranch. We'd build your mother a nice house near ours and fix up the Slash D house and barn."

"What would we do with all that land?"

"I was thinking about that. This property, the current Circle W, we'd leave as is except for the new house. We take down the fence between the Slash D and the Bar F and clean off the burned house and barn. We'd have a house and barn and bunkhouse on the Slash D and the bunkhouse on the Bar F. I figure we increase the size of the herd by rounding up as many mavericks as we can find and buying some more. We'll hire four cowhands to work the herd. I've got to learn about it anyway. What do you think?"

"I like all of it, Sam. I don't want to change the Circle W except for adding the house. Where would Anna and Max live?"

"They'd live in your Mama's house. I don't think Anna will live here very long."

"No, I don't think so, either. She's a wonderful person, Sam."

"She is. What do you think of Julia and Frank?"

"I think they're made for each other, just like we are, only different."

Sam laughed before saying, "Different is kind. I think they're both interested more in the packaging."

"That and a few other things. But at least Frank won't be deprived anymore."

"I don't think so, either. Mary, I'm going to ask you something that may come out badly but hear me out."

"Alright."

"Can you sleep in the house tonight instead of coming to see me?"

"Of course, I can. It does sound bad, though. Why? Are you afraid we'll get carried away? We were pretty close this morning and even last night I had to pretend I was asleep."

"You're a good actress because I thought you were asleep. But that's not the reason for my odd request. For two nights now, your presence has kept the nightmares away. I want to see if they'll come back tonight. I need to see if just the strong memory of you having close to me is enough."

"That's the only reason I'd stay away, Sam. And I don't care for one second if we got carried away. I want us to get carried away. I want you, Sam."

"I'm sure it's easy to tell just how much I want you, Mary."

She laughed and said, "It is. It's very, very easy to figure that out. It's one of the many reasons I want to be yours, Sam. Completely yours."

"Give me tonight, Mary. I want to see if the nightmares are over."

"I'll grant you that, but even if it's not, I'll be there every night, Sam."

Then she asked, "Sam, this is so peaceful out here and I want it to stay like this. Why does Malarkey have to come and spoil it?"

"He'll come because of his pride, Mary, just because of his stupid, selfish pride. A normal person would have realized that he's already lost and just get on with his life, but the thought of having a former Yankee prisoner so close to him who he probably believes is sleeping with his wife, is too much to take. I'm surprised he's lasted this long."

"Do you think he'll show up tonight?"

"Maybe. But we'll just have to go on with our lives. We're all armed except for Anna. You lock the doors at night in the house. That'll slow him down enough to give me time to get there."

"What about you? What if he comes after you tonight?"

"That would be a real mistake, Mary. I'll wake up in an instant if he gets close. I always have. The night that you first came to the smokehouse, I was sound asleep, but woke up and had to listen before I heard your very soft footsteps."

"I thought you hadn't fallen asleep yet."

"Besides, why would he look for me in the smokehouse? He'll head for the house."

"Then I'll be sure to lock up."

"Good."

Despite the heat, Sam pulled Mary closer and she rested her head on his shoulder as they watched the flowing water in the nearby creek that would eventually reach the Red River.

As they sat quietly, Sam revisited his preparations for Malarkey's pending night attack. He couldn't see any way to be more prepared because he simply had no idea when he would be coming. As far as he knew, Malarkey could already be in San Antonio.

———

Later that afternoon, everyone but Sophie went out to the target range. Sam brought two extra pistols for Anna and Frank. Frank had never fired a gun before, which surprised Max.

Max and Mary had increased their proficiency noticeably since their first lesson, and Julia was better, but not much. Anna did well for her first time, and Frank was simply atrocious. When they all had finished, Sam was asked again to demonstrate his skill and did so, amazing both Frank and Anna, who had never seen him shoot before.

After a late dinner and cleanup, Mary and Anna went to their room to talk about Sam's plans for the three ranches. Frank and Julia went out to the front porch where they sat on the front steps to talk. Max had taken three of the pistols into the bunkhouse to clean and reload and Sam took his and the remaining pistols into the smokehouse to service them.

It was a quiet evening at the Circle W ranch.

———

Mike Malarkey had arrived at the Bar F just minutes earlier and was climbing into a cottonwood tree in the same copse where they had buried Earl Farrell. He had his field glasses hanging from his neck as he continued higher into the foliage.

Sunset would be in just a few minutes, so he was running late and wasn't pleased about it. He clambered up to a heavy branch where he took a seat and had to lean to his left a bit to get a clearer view of Walker's ranch. He saw the Circle W in the distance and pulled up his field glasses.

There they were! Both of them, just as he suspected. They were sitting on the front steps of the house just talking, and the sight of that wife of his with the Yankee made his blood boil. He kept watching, waiting for them to return to the house to begin their part of his fantasy. He'd give them time to undress and get into bed, and maybe, if he went sooner, he'd catch them in the middle of the heat of passion.

The idea made him snicker, but even as he watched, he saw them both stand then that Walker kissed her before he waved before she walked into the house. *Where was he going? He was walking to the bunkhouse? How noble!*

The bastard was either too highfalutin' or he was a sissy. *He was going to sleep in the bunkhouse!* Then again, maybe he had sampled the boring Julia and didn't want to bother anymore. He snickered again, but thought that if he stayed in the bunkhouse, then it was going to be even easier.

Mike would simply strangle the bastard in his sleep and then walk into the house and fulfill the second part of his fantasy and take even more time. He waited for another ten minutes to make sure Walker really was going to sleep in the bunkhouse then, as he was losing light anyway, he began to climb back down. He'd give them an hour after the lamps were all out before he'd make his move. They should all be asleep by then.

Two hours later, the lights from the house were all out and Sam was lying on the bed in the smokehouse, anxious about falling asleep, and wondering if he had made the right decision by asking Mary to sleep in the house. Aside from the nightmare

271

prevention, having Mary close was an incredible incentive to be in bed.

In the bunkhouse, Max had already drifted off, and Frank was heading that way as he thought about what he and Julia had been discussing and was sure that it wouldn't be just talking soon. He was laying on the only other bunk with a mattress, the one that was the closest to the door. Max had wanted the other bunks near him empty so he could clean the pistols.

Sam finally slipped into sleep just as Mike Malarkey arrived at the end of the access road. He tied his horse to the signpost and began walking to the bunkhouse. The moon was rising, which gave him good visibility as he walked quietly, already flexing his fingers as he approached the bunkhouse. He could already feel that Yankee's throat in his hands as he fought to get air into his lungs.

———

Sam was deep into his nightmare already. He was in a familiar position. *How had he let Malarkey get so close?* He had never beaten him before and now he understood why, he was saving Sam for last so he could strangle him. His hands were around Sam's neck, choking him. Sam's hands felt like lead weights as he fought to bring them up to break Malarkey's deadly choking hands from his neck. Malarkey was laughing heinously, and his eyes glowed with hate as he continued to choke Sam. *Why won't my hands move?* Sam was losing air. He fought to breathe and knew that Malarkey finally had him now. He was going to die.

Sam shot out of his bed, sweating, his heart threatening to pound out of his chest. This was the first nightmare that was just like a previous nightmare. Why would he dream about Malarkey again if…

Like a bolt of lightning, it struck him. Malarkey! He was here!

Sam didn't put on his boots or grab his gunbelt, but simply ran from the smokehouse and stopped outside, scanning the moonlit yard, but finding no one there. The house was silent and dark. He turned to the barn and then finally to the bunkhouse. *Was that movement at the bunkhouse?*

Sam ran in his bare feet, not worrying about any small stones that stabbed into the flesh of his soles. Malarkey had to be there.

He was just fifty feet away when the shadows revealed a struggle near the bunkhouse entrance.

He kept going until he identified Mike Malarkey and quickly realized that he had his meaty hands around Frank's throat.

Mike had quietly entered the dark bunkhouse and spotted Frank sleeping in the first bunk, his head just three feet from the door. He'd grabbed him roughly by the shoulders and yanked him out of the bunkhouse door as he struggled to get to his feet, completely confused about what was happening.

By the time he realized that it was probably that man who Sam had been expecting, it was too late to cry out or even tell him that he wasn't Sam as he fought to breathe.

Max had just slowly become aware of the ruckus when Malarkey increased his pressure on Frank's neck and snarled loudly, "I've killed you, you Yankee bastard!"

Sam was just twenty feet behind him and shouted, "Wrong Yankee, Malarkey! You're a damned coward!"

Malarkey released his grip on Frank, who dropped to the hard ground, gasping for air as he reached for his throat, then spun to glare at Sam, who was walking closer.

Malarkey stalked from the bunkhouse toward Sam, fingering the Cooper Pocket pistol in his jacket and noticed that Sam wasn't armed.

"You're gonna die now, Yankee. I killed all of the scalawags in the Bar F, and now I'm gonna add a real Yankee to the list."

"You're an idiot, Malarkey. Mary, Max, and Sophie Farrell are all here and safe. So is Julia. Everyone is safe from you, Malarkey. Soon the whole world will be safe from you because you'll be dead."

Malarkey forgot about the pistol for the moment and launched himself at Sam with his arms outstretched, his fingers eager to find the right Walker's neck.

Sam was ready for Malarkey's attack and let him get close. Then, just as Malarkey's clawed hands were within a foot of his throat, Sam smashed him with a left cross. Sam's blow caught Malarkey high though, right along the right side of Malarkey's forehead.

Malarkey stumbled past, but Sam's hand was numbed by the impact with bone instead of Malarkey's face. He hoped he hadn't broken his hand, but it was too numb to notice right now.

Malarkey recovered quickly and swung a haymaker right at Sam's chin but hit his chest instead, which still knocked the wind out of Sam and sent him reeling a couple of steps backward.

Malarkey thought he had him and made another quick lunge, but Sam snapped a right jab into Malarkey's face, his knuckles crushing into the left side of Malarkey's nose, smashing it sideways splattering blood across his face.

As Malarkey instinctively grabbed for his nose, Sam buried a fist into his belly, rocking him backwards as Sam hit him with two more shots to the face. Malarkey tried to mount some defense against Sam's punishing blows by covering up, but the additive effect of all of the hard blows were telling and he knew he was going to lose, unless he had a chance to pull his pistol.

Sam made a big mistake by not chasing after Malarkey and finishing him off. It wasn't because he was being noble, but he needed to build up some reserve for the final series of blows and thought that Malarkey was too badly hurt to mount a comeback. He knew that the bastard wasn't pretending to be hurt. He was hurt badly.

But Sam's decision to pause the action was exactly what Malarkey needed.

He plunged his right hand into his jacket, his sore fingers gripped the pistol, then he let a bloody grin cross his face as he slid his index finger onto the trigger and slid the pistol from his pocket.

Sam knew he had probably committed a fatal error the instant he saw Malarkey reach into his pocket. It was too late to do anything about it, so he reached for his derringer, knowing it would be too late, but still wanted to get a shot off.

Malarkey aimed the pistol but before he squeezed the trigger he shouted, "You're a dead man, Walker!"

Just as Sam had screwed up, so did Malarkey when he felt the need to take that last bit of bravado and shout that he was about to kill him.

As soon as he saw the muzzle, Sam dropped to his knees to avoid the shot and heard the .31-caliber round buzz past his left ear. He was still struggling to get the derringer free when there was a second, louder report off to his right.

Sam recognized the sound and direction and turned toward the bunkhouse where Max stood awash in moonlight, his Colt still smoking in his shaking hand.

Malarkey had been so intent on hitting Sam with his second shot he hadn't noticed Max leaving the bunkhouse, but the roar of the Max's Colt pistol reached Malarkey's left ear almost simultaneously with the punch in the left side of his chest of the .44-caliber slug.

He turned in disbelief toward Max and with the last vestiges of his waning strength, pulled the Cooper pistol level to take

Max with him in death. Then there as a second, sharper report and Miserable Mic Mike Malarkey fell to the ground after the .41-caliber bullet from Sam's derringer hit the right side of his head.

Sam rushed not to Malarkey but to Max, slipping the derringer back into his pocket as he jogged the fifteen feet.

Max stood in the same position he had held when he had squeezed his trigger, his eyes staring in shock at what he had done.

Sam slowly took the pistol from Max's hand, dropped it to the ground, then wrapped him in his arms, making sure that he couldn't see Malarkey's body.

"Thank you, Max. You saved my life."

"I did?" he asked in a barely audible voice.

"Yes, Max. You surprised him. He was going to shoot me, but your shot surprised him."

"I killed him, Sam. I killed him," Max said as he shuddered.

"No, Max, you didn't. You may have wounded him, but I killed him with my derringer. If you hadn't shot him, I would be dead on the ground, but you did. You did what you had to do, Max. You had no other choice. It was a hard thing, but you had to do it."

"You killed him?" he asked more quietly as his shaking began to subside.

"I killed him, Max."

———

The door to the house slammed open and several forms came trotting out. They were all dressed in light-colored nightdresses, and the moonlight gave them the appearance of ghosts.

"Max, is Frank all right?" Sam asked.

"I'm all right," said a woozy Frank in a hoarse voice as he emerged from the bunkhouse, leaning against the doorway.

Max began to come out of his shock when it finally reached his conscious mind that he hadn't killed Mike Malarkey.

Sam released Max when he heard Sophie ask, "Sam, what happened?"

He guided Max to his mother as he replied, "Malarkey showed up and went into the bunkhouse. I guess he thought Frank was me and was choking him when I arrived. I yelled at him, and he stopped trying to strangle Frank and came after me. We had a fight, and when he started losing, he pulled a pistol out of his pocket. He fired once, missed and was getting ready to fire again when Max fired from the bunkhouse, hitting him in the side. When he turned to shoot Max, I shot him with my derringer, which killed him."

"How are you, Max?" Sam asked.

Max answered, "I'm all right now, Sam."

Julia went to Frank and wrapped her arms around him, and in a hoarse voice, he said, "I guess you're a widow now."

Julia looked over at Malarkey's still body and replied, "It looks that way."

Sam then said, "I'm going to go back to the smokehouse to get my boots on and take care of his body. I can see his horse over by the end of the access road."

No one answered as Sam began to walk back to the smokehouse, stopping to pick up Malarkey's small pistol as he did.

Mary followed Sam as the others waited for Sam's return.

"Sam."

Sam turned and waited for Mary to reach him. When she did, he put his arm around her shoulders, and they began walking again.

"Sam, is Max going to be all right?"

"Yes, I think so. If he had killed Malarkey, it would be a lot harder, but he didn't, so I think he'll be better soon."

"Where can you take the body tonight? It's already late."

"I'll head to the saloon and find someone who can find the sheriff."

Mary nodded as they reached the smokehouse, entered and sat on his bed. Sam reached down and after cleaning off his feet with a pair of dirty socks, put on clean socks and then pulled on his boots.

"Mary, I had another nightmare that woke me, but it wasn't like the others. It was much shorter, and Malarkey was choking me. I'd had a similar dream before, but this was so short. As soon as I awakened I felt a sense of dread. Then I knew Malarkey was here, so I ran outside and found him."

"Maybe that's the last nightmare, Sam."

"I hope so, Mary. I really do."

Sam pulled on his gunbelt and his Stetson and walked to the barn, but Mary continued to the house. Sam saddled Fire, mounted, and rode out of the barn to the end of the access road, dismounted, then unhitched Malarkey's horse and led him back to the bunkhouse.

Frank helped Sam get the body over the horse's saddle, and Sam lashed it down. He climbed back onto Fire and looked back at everyone.

"I'll be back in a few hours."

Sam didn't wait for any response but turned Fire back to the access road and headed out.

"Does anyone else need a cup of coffee?" asked Frank.

Sophie replied, "I think that would be a good idea."

She kept her arm around Max as they all walked back to the house.

———

Sam rode into Mulberry's quiet, dark streets and headed for the only building that had light. He knew that Malarkey's death would make a lot of waves in the town, but most would be good. The folks in Mulberry would sleep better now and the merchants would keep all of their profits. Sam suddenly realized that Julia was now Mike Malarkey's widow and would inherit the lumber and flour mills, the house, and Malarkey's money. Now, there was a twist!

He reached the saloon, dismounted and tied off Fire, then walked inside. He didn't need to ask where the sheriff was when he entered when he spotted him in the process of breaking up a bar fight and not doing well.

Sam stepped over and grabbed the participant who had Sheriff Morton pinned back and yanked him hard, sending him windmilling backwards until he crashed into an empty table.

The sheriff turned to Sam and smiled.

"Thanks, Mister Walker."

Then he turned back to the others and loudly said, "Now the rest of you boys calm down."

Peace was quickly restored, and the sheriff asked Sam, "Come for a drink, Mister Walker?"

"No, Sheriff, I have Mike Malarkey's body outside. He came to the ranch tonight and tried to kill my brother thinking it was me. We had a fight, and he pulled this and took a shot at me."

Sam showed him the Cooper and said, "I thought I was a dead man, but Max Farrell shot him with a Colt. I finished him off with my derringer. You need more details?"

"Nope. I'll take care of it from here. Hold on," then he looked out at the men in the barroom and shouted, "Hey, everybody! Mike Malarkey's stinking corpse is outside!"

There was a general cheer, and glasses were raised in celebration, but Sam figured they did it for anything they could imagine.

Sam just waited for it to die down and said to the sheriff, "Can I get a copy of the death certificate tomorrow?"

"Sure. I'll have the doc write up two copies. Just stop by my office."

"Thanks, Sheriff."

"Call me Ralph. You earned the right."

"Then call me Sam."

"Well, Sam, the town of Mulberry owes you one. Make that five. The Toomeys lit out earlier."

"Well, Ralph, it looks like you're going to be reelected."

"Kinda looks that way, don't it?"

Sam waved and left the saloon, mounted and soon turned south. When he arrived at the ranch, there were no lamps lit and Sam guessed it was after two o'clock in the morning. He walked Fire to the barn, unsaddled him, brushed him down, and put him into his stall.

He headed for the smokehouse. When he arrived, he tossed his Stetson onto the top shelf, took off his gunbelt, then set the Cooper pistol alongside the Colts and sat on the edge of his bed. He pulled off his boots and his shirt and then just laid back...right on top of Mary.

"Oh, I'm sorry, Mary. I didn't expect to find you here."

"Where else would I be?" she asked softly.

Sam didn't answer her question, but just slid up against her and found that her nightdress had already been removed and was on the floor near the bed.

"Sam," she asked quietly, "do you have to wear your pants?"

CHAPTER 9

Breakfast at the ranch was surprisingly upbeat. Max had recovered quickly from his shock and Sam told them what had happened in Mulberry. Anna and Sophie knew what else had happened after he had returned, but just kept it to themselves.

Mary was still euphoric about Sam's return and the extraordinary night they had spent together. And although she had no experience for comparison, she couldn't imagine anything ever matching the released passions that they had shared.

She and Sam had made love three times in the night, each more exciting than the time before. She understood the importance of the word 'love' in the term after Sam had told her that although he'd had relations with other women before, nothing equaled what he had felt last night. He told her that having sex was one thing, making love was an entirely different creature altogether, and they had made love. So much love that when they finally succumbed to much needed sleep, Mary and Sam were no longer individuals and never would be again. Each a critical part of the other.

Sam had felt the same way for the same reason. He had given all of himself to Mary and withheld nothing. He hadn't been surprised by her openness and lack of inhibition because he knew his Mary before he knew her in the Biblical sense. Even before their communal bathing, he had known she would be this way. Maybe it was because she had grown up as a tomboy and had never given in to convention, but the why was irrelevant. The unfettered Mary was a revelation in the bedroom, or in this case, the smokehouse.

They shared innumerable glances and smiles while they ate breakfast that only Max failed to notice.

When breakfast was cleared and the dishes cleaned, all six adjourned to the main room.

Sam began by saying, "This morning, I'm going to go to Mulberry to get a copy of Malarkey's death certificate for Julia. Julia, it occurred to me last night that you now own that big house, a lumber mill, a flour mill, and probably a healthy bank account. So, this afternoon, we'll need to go to Bonham and get some things changed."

"I didn't even think of that. I was concentrating on other things," she said as she looked at Frank.

Frank smiled at Julia as he said, "Sam, Julia has agreed to return to Iowa with me, and now that she's a widow, we'll get married."

"Congratulations to you both. Are you going to get married here?"

"I thought that might be a good idea, as we'll be traveling together."

Sam turned to Mary and asked, "Miss Farrell, would you consent to marrying the other Walker brother?"

Mary smiled and replied, "Do you really need to ask, Mister Walker?"

"I did have to ask because your mother is sitting right there. Shall we make it a double ceremony, then?"

"That would be wonderful," Mary replied.

"When do you want to have this done, Frank and Julia?" Sam asked.

"How about Friday morning at ten o'clock?"

"At the county courthouse in Bonham?"

"That'll work."

"Okay. We have three days to arrange everything. When will you be going back to Iowa, Frank?"

"Right after the wedding. We'll stay in Bonham in the hotel and leave in the morning on the stage to Clarksville. We'll catch the train from there."

"Okay. So, we need to get a lot of things done before then."

Sophie said, "I'll help Mary and Julia with their dresses for the wedding. I'm not sure Mary has anything close to appropriate."

"I have some dresses in the trunk that would work, I think," said Anna, "They'd have to be let out a bit around top, but they should be right other than that."

"Thank you, Anna," Mary said with a smile.

"I'd be honored, Mary."

"My nice dresses are still at the house," said Julia.

"We can pick them up today if you'd like. We'll take the buggy."

"I can drive the buggy, Sam," offered Frank.

"That's fine. I'll ride along and bring a packhorse just in case. Once we get the death certificate, we can stop back here for lunch and then head to Bonham and see the judge about a court order making Julia the heir to all of Malarkey's holdings. We can stop at the land office and get the deeds changed and then pick up anything we need, like wedding rings, while we're there. Tomorrow, Julia, we'll need to go back to Mulberry to have them give you a draft for the money in Malarkey's account. Do you have any idea how much that is?"

"I'm not sure. It could be quite a lot. He just took money from everyone, but never spent much of it. He just took what he wanted whenever it suited him."

By the end of the conference, the wheels were set in motion for the double wedding and Frank and Julia's departure.

———

An hour later, Sam was riding alongside the buggy being driven by Frank with a smiling Julia tucked in close beside him. He was trailing a packhorse in case Julia wanted to take more than just her clothes. Sam hoped that Joe would have approved of what had transpired in the last month. He felt he had done what he could for Julia. She wasn't the sweet, shy woman that Joe had described, but Sam had freed her from her bad situation and given her the means to get on with her life. Frank was a good man, but not in Joe's class because few were. But Julia seemed happy, and that was all that mattered.

They reached Mulberry, and the buggy turned off to the big house while Sam and the packhorse turned to the sheriff's office, where he stepped down, tied off Fire, and walked inside.

"Morning, Ralph," Sam said to a grinning sheriff who sat with his boots on the desk.

"Howdy, Sam. Got that death certificate for you. You say that was a derringer that got him in the side of the head?"

"Yes, sir. Got it right here," Sam replied as he pulled out the Remington and showed it to Ralph.

"How far away was it?"

"About ten feet or so."

"At night? That's some good shooting with that little peashooter."

"It's a lot more accurate than you might think. It's a good thing to carry around in your pocket."

"Maybe I should get me one."

"Here," Sam replied as he tossed the small gun to the sheriff.

He caught it, looked at the pistol and asked, "Thanks, Sam. Is it reloaded?"

"Never got around to it. The first chamber needs a reload."

"Cartridges easy to find?"

"Yup. Remington .41-caliber rimfires."

"Nice pistol," Ralph said as he slipped it into his pocket and pulled his feet down.

He slid the death certificate across the desk and Sam caught it just as it floated off the edge.

"Thanks, Ralph. I'll give this to Julia."

"You take care, Sam."

"I'll be seeing you around, Ralph."

Sam waved as he left, folding the death certificate and sliding it into his vest pocket. He had recovered the vest from the trunk of his belongings that Anna had brought with her. The trunk also contained his only suit. It was older but still was a reasonably decent fit. It was tight around the chest and shoulders, but he'd only have to wear it once more anyway.

He stepped up on Fire, then trotted back east and then north to Malarkey's house. He saw the buggy out front and tied off Fire, removed two panniers from the packhorse and walked to the house. When he entered the open door, he heard Julia and Frank engaged in something other than finding clothes, so he loudly cleared his throat and waited for the sound to subside.

It was more than five minutes before Frank walked into the room from the office and smiled.

"Julia was showing me the library. She said it was funny because Malarkey couldn't read."

Sam avoided making any comments, especially considering how he and Mary had spent the night, but said, "Here's his death certificate. Julia may want to keep that in her purse. It's a very important piece of paper."

"Sure. She'll be out in a second."

It was more than a minute when a red-faced Julia exited the office and smiled at Sam, saying, "We were busy."

Sam simply replied, "I can see that. I gave the death certificate to Frank."

Frank handed it to Julia, who put it in her purse. She was still correcting little mistakes in her wardrobe as they went upstairs to her bedroom.

She filled the panniers with her clothes and other items and still had some that she decided weren't worth taking along.

"You can just use the trunk that Anna used to bring my things," Sam suggested.

"Anna has already emptied hers, and we'll be using that one," said Frank.

"Good, I don't have any place to put my things right now anyway," Sam said with a laugh.

———

They returned to the ranch an hour later and unloaded Julia's things into her bedroom. After lunch, Julia and Frank boarded the buggy again, and Sam mounted Fire. Mary and Anna were riding with them to Bonham because Mary and Sam needed to pick out their wedding band set and Anna needed her Stetson. She would inherit Julia's gunbelt.

When they arrived in Bonham, Frank and Julia went to the county courthouse with Max. The judge read the marriage certificate and the death certificate and signed the court order to speed access for Julia. It didn't hurt one bit when Julia flashed a smile at the judge.

When they left the courthouse, Frank and Julia went to the land office and Sam told them he'd meet them at Parson's after they finished.

While they were in the courthouse meeting with the judge, and Anna and Mary were at Parson's, Sam stopped by the bank and asked to see the real estate officer. He was shown to the office of Mister John Bristow and it didn't take long to negotiate a price on the Slash D.

It had been on the market for years with no takers. It wasn't that it was a bad ranch, it was just that there was so little cash available, and the bank couldn't find too many buyers with steady income for a mortgage. The asking price of twenty-four hundred dollars wasn't even a starting point for Mister Bristow. He started at two thousand and Sam was able to buy the property for fifteen hundred and fifty dollars. Cash spoke very loudly to the bank.

He left with the completed sales contract in his vest pocket and figured that he'd visit the land office on the day of their wedding. He figured Frank and Julia were keeping the clerk busy with three transfers, so he headed for Parson's.

When Sam entered the store, he found Anna already sporting her new Stetson.

Mary and Anna smiled at him as he told Anna that she looked like a 'right handsome filly', then he took Mary's hand and had John Parson show them his selection of wedding bands. They found a nice set, and Sam paid for the rings and the hat.

Ten minutes later Frank and Julia arrived and quickly picked out their wedding bands as Sam recalled that he had never seen Julia wearing one before.

—

The work in town completed, they returned to the house and continued the preparations for the double wedding. Mary and Anna had selected Mary's dress and were soon making the necessary modifications, while Sam, Frank and Max had to enlist Sophie's help to get their suits reasonably presentable.

That night, even before Sam and Mary did anything romantic, Sam told Mary about his purchase of the Slash D, and she was thrilled with the idea and wanted to go and see the ranch tomorrow, but tonight, she had other much more desirable intentions on her mind that seemed to mimic those of her fiancé.

———

The next morning as they had their breakfast, even Max had figured out what was going on in the smokehouse, then winked at Sam like they shared a secret. Sam winked back and smiled. He was glad to see Max bounce back as he had been concerned about him since the night of the shootout with Malarkey.

When Sam and Mary rode out of the Circle W to inspect their new ranch in the early morning, it was already hot, then as they turned down the access road, Sam noticed smoke coming out of the cookstove pipe.

"Looks like we've got squatters, Mary."

"Did you want me to come along, Sam?"

"What do you want to do?"

"Honestly? I'd rather just wait near the bunkhouse."

"Smart move, Mary. You do that, and I'll see what's cooking."

"Even now, Sam?" she asked as she smiled.

"Always the best time to use a little humor."

They walked their horses to the bunkhouse, and Mary stopped. Sam continued to keep Fire at a walk and found two horses parked behind the house and immediately recognized the horses of the Toomey brothers.

Sam pulled up, dismounted and left Fire standing unhitched as he pulled his right-hand Remington. He walked steadily toward the back of the house, then stepped quietly onto the back-porch steps, hoping that they hadn't bought more pistols. He had noticed that the horses didn't look healthy, so it wasn't likely that they'd used their meager resources to buy more weapons.

He didn't do anything fancy when he reached the door, but just yanked open it open and quickly stepped inside.

"Morning, boys," Sam said as he leveled his pistol.

Jimmy and Pat Toomey both stopped in midbite and jumped at Sam's sudden appearance.

"We ain't doin' nothin'!" shouted Jimmy.

"You're both trespassing on my ranch, Jimmy."

"This ain't nobody's ranch," argued Pat.

"I bought it yesterday. It's mine now, and you boys are trespassing."

"Mister, we ain't got any money, and nobody will hire us. We were gonna go back to Mulberry but had to get something to eat first."

"Well, finish your beans and then leave. I don't think you'll want to go to Mulberry, boys. Mike Malarkey is dead. I killed him the night before last when he showed up and tried to do me in."

"Mike's dead?" asked Jimmy in disbelief.

"Yup. Two bullet holes. Now, I suppose I could be a kind man and offer you both a job or give you some money, but you both were responsible for killing Earl Farrell and damned near killing his wife. I won't kill you because you're both unarmed. You eat your beans and get out, but if I ever see you anywhere close to me or mine again, I will kill you both. That is all the mercy you will get from me."

They needed no more inducement as they wolfed down their remaining beans and ran from the kitchen, Pat still wiping some bean juice from his mouth.

Sam trailed after them and watched as they hurriedly mounted, then rode away from the house. They passed by Mary as if she didn't exist and kept going. He saw them pause at the end of the access road and then head north toward Mulberry.

Mary had watched them fly past then walked Venus to where Sam was standing, dismounted and asked, "Was that the Toomeys?"

"It was. They were in bad shape and had no money, no food, and no future. I remember a talk I had with Max on the night we met them and the other two Malarkey boys. He asked me why I didn't shoot them, and I told him it would have been murder. It was true and what he needed to understand at the time, but I wonder now if getting shot wouldn't have been a better fate for those two. Their lives are forfeit, Mary. Now they may eventually catch up with another band of outlaws, but they'll be hunted their entire lives. It's no way to spend your life, Mary."

"Let's go and look at the ranch, Sam."

Sam smiled and replied, "Let's do that."

After they were back in the saddle they rode east and began the tour of their new acquisition for three hours before returning to the house and doing a more thorough inspection of the place. It looked like some repairs had already been made and was in good condition, considering.

They returned to the Circle W for lunch and told everyone about the chance encounter with the Toomey brothers and then what they had found on the ranch, although all of the Farrells had a pretty good idea of the layout and condition of the ranch.

———

The next day was surprisingly normal. Julia packed her things into the trunk and Anna had given her the travel bag she had used when coming to Texas and said it was only fitting that it should return to its birthplace in Iowa.

Sam, of course, pointed out that it had been manufactured in Cleveland, Ohio and Anna called him a smarty-pants and smacked him on the head, which he told Mary was almost a family tradition.

Sam, Frank, and Julia rode back to Mulberry. When Julia closed Malarkey's account, she was given a draft for a staggering $5,432.10, which was even more than she had expected. The way the clerk behaved when he handed it to her, the withdrawal would put the bank in jeopardy of closing its doors, but none of them really worried about it.

———

Friday arrived with little fanfare. Sophie, Julia, and Mary took the buggy because all were wearing dresses. Sam had confessed to Mary privately that she looked beautiful in her dress, just as she did in her tomboy clothes, or nothing at all. Mary took it as the compliment that it was.

They arrived in Bonham during the midmorning and parked the buggy and horses outside the courthouse. They all entered and went to the judge's offices, where they completed the paperwork. Anna and Sophie would serve as witnesses for both marriages.

The ceremony was brief and legal without organ or flowers, no large crowd of well-wishers and only a modicum of weeping. The two couples were joined in legal matrimony before noon, but to Sam and Mary, it was little more than an acknowledgement by the state of Texas of the marriage that they had promised to each other days earlier.

Frank and Julia acted more like traditional newlyweds, even though both had been married before.

After they had completed all the forms and exited the courthouse, Sam took them all to the restaurant for a wedding luncheon. After they had finished their quick meal, Frank and Julia said they needed to get to the hotel and make sure everything was ready for the next day's journey. It was a weak excuse, but everyone understood the almost desperate need for privacy, even Max.

The rest of the group made their farewells to Frank and Julia and then watched as the couple disappeared into the hotel. Sam dropped off the trunk at the stage depot, and they marked it with Frank's name.

Sam's next job before they returned was to have the deed for the Slash D registered. While they were in the land office, Sophie had the Bar F transferred to Sam and Mary Walker. Mary smiled and watched as the clerk wrote her new name down. It was the first time she had seen it written.

She saw it again and got to write it herself when Sam had Mary added to the bank account less than an hour later.

All the legalities completed, they finally returned to the Circle W arriving in mid-afternoon.

When they returned, Mary pulled Sam aside as Anna, Max, and Sophie walked into the house.

"Sam, did you want me to change before tonight?"

"If you don't mind, Mary, I'd kind of enjoy getting you out of that dress."

"That's what I thought, you lustful man."

"Your fault, my beautiful bride."

She kissed him and smiled, walking with an exaggerated hip sway as she left him, then glanced back and winked. Sam knew it was going to be a wonderful life with his Mary.

The night didn't come fast enough for Sam and Mary. When they finished dinner, they hurried outside and into the smokehouse.

Sam quickly closed the doors as Mary lit the lamp, there was no reason for darkness this time.

"I imagine that not too many newlyweds have spent their wedding nights in a place that used to be filled with ham and bacon hanging from the rafters," said Sam.

"How do you know? I think smokehouse wedding nights are the tradition in Iceland."

Those were the last words that Mary would speak, at least the last words that could be repeated in mixed company, for two hours, but it was difficult for those in the house or even Max who was two hundred yards away in the bunkhouse to not hear the loud cries and other more exotic sounds that echoed from the smokehouse that night.

———

The next morning, they were all sitting around the breakfast table. Mary was wearing britches and a tighter shirt at the request of her husband as Sophie sat down and placed a large envelope on the table.

"Julia said to give this to you today. I don't know what it is."

Sam glanced at Mary, then picked up the envelope and used a kitchen knife to open it.

Sam slid the papers from the thick envelope, unfolded them and sighed when he saw the contents.

"They're the deeds to the house, the lumber mill, and the flour mill. They're all in my name. She left a letter, too."

He read:

My Dearest Sam,

I have no use for these because I'll be in Iowa. I know if I give them to you, you'll do right by the workers, because Malarkey wasn't. I think the house will be perfect for Anna when she marries, too.

I know how much you sacrificed to come to Texas to fulfill your promise to Joe and can think of no other man with the courage or conviction to do what you've done. But you've found your Mary, and Joe certainly had that right. So, your sacrifices have been well repaid by that alone.

I loved Joe and didn't think I would ever know any other couple who had what he and I shared. I was not only wrong; I found another couple that has even more in common than we did. I may have had designs on you from the start, but it didn't take long to see how perfectly matched you are with your Mary.

Do what you wish with the properties. Write to us often and tell us what is happening in your new home back in Texas.

With all my love,

Julia

Sam handed the letter to Mary and already began to wonder about what he would do with what he held in his hand. *What was he going to do with a lumber mill and a flour mill?* At least he knew where he could get lumber for his projects now. The house was a bit of a problem, though. It would have to have a caretaker, or maybe not.

Mary handed the letter to Sophie as she asked, "Sam, what will we do with these things?"

"Monday we'll ride over to the two mills and sort out what's what. I'll make sure we have a good foreman who knows what he's doing at each location. We'll make improvements as necessary and make sure the workers know that things won't be the way they were when Malarkey was the boss. We'll find out if they're being paid a fair wage. The house will be a problem for a little while, so we may need a caretaker. I will abscond with some of those books, though."

"There are books?" Max asked.

"Hundreds of them. Malarkey couldn't read, but Julia told me that they were there when he bought the house, and he thought they made him look smart."

Sam looked at Max. He'd spent so much time these past few days with Mary that he felt he had neglected Max.

"Max, I think you need a bath."

Max smiled and replied, "I think so, too."

"Ladies, if you'll excuse us, we are going to bathe."

"About time, too," said Mary.

"I'll make the same offer to you tomorrow, Mrs. Walker."

"And you'll get the same enthusiastic response, Mister Walker."

With her promise that he was sure she would satisfy, Sam and Max headed for the swimming hole.

As they walked east, Max said, "Sam, remember the other day when I said I didn't think I wanted to be a rancher?"

"I did. Do you have an idea what you want to be now?"

"Yes, sir. When I had to shoot Mister Malarkey the other night, I thought how terrible it was that I had to have to do that. It shouldn't be a kid who stops bad men. It should be the law. I want to be a lawyer. Is that okay?"

"That's a great thing to want to be, Max. You have all the tools to be a great lawyer. You're smart, and you have a good amount of common sense. I think you'll do well."

"Can I go to college?"

"You can. You have to get admitted, which means you have to do well on the entrance exams. That means a lot of study and reading."

"Can you help me?"

"I'll always help my brother, Max."

Max nodded and felt an incredible sense of direction and opportunity fill his mind.

———

They had a great time in the pool. Max had worried that Sam might be disappointed about not wanting to stay on the ranch, but after Sam's strong endorsement of his career choice, Max was free to be a twelve-year-old boy again.

They spent most of that time talking about Joe, which had been a common topic when they'd been waiting near the ranch sign those two dark nights.

On their return trip, Max asked if he could tell the ladies about what he was going to do.

"It's your news, Max, so it should come from you."

"Sam, do you think I'll ever meet a girl who I can like as much as you like Mary?"

"You will, Max. Just make sure you pay attention to what's inside the package."

"What's that mean?"

"Now, your sister, Mary, Julia, and Anna are all very pretty. That's the package, do you understand? It's what you see on the outside. But even Mary would admit that Julia is prettier than she is. But why do I love Mary and not Julia?"

"Because she's your friend."

"You know, you're exactly right, Mary is my friend. We understand each other. We are so much alike. She's a wonderful person inside that package, and that's what's more important. I just had the added bonus of having the wonderful person stuffed inside an equally wonderful package."

"Oh. So, I should talk to them and see if they're good inside, too?"

"It's more than that, Max. I knew a lot of pretty ladies who were good people, but none were right for me. You know how Mary and I are always having fun when we're talking? We make fun of each other."

"It's really funny."

"It's more than funny, Max. It means that we share the same sense of humor and share the same values. We share everything, Max. When you find a girl that shares everything with you, don't let her go. Don't let anyone get in your way."

"I won't, Sam."

"Good. You'll be as happy a man as I am when you find her, Max."

———

Two hours after they left, the two smiling males entered the kitchen and met with three smiling women.

"I'm gonna be a lawyer," announced Max.

"Well, good for you!" Mary said as she hugged her brother.

Sophie and Anna added their support as well as Max beamed.

———

After the incredible day of two marriages, one couple's departure and the transfer of all the property, came the busy days.

On Monday, Sam and Mary, accompanied by Anna, visited the lumber mill and the flour mill. The flour mill seemed to be in decent shape, although the workers seemed less than pleased with their working conditions.

After Sam talked to them for a while though, their mood improved. He found their wages were less than half of what they should be and doubled them, then he saw the changes that needed to be done and wrote them down. He asked who the foreman was and was told that Malarkey didn't have a foreman. He asked them who should be the foreman, and it came down to two men.

The deciding factor was that one could read and the other couldn't. He gave the job to the literate worker with an explanation to the one who wasn't chosen. It seemed harmonious when he left, then he gave the list of repairs to the foreman and told him to get the work done and to bill it to the company.

The lumber mill was a bit more of a mess. The workers were in the same state of disharmony as the flour mill workers, because of failing equipment, dull blades, and poor wages. Again, Sam sat with them and listened to their complaints, writing notes as he did. At the lumber mill, he didn't need to take a vote among the workers as he had at the flour mill. There was a young man, maybe the youngest one there, who seemed to take charge by nature.

Sam appointed Will Everson as the foreman, and no one objected. He doubled their wages as well and called Will Everson over before he left.

He handed him his list and said, "Will, I have a list of repairs that need to be done. Go ahead and contract out for the repairs. If the blades can't be sharpened, buy new ones."

"I'll take care of it, Mister Walker, but there is one other thing. Malarkey fired one of the men ten days ago when he cut himself. He's in kind of a bad way with money, and he's got a wife and baby. Do you think we can bring him back?"

"Bring him back and pay him back wages at the new wage rate. How about you, Will? Do you have a wife?"

"No, sir, I don't have the time. I've been working and studying to try and get into college. I should have enough money sooner now that you've raised our salaries."

"Call me Sam, by the way. What do you want to study?"

"Animal husbandry. I used to work at the Slash D ranch until it went under."

"Well, Will, guess who owns the Slash D ranch now? I'll be needing to get it started again, and I don't know anything about cattle. We're going to merge it with the Bar F, too."

"That'll be fifteen sections! You could run a few thousand head on that much land. You couldn't do it in West Texas, but we have better grass and water here. That's quite a project, Sam."

"I'll need help, Will, but put that in your head for a while. Right now, let's get the mill running normally."

"Yes, sir!" exclaimed a smiling Will Everson.

Sam shook his hand and then turned to escort Mary and Anna outside.

They had been watching as he had talked to Will, and Anna asked, "Who was that, Sam?"

"Your future husband, Anna," Sam asked as he took her and Mary's arms, smiled and started walking.

Anna remained speechless even after they mounted their horses while Mary just smiled.

Once in the saddle, Mary looked at Sam and raised her eyebrows, then Sam winked at her as they rode away.

The ride back to the Circle W was only the first day that would herald a long string of events that would mark the coming months.

———

The new cottage was completed and the repairs on the Slash D ranch house were done the same week as was the removal and clearing of the burned-out rubble from the Bar F. Sam had consolidated all three ranches into the Circle W and the Circle W extended.

The lumber mill and flour mill were both humming by the end of July, and Anna and Will Everson began seeing each other socially that month as well, which surprised no one. After just that initial brief conversation, Sam believed that he and Anna were just made for each other.

Mary announced her pregnancy in August, and they received a letter from Iowa announcing Julia's pregnancy as well. That surprised both Mary and Sam, because Julia hadn't become pregnant in more than a year of marriage with Malarkey.

Will moved into the old Slash D ranch house after he gave up his position at the lumber mill and began to work with Sam to improve the herd. They hired four ranch hands, and Will was made the ranch manager. After rounding up every maverick they could find in the area and pulling the Bar F cattle together, the herd amounted to almost six hundred animals, which was a good start.

Sam learned a lot from Will about cattle and rode as a regular ranch hand, without the pay of course. Will had selected good men, three of whom had worked the ranch with him when it was the Slash D. Will decided to forgo college, as he would already be doing what he wanted to do and where he wanted to do it.

Then there was the other reason for his decision…Anna. If he had gone away to college, he couldn't be married, and he wasn't about to let Anna get away. He didn't realize that she had no intention of letting him get away, either. She endured the occasional reminder from Sam about his first comment to her about Will and would return his remark with one about Barbara Jean.

Max returned to school in September with renewed enthusiasm and astonished his teacher with his new attitude, and at mid-term, received his first report card with straight A's in his life. Sophie was ecstatic with her son's improved academic performance and his overall positive outlook on life. He would only receive one B for the rest of his schooling and that was in physical education.

Mary's pregnancy was going well, but they didn't let that get in the way of their nighttime, and sometimes daytime, pursuits. And now that they had the whole ranch house to themselves, they could engage in more enthusiastic expressions of their love.

They exchanged letters with Julia almost weekly. She was happy about her unexpected pregnancy, and both she and Mary had due dates in February.

On October 11, Anna and Will were married. Anna moved out of the cottage to the ranch house on the old Slash D with Will.

There was still the question of the big house in town. The books had been moved, and Anna had cleaned it out of its cooking utensils and dinnerware. Nobody seemed to want it, until, of all people, Sheriff Ralph Morton approached Sam and told him that his wife had been admiring the house for years and that if they ever wanted to sell, to let him know.

Sam guessed the market value of the fancy house to be almost two thousand dollars, so he asked Ralph how much he was willing to offer. Ralph said they had an offer on their house for six hundred and had saved another four hundred dollars, so Sam said he'd let it go for eight hundred. Ralph almost peed his pants and shook Sam's hand until it was numb. They closed the deal at the bank an hour later. Sam had the draft made out to Anna Everson, then left the bank and rode south, stopping at the ranch house to find Anna in the house cooking lunch.

"Sam! What brings you around?" she asked as he entered.

"I just sold the big house to Sheriff Morton."

"Well, that's good news. I thought you'd be stuck with it for years. What priced did you give him?"

"I only asked him for eight hundred dollars. That's less than half of what it was worth, but it would make Morton and his wife happy."

"You're still the wonderful brother I've always known," she said as she kissed him on the cheek.

"Anna, remember what Julia wrote in her letter about the house?"

"I do. She just couldn't have guessed that I'd find Will and live on the ranch. I couldn't be happier, Sam."

He handed her the draft and said, "Anna, here. I had them make out the draft to you for the house. You'll be able to do a lot of things with the money."

"Sam, we don't need the money. We have a nice house, and you're paying Will a very generous salary."

"Anna, you'll be needing all those baby things soon. You know, a crib and diapers. All of the things we've been buying."

"How did you know? I haven't even told Will yet."

"I know because you're my Anna," he said as he wrapped her in a hug.

"I love you, Sam."

"I love you too, Anna. Now, take the money, and you'll have a nice cushion for when the baby arrives."

"All right, you convinced me."

"Do you mind if I tell Mary?" he asked.

"As long as I get to tell Will first."

"All right. It's a deal."

He kissed his sister on the cheek again before leaving.

———

When he returned to the Circle W ranch house, he found Mary and Sophie in the kitchen and gave them the news of the house and an explanation of why he gave the money to Anna, along with a caution about telling Will.

Both women were overjoyed with the news. Mary was especially happy, knowing that their baby would have a cousin and a playmate.

They went to bed on the evening of February 7th, and Sam was affectionately rubbing Mary's swollen belly as they drifted off to sleep.

Sam was having a dream about the prison camp that wasn't a nightmare when Mary shook him awake. It was time for a new Walker to enter the world.

Sam quickly left the room and retrieved the midwife, Lizzie Wilcox, who was sleeping in the cottage with Sophie.

Sam was worried, despite the midwife saying everything was perfect. Mary was in labor for a long time and Sam could tell that even the midwife was getting a little nervous.

But after all the worry and concern, Mary finally gave birth to a baby boy without any difficulties. Joseph Max Walker announced his arrival with loud wails at 4:28 p.m.

When he was allowed to enter the room, Sam went to his tired wife's side, and she smiled at him.

He touched her sweaty, but still joyful face with his fingertips, smiled and she said, "He's a beautiful boy, our son."

Sam nodded and replied, "He is, Mary. Want to go and take a bath now?"

"In February? You must be joking. Now, if I'd had him in July, maybe," she replied softly with a smile.

Sam knew she was tired, so he kissed her gently on the forehead then stood, smiled down at her, then turned and left the room to let her sleep.

———

The next morning, Sam sat next to Mary as she fed little Joe and smiled at her.

"Well, Mary, it looks like everything is complete now and our world has been restored as it should be. You know, Mary, I don't have nightmares anymore, but I did have a dream when you went into labor. I remember it so vividly because you woke me up to tell me it was time.

"I was sitting in the prison camp with Joe at my back. It was unusual because I wasn't hungry. It was a beautiful, warm day, and I felt content, which wasn't possible at that place. We were having our usual conversation about going home, and I said that I was going home to marry Barbara Jean, and he told me I was wrong. I'd go to Texas and marry his sister, Mary.

"I then asked him why he was so sure, and he told me that he'd always known that I would marry you because I had to marry you. I thought that it was a strange thing for him to say, so I asked again why he thought I had to marry you. He was a strong and happy Joe and not the man in the prison camp who looked at me and said, "Because how else could you have little Joe?"

EPILOGUE

A week later, Mary was up and around and happily feeding her baby. They received a letter from Frank saying that Julia had given them a beautiful baby girl at ten o'clock in the morning on February 8th and named her Mary Rose Walker.

Anna gave birth to a baby boy on August 5 and named him Sam William.

The Toomey brothers were hanged in Waco, Texas, for murder on September 4, when they tried to hold up a bank and after shooting a clerk, were taken down by the sheriff's shotgun.

Mary went on to have three other children, all girls.

The Circle W prospered and had eight full-time hands to handle the large herd.

Max Farrell became an attorney and the prosecutor for Fannin County, and with the help of Sam and Mary, bought a ranch just north of Bonham in 1880 and even managed to get the Bar F brand.

Sophie Farrell died on March 1, 1882, from pneumonia. She was buried next to her husband on the old Bar F property, having never made Sam a pecan pie.

For many years afterwards, Mary and Sam would still go and visit the swimming hole and enjoy private, passionate time in its cooling waters. Each time they visited the pool, they would tread water, kiss, then slowly descend beneath the surface, linked to each other and think the same thing: Joe had been so right.

1	Rock Creek	12/26/2016
2	North of Denton	01/02/2017
3	Fort Selden	01/07/2017
4	Scotts Bluff	01/14/2017
5	South of Denver	01/22/2017
6	Miles City	01/28/2017
7	Hopewell	02/04/2017
8	Nueva Luz	02/12/2017
9	The Witch of Dakota	02/19/2017
10	Baker City	03/13/2017
11	The Gun Smith	03/21/2017
12	Gus	03/24/2017
13	Wilmore	04/06/2017
14	Mister Thor	04/20/2017
15	Nora	04/26/2017
16	Max	05/09/2017
17	Hunting Pearl	05/14/2017
18	Bessie	05/25/2017
19	The Last Four	05/29/2017
20	Zack	06/12/2017
21	Finding Bucky	06/21/2017
22	The Debt	06/30/2017
23	The Scalawags	07/11/2017
24	The Stampede	07/20/2017
25	The Wake of the Bertrand	07/31/2017
26	Cole	08/09/2017
27	Luke	09/05/2017
28	The Eclipse	09/21/2017
29	A.J. Smith	10/03/2017
30	Slow John	11/05/2017
31	The Second Star	11/15/2017
32	Tate	12/03/2017
33	Virgil's Herd	12/14/2017
34	Marsh's Valley	01/01/2018
35	Alex Paine	01/18/2018
36	Ben Gray	02/05/2018

37	War Adams	03/05/2018
38	Mac's Cabin	03/21/2018
39	Will Scott	04/13/2018
40	Sheriff Joe	04/22/2018
41	Chance	05/17/2018
42	Doc Holt	06/17/2018
43	Ted Shepard	07/13/2018
44	Haven	07/30/2018
45	Sam's County	08/15/2018
46	Matt Dunne	09/10/2018
47	Conn Jackson	10/05/2018
48	Gabe Owens	10/27/2018
49	Abandoned	11/19/2018
50	Retribution	12/21/2018
51	Inevitable	02/04/2019
52	Scandal in Topeka	03/18/2019
53	Return to Hardeman County	04/10/2019
54	Deception	06/02/2019
55	The Silver Widows	06/27/2019
56	Hitch	08/21/2019
57	Dylan's Journey	09/10/2019
58	Bryn's War	11/06/2019
59	Huw's Legacy	11/30/2019
60	Lynn's Search	12/22/2019
61	Bethan's Choice	02/10/2020
62	Rhody Jones	03/11/2020

Made in the USA
Monee, IL
12 March 2021